# DEEP
# SIX

# Also by D. P. Lyle

## The Dub Walker Series
*Stress Fracture*
*Hot Lights, Cold Steel*
*Run to Ground*

## The Samantha Cody Series
*Original Sin*
*Devil's Playground*
*Double Blind*

## The Royal Pains Media Tie-In Series
*Royal Pains: First, Do No Harm*
*Royal Pains: Sick Rich*

## Nonfiction
*Murder and Mayhem*
*Forensics For Dummies*
*Forensics For Dummies, 2nd Edition*
*Forensics and Fiction*
*Howdunit: Forensics; A Guide For Writers*
*More Forensics and Fiction*
*ABA Fundamentals: Forensic Science*

## Anthologies
*Thrillers: 100 Must-Reads* (contributor); *Jules Verne, Mysterious Island*
*Thriller 3: Love Is Murder* (contributor); *Even Steven*

# DEEP SIX

## A JAKE LONGLY NOVEL

## D. P. LYLE

**Oceanview Publishing**
Longboat Key, Florida

ISBN  978-1-60809-181-2

Published in the United States of America by Oceanview Publishing
Longboat Key, Florida

www.oceanviewpub.com

10 9 8 7 6 5 4 3 2 1

PRINTED IN THE UNITED STATES OF AMERICA

*To my late mother, Iris Elaine Campbell Lyle, who taught me the power and healing nature of humor. A day doesn't go by that you are not greatly missed. And to my father Victor Wilson Lyle, who taught me that work is its own reward.*

# ACKNOWLEDGMENTS

To my wonderful agent and friend Kimberley Cameron of Kimberley Cameron & Associates. KC, you're the best.

To Bob and Pat Gussin and all the great folks at Oceanview Publishing for your friendship and always spot-on insights and help, making my writing the best it can be.

To Nan who supports me through the madness of writing.

To The Bean, our wonderfully noisy and nocturnal Bengal, who makes sleep a rare commodity and work, a more or less twenty-four-hour-a-day event, the only real option.

# DEEP SIX

# CHAPTER ONE

IT WAS PRECISELY 12:12 a.m. when the window shattered. A crack-crunch, an eardrum-concussing pop, and a spray of glass shards. It didn't explode by itself, mind you, but rather courtesy of a cavity-back, perimeter-weighted two-hundred-dollar five iron. A Callaway. I recognized it because it was mine. Or at least it had been.

I knew the exact time because the flying glass yanked me from sleep, my forward-slumped head aligned squarely with the dashboard clock. Took a couple of seconds to gain any sort of perspective on what had happened.

Of course, sleep wasn't part of the job. Watching the house two doors down and across the street was. In my defense, nothing had moved in the house, or even along the street that snaked through the high-dollar neighborhood, for at least a couple of hours. But sitting in the dark, behind the wheel of my car, boredom did what boredom does. Knocking back the better portion of a bottle of Knob Creek hadn't helped either. Stakeouts were mind numbing and a little more numbing of the mind couldn't be all bad. Right?

"Jake, what the hell are you doing?" the reason for the glass explosion screeched through the jagged hole.

This wasn't just any window. It was vintage; the reason it shattered rather than simply spider-webbing. The original passenger window of my otherwise spotless 1965 Mustang. Burgundy with black pony interior, now littered with glass shards. Going to be a bitch to find a replacement.

Speaking of bitches, I recognized the grating voice even before I looked up into the face of my ex. Tammy's the name; crazy's the game. I'd lost four good years listening to it. Mostly whining and complaining, sometimes, like now, in a full-on rage. She had a knack for anger. Seemed to need it to get through the day.

She gripped the five iron with both hands, knuckles paled, club cocked up above her shoulder, ready to smash something else. If history offered any lesson it was that she might graduate from the side window to the windshield and so on until she got to me. Tammy didn't have brakes. Or a reverse gear.

Cute according to everyone, except maybe me, she was a beach-blond with bright blue eyes, a magic smile, and a perfect nose. Some plastic surgeons were gifted. Expensive, but gifted. I knew. I'd paid for the nose.

But cute Tammy had a short fuse. She could go from zero to C-4 in a nanosecond.

Like now.

"Funny, I was just fixing to ask you the same thing," I said.

Still shaking the cobwebs loose and trying to get oriented to person, place, and situation, I managed to get the characters involved sorted out pretty quickly. Staring at a cocked five iron in the hands of your ex-wife will do that. The place came along in short order. Peppermill Road. A loop off Perdido Beach Boulevard that arched through The Point, a megabuck enclave nestled into another expensive enclave known as Perdido Beach. Very high up the financial food chain, The Point was a row of seven-figure, stilted homes that hung off Peppermill like charms on a bracelet, each facing the Gulf over a wide, sugary beach.

Okay. Two down, one to go.

Person, check. Place, check. It was the situation I struggled with.

"Why are you parked in front of my house?" she asked, chin jutted forward, eyes flashing that anger I knew so well.

Well, there was that.

"I'm not. I'm parked across the street."

The five iron cocked another couple of inches. Her knuckles whitened even more and her Pilates-pumped forearms tensed. "Don't mess with me, Jake. Why the hell are you here?"

"Is that my five iron?"

Tammy's face flushed and the rage that rose up in her chest was almost palpable. I knew I could be infuriating, could push her buttons like no one else. Lord knows she had told me often enough. Truth was I did sort of enjoy it. She actually was cute when she was mad. Dangerous, but cute.

That little vein that ran down the middle of her forehead expanded as she spun, switching to lefty, and shattered the Mustang's small rear passenger window. Also original. Probably even harder to replace.

"Whoa, whoa, whoa. What's wrong with you?" I was smart enough not to add "other than the usual," but it did cross my mind. Did I mention the woman never could find her own brake pedal?

She pointed the five iron at my face. "Why are you spying on me?"

I now noticed that she was wearing black sweat pants and a cropped pink t-shirt, exposing her tight belly. She would be hot if she weren't so insane. I'd married the hotness, and divorced the insanity.

I began brushing glass snow from my shirt and shaking it from my hair. "I'm not."

"Really? You going to go with that?" At least she had lowered the five iron. "You're parked across from my home, clear view of my living room, and you have your pervert glasses with you." She nodded toward the binoculars on the passenger seat. They were also frosted with shattered glass.

"Night vision. I need them for my work."

"Work?" She didn't even make a feeble attempt to cover the sarcasm in her voice.

"I'm on a case. For Ray."

"Just great. The only person I know who makes you look smart."

Ray, my dad, actually was smart, sometimes frighteningly so, but Tammy and Ray had never really hit it off. Ray didn't play well with most people. Neither did Tammy. So they mixed in an oil-and-water, cat-and-dog, fire-and-ice kind of way.

"You remember him?" I said. "He'll be happy to hear that."

Another button pushed.

"Don't be an ass. I tried for four years to sweep him out with the trash, but some lint you just can't get rid of."

I smiled. "And he always speaks so kindly of you."

She bent forward at the waist, her eyes now level with mine. "Right. So why are you working for Ray?"

"He needed someone to do a bit of surveillance work."

Her expression said she wasn't buying it. Like I was lying. Can't imagine where she got such an idea. She gave a soft snort as if to add an exclamation point. "Why not that redheaded behemoth that follows him around?"

"Pancake's busy."

Another snort. "Probably eating."

"Or sleeping. He tends to do that about this time every night."

She shook her head. Sort of a disgust shake. "And here I thought you swore you'd never work for Ray." She shrugged. "Guess that's like every other promise you ever made."

"Doing a little surveillance isn't exactly working for him."

"Surveillance? A big word for snooping." I started to say something insightful about collecting evidence and not snooping, but Tammy wasn't finished. "I don't really give a good goddamn who you snoop on as long as it's not me."

"It's not."

"Right." She took a step back and the five iron rose again. She searched for another target. Her gaze settled on the windshield.

"Put the club down and listen." She lowered it a notch, but her tight jaw didn't relax an ounce. "I know most things in your world revolve around you, but this has nothing to do with you."

Her head swiveled one way and then the other. "Who? What did they do?" She was now in full gossip mode. A Tammy staple. "I bet it's Betsy Friedman, isn't it?" Not waiting for a response she continued. "Is she humping someone?" She looked toward a gray house with a large fountain in front just ahead of where I was parked. "I bet she is."

"I can't talk about it."

"Sure, you can."

"No, I can't."

"Right. All that private eye protect the client shit?"

"Exactly."

Longly Investigations, my father's PI outfit. Ray Longly had been a lawyer and a former FBI special agent and then did some kind of spook work for the Feds he would never talk about and now for the past five years a PI. Ever since he split from the alphabet soup of D.C. agencies. Or they split from him would be more accurate. Part of Ray's "never playing well with others."

"And your antics aren't helping the investigation," I said.

A quick burst of laughter escaped her collagen-plumped lips. "That's rich. You couldn't investigate a flat tire. You're an idiot."

Sort of explains the divorce, doesn't it? Partly, anyway. Before, back when I played major league baseball, she'd thought I hung the moon. Could do no wrong. Took her to the best restaurants and nightclubs and vacations down in South Beach, sometimes Europe. Tammy loved Paris. And loved playing a Major League wife. Rubbing shoulders with big-name athletes, believing that she could be a *Sports Illustrated* swimsuit model. Truth was, she probably could. Even today at thirty-one.

But four years ago, after my career ended, after I pitched eleven innings on a cold Cleveland October night and never recovered from the rotator cuff injury that followed, and after the paychecks dwindled to nothing, she moved on. To a lawyer. The guy who owned the seven-figure, six-bedroom hunk of steel, glass, marble, and designer furniture across the street.

Circle of life on the Riviera. Not that one. The redneck one. Gulf coast style.

"If it's not Betsy, then who?" she asked.

I shook my head. "At the risk of being redundant, I can't tell you."

"Can't or won't?"

"You pick. Either works for me."

The five iron elevated again. I uncoiled my six-three frame from the car and stood, looking at her over the roof.

"Take a breath, Tammy."

That's when the police cruiser rolled up, settling near the curb maybe twenty feet from my Mustang. A uniformed officer stepped out, remaining behind the open door, right hand resting on the service weapon attached to his hip. He was trim and fit in his perfectly applied uniform and spoke in a calm, even voice.

"You folks want to dial it back a bit?" he said. "Maybe tell me what's going on here?"

After the niceties and introductions, him—Officer Blake Cooper, me—Jake Longly, her—Tammy the Insane, she told her story. Amazing how it had no relationship to reality. She began slowly but quickly built momentum, telling the good officer that I was pond scum—her words—and that I was a despicable piece of crap—more of her words—and a couple of other monikers that are better left unsaid, finally stating that I was stalking her. Spying on her. In the middle of the night.

Welcome to Tammy's world.

While she spoke, Cooper's gaze moved over her, stopping at the most interesting parts. When he was finally able to extricate himself from all things Tammy, he looked at me. "Sir, were you spying on her?"

"If I was, I'm not sure parking in plain sight right across from her front door would be the wise choice."

"You want to explain that?"

I did.

"Surveillance? On who?"

"Can't say. It's a private matter."

Cooper walked around the door to the front of his cruiser, hand now off the gun, thumbs hooked beneath his service belt. "You live here? In the neighborhood?"

"That's a hoot," Tammy said. "He lives in a cardboard box behind the shopping center."

She can be so endearing.

"No, sir, I don't. I'm on a job. For Longly Investigations."

"Ray Longly?"

"Correct."

"You work for him?"

"He's my father."

Cooper nodded. "That explains a lot."

Ray didn't restrict himself to only the FBI shit list. He and the local gendarmes didn't play well together, either. Seems he frequently butted heads with them over one thing or another. Usually stomping on their turf. Or at least they tended to see it that way. And more often than not that was the truth of it.

Tammy jumped in. "See, I'm not the only one that thinks your father is a goofball."

Cooper turned her way. "Ma'am, that's not exactly what I said."

She shoved one fist against her hip, staring at him. "Sounded that way to me."

Again he looked her up and down before getting back to me. "Want to tell me what this's all about?"

Boy, did I ever. "I'm on a job. Doing surveillance work for a licensed private investigation firm. I wasn't doing anything until she went Tiger Woods on my car."

"I take it you two know each other," Cooper said. Not really a question.

"We used to be married," I said. "Probably not hard to figure why it didn't work out."

Again the five iron elevated.

"Ma'am, please don't do that," Cooper said.

She shook her head and lowered the club. "I want him arrested."

"I don't think that'll be necessary." Cooper eyed me. "So, you're Ray Longly's son? The baseball player?"

"Ex-baseball player," Tammy said.

"I am," I said.

"You were great in the day."

"That day is long gone." Tammy again.

Cooper took a deep breath and puffed out his cheeks as he exhaled slowly. I think he was finally beginning to realize just how difficult communication with Tammy could be. When he spoke it was calm and measured. "I got a call. One of your neighbors said there was a fight going on. Complaining about the racket."

"So, arrest him for disturbing the peace," Tammy said. "Or something like that."

Cooper sighed. "I think I have a better solution. Why don't you run on back home," he said to Tammy. And then to me, "Maybe you should shut down your surveillance for the night."

Tammy's chin came up and her shoulders squared. "And get off my street." Always the last word.

"Will do," I said.

"Ma'am?" Cooper waved a hand toward her house.

She hesitated, turned, started across the street.

"Can I have my five iron?"

"Bite me, Jake." She extended a middle finger skyward but never looked back as she marched across the street, up the walk, and into her house. The door slammed hard.

"That was fun," I said.

"Want to file any charges?" Cooper asked, his head tilting toward my Mustang. "For the damages?"

"Wouldn't do any good. Her new husband's an attorney."

He nodded. "I see." He looked around. "Anything going on I should know about?"

"Not really. It's a domestic issue."

Again he nodded. "Not much I can do since it doesn't seem that you broke any laws, but I'd suggest you vacate the premises." He shrugged. "To avoid further problems."

"My thoughts exactly."

"One question," Cooper said. "How'd you get in here? Past the guard gate?"

"I have a nice smile." I smiled. Cooper didn't. "They know me."

Cooper hesitated, then nodded and handed me his card. He climbed in his cruiser and left.

# CHAPTER TWO

AFTER THE EVER-PLEASANT Tammy and the all-business Officer Blake Cooper vacated the premises, I surveyed the damage to my car. The shattered windows were essentially irreplaceable. Seems Ford doesn't make windows for fifty-year-old cars. The nerve of them. I began knocking away the toothy window remnants from the frames and picking up the larger pieces from the seats, dropping them on the floorboard. The floor mats were expendable, the pony interior not.

As if to prove that any situation could go from bad to worse, the wind kicked up, dragging with it the smell of rain. Out over the Gulf a bank of dark clouds, tops silvered by the moonlight, innards flashing bright white with lightning, marched toward shore.

Just great. Twenty miles from home, no right-side windows. Didn't bode well for my pony interior.

Headlights washed over me, and I looked up the street. Now what? Did Cooper have more to say? Maybe he called it in and his boss gave him the green light to haul my ass downtown. To tweak Ray if nothing else.

I raised one hand to shield my eyes from the headlight glare. The car, a shiny new red SL Mercedes, rolled to a stop. The deeply tinted window slid down, revealing a young woman. Her straight blond hair hung like silk curtains to her shoulders and framed a face that could grace the cover of *Vogue*. Definitely not what I expected.

"That was interesting," she said.

"You saw that, huh?"

She laughed. Soft, almost musical. "Hard to miss a woman beating the hell out of a classic Mustang with a golf club."

I looked back up the street, from where she had come. "You live around here, I take it?"

She brushed a wayward strand of hair from her face. "Just back around the bend."

"You on a beer run or something?"

Another soft laugh. "Heading out to see a friend."

"A little late, isn't it?"

"He's a bartender. Doesn't close up until one. But he's not nearly as interesting as this."

"Bet he'd be happy to hear that."

She shrugged. "He'd get over it."

I reeled in my first response—that a woman as beautiful as her probably didn't have to worry too much about pissing him off. No one would put her on the road for being late. Instead, I smiled.

"So what was that about?" she asked.

"My ex. She's insane."

"Obviously."

"I'm Jake."

"Nicole."

She extended a hand out the window, and I shook it. Soft skin, firm grip. The first drops of rain peppered my face.

"You better get that beauty under cover."

"My thoughts exactly. Problem is, cover is about twenty miles away."

She hesitated, examining me as if trying to decide something. "Or just up the road. My place. You can stick it in the garage until this blows over."

"What about your friend?"

"Sean the bartender? Like I said, this is much more interesting."

She smiled. Perfect teeth. Perfect smile. Just perfect. *Down boy.*

"Glad I could brighten your evening," I said.

"A girl's got to find fun where she can."

"You have an odd definition of fun."

"I hear that a lot."

The rain picked up, fat drops now smacking the Mustang's roof and windshield.

"Follow me," she said.

Not waiting for an answer, she pulled ahead, flipped a U-turn, and blasted up the road. I cranked up the Mustang and followed, but by the time I made the U, she was already out of sight around the curve. It crossed my mind that maybe this was all a game. That she was trying to ditch me. That maybe, just maybe, this would all be a good story for her to share with her friends over lunch tomorrow.

I realized that this was a rather dim view of the fairer sex, but with rain slanting through my Mustang's shattered windows, courtesy of one member of that sorority, I suspect I'd be forgiven.

I navigated through the sweeping bend and on to a quieter stretch of Peppermill Road. No sign of the Mercedes. Where the hell did she go?

Here on The Point, the homes were widely spaced, separated by hundred-foot wide natural areas that consisted of sea oat-topped sand dunes and clusters of pine trees. Zero lot line was not part of the residents' vocabulary. And here, on the point of The Point, the spacing was even more generous, the road even darker.

I slowed. Still no sign of the Mercedes. Then on my left, taillights winked through the sea oats that topped a broad sandy mound. Beyond a wide drive, her Mercedes nudged near a garage door that was rolling open. She pulled in. I slid my Mustang in next to the SL.

"Anybody ever tell you that you're hard to follow?" I asked.

"Everyone."

The massive house was two stories of glass and stone and wood. Substantial was the word that came to mind. As well as expensive. Four broad, curved, stone steps led to the intricately carved wooden double front door. I followed Nicole inside.

The interior was equally impressive. And substantial. And expensive. The living room seemed as big as my entire home. Deep sofas, a river rock fireplace, a massive flat screen TV that would do most movie theaters proud, and a wall of French doors that looked out over a wide deck, the beach, and the now churning Gulf. Rain hammered the glass. Lightning skittered in the distance, followed by a low rumble of thunder.

"Something to drink?" Nicole asked.

"Sure."

She navigated to the bar, a hand-carved oak monstrosity that filled one corner of the room. Behind the bar, dozens of liquor bottles stood like soldiers before a long mirror. She wore strategically frayed jeans and a red Ferrari t-shirt, both welded to her body as if shrink-wrapped. And what a body. Long and lean, curved where it should be. A West-Coast strut that looked like she had been runway trained.

"You look like a bourbon drinker," she said.

"What does a bourbon drinker look like?"

"Rugged, studly."

"That's me, all right."

She laughed. "What'll it be? Bourbon?"

"Whatever you're having is fine."

"Tequila it is." She snagged a bottle of Patrón Silver and two glasses, splashing a healthy dose in each, handing one to me. She touched her glass to mine. "Welcome."

"Nice place. Much better than mine."

"Mine, too." She took a sip. "This is my uncle's vacation home."

She placed the Patrón bottle on a coffee table that looked long enough to handle an F-18 landing.

"I can't imagine what his primary must look like," I said.

"Bigger."

"What does he do?"

"Movies. Producer, director, writer, all the usual Hollywood tags."

I gave the room another onceover. "Seems to pay well."

"Especially at his level. Won a couple of Oscars, a half dozen Emmys."

"Why here? Why not Malibu or someplace like that?"

She kicked off her sandals. "That's where he lives most of the time. Malibu. The Colony. He's originally from Pensacola. Not big on Hollywood folks so he likes to come hang here."

"And you?"

"My condo's in California. Orange County. Newport Beach. You know that area?"

"Been there a few times. Very nice."

"Too crowded. Much quieter here."

"Where is he now? Your uncle?" The thought crossed my mind that maybe we weren't alone. Maybe Uncle Joe, or whatever his name was, was upstairs asleep. Or loading a gun.

Her delicate fingers held the glass of tequila near her chest, the Ferrari logo distorted through it. "Europe. He'll be there for a few months. Shooting his next film."

"So you're on vacation?"

"Sort of. Working on a screenplay."

"Isn't everyone in California working on a screenplay?"

She laughed again. "Seems so. But I've actually had a couple produced."

"I'm impressed."

"Don't be." She stirred the tequila with one finger and then sucked it clean. "They were short films. Though one was shown at Sundance."

"Congratulations."

"Yeah. With that and six bucks I can get a latte at Starbucks." She sat on the sofa, patting the cushion beside her. "Come. Sit."

I couldn't think of a reason not to, and if I had, I would have hammered any such impulse into submission. I sat. She twisted toward me, folding her legs, her knees against my thigh.

The rain drummed the windows in waves. A long, stuttering flash of lightning lit up the room, followed by palpable thunder.

She flinched and said, "Looks angry out there."

"It'll blow through."

"I guess I'm stuck with you until it does." She flashed a smile. "But since we have some time, tell me the story?" She refilled our glasses, returning the Patrón to the table.

"What story?"

"All that golf club business."

"The usual. Marriage, divorce, crazy woman. You live in California. I'm sure you've seen it before."

"True." She brushed her hair back over her shoulder. Even her neck was beautiful. Or maybe it was the emerald hanging from the wound gold chain. "Are you a stalker or something?"

"No. But, that's what she thought. Then again, in her world everything is about her."

"What were you doing in this neighborhood in the middle of the night?"

"Snooping. Just not on her."

"Interesting. There's a story there."

Her eyes were so deeply blue they seemed bottomless. Like a calm tropical lagoon. Maybe a blue iceberg. But not cold. Definitely not cold.

"My father's a PI," I said. "I was doing some work for him."

"And the story gets better. Now I'm definitely intrigued."

"Another old story. Some dude thinks his wife is seeing someone every time he leaves town. Wants her watched. Find out who she's fooling around with."

"That's more mundane than I hoped."

Nicole was far from mundane. Painfully beautiful but obviously bright. Not one of the vacuum-headed blonds I usually ran into on the local beaches and at my bar.

"PI work is mostly mundane," I said. "And boring. Lots of time eating junk food, waiting for something to happen."

"Like getting your windows smashed?"

"That's a first."

"I guess real PI work isn't like the movies? Sam Spade and all that?"

"Not even close. I suspect your uncle would say the same thing."

"Probably." She stretched and suppressed a yawn.

"Am I keeping you up?"

"You stole my line." A wicked smile.

I shook my head. "Funny."

"That's what I was going for."

"What's his name?" I asked. "Your uncle?"

"Charles Balfour."

"Really? I know him. Know of him, anyway."

"Who doesn't? He's my mother's brother. She and Dad are in the business, too. Mom's in costume design. Dad's an editor. Both have also won awards."

"And you're a screenwriter. Very talented family."

She tilted her glass toward me and shrugged.

"You should be an actress," I said. "You definitely look the part."

"What? Drug-addled and stupid?"

"I was thinking more beautiful and photogenic."

"And I thought my eyes were too big."

I looked into those blue eyes. "Not big. Maybe deep."

She stared at me, then reached out and laid her hand on my arm. "That's sweet." A soft squeeze. "I was an actress. Sort of. Did a couple of movies. Bit parts. The girl in the bikini. Sometimes cutoff jeans. Eye candy. Always in the background."

"Bet you stole the scenes."

"Are you hitting on me?" she asked.

"Just making an observation."

"Pity. I could use being hit on about now."

"I can't imagine you going through a single day without some guy making a play."

She smiled. "That's very kind. Unfortunately, I seem to attract losers."

"Don't we all."

She snagged the tequila and refilled our glasses again. The bottle now half empty. Felt like most of it was swirling through my head. Should have had more than a granola bar for dinner.

"So, why screenwriting and not acting?" I asked.

"Ever been on a movie set?"

"Not really. A few TV interviews. That sort of thing."

"Whole different animal. Movie sets are boring. Tedious. A lot of people doing mostly nothing. I don't do tedious and boring well."

"How old are you?" I asked.

She frowned. "You should never ask a lady her age." Then she laughed, those baby blues sparkling. "I'm just kidding you. I'm twenty-seven. Why?"

"You look younger, but act older."

"That's a compliment of sorts, I suspect."

"It is."

"And you?"

"Thirty-two."

"So why the divorce?" she asked.

"Like I said, she's crazy."

"Crazy usually goes both ways."

I nodded. "And crazy isn't all bad. Just when it reaches the level of true insanity."

"And?"

"And what?"

She flipped her hair back again. "I bet there's more to the story."

I shrugged. "I wasn't very discreet."

"Banging some bikini blond on the side?" She raised an eyebrow. "Or were there several?"

I shrugged again. Not really wanting to get into it.

"So you're an admitted bad boy?" she said.

"You sound like her."

The phone rang.

"I should get that," she said. "It's probably Sean wondering where I am."

She stood and walked to the bar where her purse sat. She retrieved her cell phone, bringing it to her ear.

The side of the conversation I heard went like this:

"Sorry, I fell asleep."

"I didn't hear it. My cell was in the other room."

"No, it's too late. Tomorrow?"

"I'll call you then."

She hung up the phone. "Sorry about that."

"Hope he's not mad."

"He'll get over it." She sat. "Or not."

For the next hour or so, the rain never let up though the lightning seemed more muted, the thunder more distant. We destroyed the tequila bottle and shared histories.

She was born in Beverly Hills; I'm a local boy who, except for a couple years in the big leagues, had lived on the Gulf my entire life. She earned a degree in literature at UCLA and a MFA in film from USC; I managed two years at the University of South Alabama on a baseball scholarship, up to the bigs, then back to South Alabama to finish my degree in business administration. She hung on the Hollywood circuit but never could catch the big break so moved down to the OC to distance herself from the LA madness; I bought a beach bar, and occasionally worked part-time for my dad. Like tonight.

Soon she placed her empty glass on the coffee table and stretched out on the sofa, her head in my lap. "You're easy to be with, Jake Longly," she said.

"As are you."

She wiggled deeper into the sofa, getting comfy. My head dropped back on the cushion, and I stared up at the pressed-copper ceiling. She took my hand in both of hers, lacing her fingers with mine, and soon her breathing became soft and shallow. My eyes grew heavy.

That was the last thing I remembered.

# CHAPTER THREE

THE NEXT MORNING I woke groggy and more than a bit disoriented. My head had settled into the sofa's deep cushions, my gaze up toward a ceiling I didn't recognize. My heartbeat pulsed in my eyeballs and even my teeth and scalp hurt. I tried to move, but my neck and back protested. Took me a couple of minutes to remember where I was. One glance at Nicole and it all came back. Tequila. The devil's liquid. I never handled white whiskey well, anyway. Gin, vodka, tequila always did a number on my brain. And every time, like now, I promised myself I'd stick to bourbon and beer. Why could I never remember that?

Neither Nicole nor I had moved. She was still stretched out on the sofa, curled on one side, her exquisite face in profile on my lap. She had apparently pulled an afghan throw over us sometime during the night. Or maybe I had. I had no memory of that. I glanced at my watch. Eight a.m.

I slipped from beneath her, settling a decorative pillow beneath her head. She murmured something but didn't wake up. I arranged the throw over her, snugging it up to her neck, and walked to the windows. Clear and sunny. My eyes felt as if someone had sandpapered them. I blinked a few times, but it didn't help. The Gulf was calm and the beach empty except for a few early risers, staking out their plots of sand for the day.

After I found my shoes—one near the bar, the other propped against a chair, no memory of how they got there—I slipped them on and kissed Nicole on the cheek, saying something stupid like, "I had a good time." Totally lame. But, hungover, it was the best I could come up with. She never opened her eyes but offered a weak smile and muttered, "Call me later."

How could I refuse that offer? But I didn't have her number and said so.

She told me and I added it to my phone's call list. I let myself out.

Next stop, Alberto's Exotic and Vintage Cars. Alberto Garcia, the owner, was the best mechanic around. Could fix anything. And if anyone could find windows for a '65 Mustang, Alberto could. His shop was in Gulf Shores, a mile from the beach, in a mostly light industrial area. The low cinder block building was painted bright yellow and had an aged corrugated metal roof and four work bays. He specialized in exotics and Detroit muscle cars.

When I pulled into the gravel lot, Alberto walked from one of the open bays where a light blue vintage Chevy Malibu hovered on a lift, two of his guys beneath trying to pry something loose. Alberto smiled while wiping his hands with a grease-stained towel.

"Jake. How goes it?"

"Lost a couple of windows last night."

He leaned into the car, eyeing the glass bits that still covered the floorboards. "What happened?"

"You don't want to know."

"A woman. Got to be."

I shrugged. "Tammy."

He laughed. "That woman's going to do that to your head someday."

Alberto knew Tammy all too well. She had thrown a few tantrums in his direction over some perceived failures to repair her car properly. Wasn't the case, but she never let reality get in the way of a good explosion.

"Might be hard to find windows for this thing," I said.

He nodded. "I'll make a couple of calls and see what I can dig up."

"Thanks."

"You need a car to drive?"

"Maybe just a ride over to Ray's place."

Alberto rounded up one of his guys, a young kid named Robbie, who looked more like a surfer than a mechanic. He had shaggy blond hair that half covered his eyes and wore jeans and a faded green t-shirt, sleeves ripped off at the shoulders, exposing sinewy arms. We climbed in his red pickup and ten minutes later reached the two-story, stilted structure on the sand in Gulf Shores that served as Ray's home and the offices of Longly Investigations. Ray's black 1966 Camaro SS and his black Chevy dual cab pickup were wedged among the support poles. I thanked Robbie and climbed the stairs to the first floor deck.

Longly Investigations occupied most of the lower floor, taking up what had originally been the living room, dining room, and den. The kitchen was at the far end; living quarters upstairs. The aroma of cooked bacon and fresh coffee filled the air. In the kitchen, I found a plate with two strips of bacon and a piece of wheat toast. I poured a cup of coffee, and then folded the bacon in the toast, taking a bite as I headed out to the deck, where Ray did most of his work at an umbrella-shaded teak table. Near his elbow rested a plate with the remnants of his typical breakfast—eggs, bacon, toast. He held a cell phone to his ear and a Mountain Dew in his free hand. Always a Dew. Part of Ray's so-called "breakfast of champions."

I sat across from him.

Ray was one tough SOB. Fifty-eight, still very fit, with short-cropped graying hair and pale-blue eyes that could ice over with little provocation. Ran on the beach and pumped iron at a local gym every day. Rain or shine. He'd been a Marine before all the law school, FBI, spook world, and PI stuff. He was straightforward, no BS, and many folks didn't like his in-your-face attitude. Usually those he was investigating. Sometimes the local police. He seemed to step on their turf more often than not. They weren't usually happy. But as he always said, "Screw 'em. If they did a better job, I wouldn't be needed."

Those who didn't tolerate Ray's aggressive and direct approach to life included me. Went back as far as I could remember. He'd always run the family like a military unit. When I slacked off at school, as I often did, Ray would go ballistic. "Make something of yourself, boy," being one of his oft-used lecture punchlines. Had it not been for my baseball prowess, Ray and I would likely have split long ago. But athletic ability made up for a lot of sins in his eyes, so we fell into an uneasy truce. Not that he didn't constantly try to drag me into his business, where he could again be in control, but I resisted. But this time, when Ray asked me to do a little stakeout work for him, he had actually used the word *please*. Not part of his usual vocabulary. So I decided what the hell. Right now though, being down two car windows, I wished I'd said no from jump street. Too late now.

Ray wrapped up his call by saying, "Tell that son of a bitch I ain't coming to Miami. No way." He listened and then said, "Just tell him." He ended the call, not waiting for a response.

"Problem?" I asked.

"That divorce case down in Coral Gables. Going to trial next week in Miami. They want me to come down and testify. Don't want to pay for it though. Fuck 'em." He drained the Dew. "How'd it go last night?"

"Interesting."

"Yeah?"

"Not with Barbara Plummer. Nothing there. Looks like she

crashed around ten. At least that's when all the lights went out. No one came by."

Barbara Plummer was the target of our investigation. Our? I mean Ray's. Henry Plummer, Barbara's husband, a wealthy software developer who used his countless millions to move into real estate development, had hired Ray to catch his wife cheating. He was "absolutely sure" she was and needed ammo. Not for a divorce or anything along those lines. More to "yank her back in line" was the way he put it.

"That doesn't sound interesting."

I told him the rest of the story. The Tammy story. Not the Nicole one. Nothing to hide there, not really, I just didn't want to get into it. Didn't want to listen to Ray ranting about my dick leading me around. An old and repetitive argument between us. Ray was of the opinion that running a bar and chasing bikinis was not a career. I disagreed.

"Shouldn't have parked in front of her house," Ray said. "Her being insane and all. Maybe on down the way a bit would have worked better."

Ray could always do things better.

"The view of the Plummer place was clearer from where I was."

Ray nodded and then rubbed his neck. "Give Pancake a call. Henry will be away a couple more days and he's sniffing into some things on the good wife. Last I heard she has some gig tonight and last time she had one of those she had a visitor. Either planned or picked up at the party."

"Will do."

"Guess you'll have to use the pickup until your car's fixed."

"Thanks."

"Don't park it in front of psycho Tammy's house, though."

"I'm thinking the beach might be a better approach, anyway," I said. "Good view of the back doors and the bedrooms from there."

"Better get some sleep today. You look like shit."

"Thanks. Glad you noticed."

He shrugged. "Is what it is."

# CHAPTER FOUR

I SLEPT UNTIL around four and then rolled out of bed, showered, shaved. That cleared my head a bit so I answered a few emails and made two calls. One pleasure, one business. The pleasure call first. Priorities. Nicole answered after a single ring.

"Drinks and dinner?" I asked.

"Please. I'm starving."

"Miss me, huh?"

"That must be it." She laughed. "Quit screwing around and get your tail over here."

"Anxious, I see."

"Hungry. Get moving."

I then called Pancake. Arranged to meet him at five.

Twenty minutes later, I pulled into Nicole's drive. The garage door rattled open. She stood next to her car. She wore cutoff jeans, form-fitted to her hips, exposing legs that went all the way from here to there, and a dark-green tank top. Sunglasses as big as saucers. *My, my.*

"It's about time," she said.

"Got here as soon as I could."

"Got to teach you to drive faster."

"Still couldn't keep up with you."

"That's why I'm driving." She settled in the SL and backed from the garage. I climbed in. The top was down and the late afternoon sun warmed my face. She spun backwards from the drive and into the street. I held on, and we were off. The Gs pressed me into the seat.

"Where to?" she asked.

"Captain Rocky's."

"The dive down in Gulf Shores?"

"That would be it."

"I love dives," she said.

"Me, too."

"You go there often?"

"I have to. I own it."

The full name was Captain Rocky's Surf and Turf. I had purchased the beachfront bar/restaurant five years earlier from Rocky Mason, the original owner. Thanks to the money the Texas Rangers had paid me to toss ninety-mile-an-hour fastballs. Didn't change the name since it had a strong local and tourist following. Besides, I liked Captain Rocky's. Sounded perfectly beachy.

It was one of the few things that ended up on my side of the table during the divorce. Tammy's take on Captain Rocky's? She wanted nothing to do with "that den of sex and alcohol." I couldn't really argue with that, though to me Rocky's did serve good seafood. Ribs and steaks, too.

Nicole drove like she was at Talladega. Tires whining, whipping through traffic, more than a few horn blows, from her as well as irritated motorists, until she finally crunched into the shale lot of Captain Rocky's and slid to a stop in an empty space near the front door.

"You fly here often?" I asked.

"Wimp."

As soon as we entered, I saw Pancake. Couldn't miss him. He was the massive redheaded, freckle-faced block balanced on a barstool that, even though new and fairly sturdy, looked as if it might give up and collapse at any minute.

Bartender Carla Martinez, my manager, bookkeeper, and everything else, looked up. "Better shape up, the boss man's here."

Pancake spun on the stool. It groaned like an old man shouldering a sack of cement. "Well, well, who do we have here?"

I knew he didn't mean me.

He stood and wrapped his thick arms around Nicole. "Welcome to my office, darling."

Pancake did do most of his work here. Why not? Free rent, free food, free booze, and lots of people to talk to. Pancake loved to talk.

Nicole laughed. "Working in a bar sounds like my kind of job."

"This is Pancake," I said. "He works for my dad. If you use the term *work* loosely."

Pancake released Nicole from his bear hug, pushed her back a step, and looked her up and down. "Mighty fine. Much too fine for old Jake."

"I hate to break up this little lovefest," Carla said. "But what can I get you guys?"

"We'll grab a table," I said. "Got some things to discuss."

Carla shook her head. "Work, work, work. That's all you guys do."

She can be such a smart-ass sometimes. But the truth was the place would collapse without her. She really ran the business. Took care of payroll, inventory, and snapped the employees into place with a look, and if necessary, sharp words and walking papers. Getting good, stable help on the beach wasn't all that easy, but Carla managed. At only five-four she was fit and borderline muscular, a remnant from her early years as a fitness model. She still worked out religiously and worshipped the sun, the reason she was so deeply tanned. She had dark, curly hair, always pulled back into a thick mane, and black eyes that could be friendly or menacing, your choice.

Nicole, Pancake, and I settled at a corner table, overlooking the outdoor dining deck and beach, still packed with sunbathers, swimmers, and families gathered beneath large yellow umbrellas, which now cast long shadows across the white sand. Tourists, trying to squeeze in as much beach time as possible.

Carla took our orders: beer and fried shrimp with fries, coleslaw, and hush puppies. Manna from heaven.

"So why do they call you Pancake?" Nicole asked.

"Jake, I'll let you tell her. I'm going to hit the head," he said. "You only rent beer, and I got to go make a payment."

After he left, Nicole said, "So, tell."

I did.

Pancake's real name was Tommy Jeffers. Most people thought "Pancake" came from his ability to demolish a stack of pancakes. And then march through a mess of bacon, eggs, and grits. Truth was he could pretty much demolish anything put in front of him. Pancake's football prowess was legendary. In high school, he played left tackle and specialized in pancake blocks. The ones that flattened some undersized, terrified defensive lineman. People along the Gulf Coast still told Pancake stories, some true, some made up, all involving some poor soul getting roadgraded.

Then on to the University of Alabama where he started for three years before tearing up a knee, ending his career and any chance to move up the food chain to the NFL. He transferred from Tuscaloosa to the University of South Alabama over in Mobile where he completed his criminal justice degree while working for Ray, and Longly Investigations.

Pancake returned as I was finishing the story.

"I wouldn't have liked the NFL, anyway," Pancake said. "Too

much business and BS. Not enough fun. Game's supposed to be fun." He finished his beer and waved the empty toward Carla. "Truth is, I'm exactly where I'm supposed to be, doing exactly what I'm supposed to be doing."

"That's so sweet," Nicole said.

"That's Pancake," Carla said as she placed a fresh bottle of beer on the table and snatched up the empty. "He's sweet." She ruffled his red hair.

"You got that right, darling."

Carla rolled her eyes and walked away.

"Speaking of what you're supposed to be doing," I said, "Ray said you had some new info on our target."

He glanced at Nicole.

"It's okay. She knows about it. Some of it, anyway."

"Ray on board with that?"

I shrugged. "Not yet. But I'll deal with him."

"Better you than me."

"If it's a problem I'll go sit over there." Nicole pointed toward a nearby empty table.

I laid a hand on her arm. "Stay here. It's okay."

Pancake took a slug of beer. "Seems the wife has some fundraising deal tonight. A dinner at Sophia's."

Sophia's, a high-end restaurant about a half mile down the beach, was nothing like Captain Rocky's. All crystal, linens, French delicacies, and a twenty-page wine list. My place had a better view and cold beer, though. And, of course, hush puppies.

"My sources say it'll be done by nine," Pancake continued. "I suspect she'll be back home by ten and ready to receive visitors." He grinned.

"Might be too late," I said.

He shook his head. "Apparently one of the things that got hubby to thinking something was going on revolved around a similar event."

"I take it she does these fundraising events often?" I asked.

"Yep. She's rich and bored. What else is she going to do?" He opened his big hands and shrugged. "Apparently she's a real social butterfly." He took another gulp of beer. "Anyway, Henry came back from a trip the day after one of her events. Said something was off. Couldn't be specific. Said she acted weird, guilty, and the house didn't feel right. Whatever that means. Even said their bedroom had an odd smell."

"He was probably smelling the alpha dog," Nicole said.

Pancake and I looked at her.

"You know what I mean." She laughed. "You two are alpha all the way."

"You can bet on it," Pancake said.

"Henry thinks she hooked up with someone at the event?" I asked. "That sort of thing?"

"You got it."

"He's returning when?"

"Day after tomorrow."

"So tonight . . . ?"

Again, Pancake opened his hands and shrugged.

I nodded. "Okay, we're on it."

"On what?" Nicole asked.

"Looks like another stakeout."

"Cool. Never done that."

"You'll have to hide some of that," Pancake said.

"That what?" Nicole asked.

He waved a hand toward her. "All that wonderful skin. Attracts too much attention."

She laughed. "I like this guy."

"Most women do," Pancake said.

Nicole tilted her beer bottle toward him. "I don't doubt that at all." Then she looked at me. "This stakeout. You weren't planning on parking on the street again, were you? I don't want to get hammered by a golf club."

"You sound like Ray," I said.

"Don't look nothing like him though," Pancake said.

Not even close.

# CHAPTER FIVE

"WHAT'S THAT?" I motioned to the large tote bag Nicole plopped down on her living room floor. Lime green with a multicolored beach scene—two blue-and-white-striped beach chairs resting on yellow sand, a bright green umbrella, and a red pail and shovel—beneath pale-blue script that read: *Destin, Florida, Jewel of the Emerald Coast*. Nothing stealthy about it.

"You have your spy bag," Nicole said. "And I have mine."

My "spy bag" was an incredibly stealthy black canvas duffel filled with electronic and surveillance goodies I had raided from Ray's closet. Actually closets. He had three filled with gadgets.

"Spy bag?" I asked.

She propped her hands on her hips. "Yours has all that night vision and other fancy stuff. Mine has the essentials."

"Such as?"

She nudged the bag with a sneaker toe. "Blanket, tablecloth, a wonderful Stilton cheese, French bread, strawberries, and wine. Two bottles. Good stuff I snagged from my uncle's wine cellar."

"Two bottles?"

"You said it could be a long night."

"Not if we drink two bottles of wine."

She rolled her eyes.

"Besides, this isn't a picnic," I said.

"Doesn't mean we can't have fun. I mean, you did say that stakeouts were boring so I'm just adding a little interest."

Which she had already done with her outfit. We both wore all black but my sweatpants and t-shirt were downright pedestrian compared to her painted-on tights and tank top. Maybe wine wasn't such a bad idea.

I glanced at my watch: 9:30. "Let's get moving."

Nicole saluted. "Roger that, General."

"General?"

"You're in charge so why not be a general? General Jake Longly." She laughed. "Sounds like one of those Civil War dudes."

"So what's your rank?"

She glanced toward the ceiling, her forehead furrowed in thought. "Maybe Major."

"Like Major Major?"

She laughed. "*Catch 22*, right?"

"You got it. Actually his name was Major Major Major so with his rank he became Major Major Major Major."

"I'm impressed," she said.

"That I knew that?"

"That you can read." She gave my arm a playful punch.

We tugged on black windbreakers and grabbed our "spy bags." Down the wooden deck steps, across the deep sugary sand until we reached firmer footing near the gently lapping waterline, where we turned around the point and headed up the beach. Most of the homes we passed were dark, vacation homes that sat empty much of the year, while others showed signs of life. On one massive deck two couples sat around a fire pit, their voices and laughter spilling down the beach toward us. They seemed to give us little notice.

Soon we eased past Tammy's place, dark except for a single lamp in the den. The nightlight she always left on. She and hubby Walter were either out or had turned in early. Early for Tammy, anyway.

Two houses down sat the massive two-story Plummer home. It was dark.

I stopped and pointed. "That's it."

"Who are we spying on anyway?"

"Not spying. Surveilling."

"Potatoes, po-TAH-toes. So, who are we *surveilling*?"

"The Plummers."

"Plumbers live there?"

I laughed. "Not plumbers. The Plummers. Henry and Barbara."

Now she laughed. "I knew plumbers made good money but I didn't think that good."

"You obviously haven't had clogged pipes lately. I pay my doctor less. Do you know them? The Plummers?"

"No."

"Henry made a gazillion bucks in software and took up real estate development as a second career. Apparently a very lucrative endeavor. Shopping centers, condo projects, and a couple of gated communities, I understand."

"Not bad for a second career."

I began walking again. "We'll set up among those dunes." I pointed to a series of sea-oat-topped wrinkles in the sand just beyond the Plummers' home. "They'll supply good cover."

We settled in a sandy depression between two low mounds. While Nicole spread out the blanket and retrieved bread, cheese, and wine from her bag, I set up the camera and laptop Ray had given me. He had said that since I was "going mobile," meaning not sitting in the car, this rig would help. I screwed the camera to a sturdy tripod, whose legs I wiggled into the sand to stabilize it. Satisfied it wouldn't topple over, I extended the tripod's neck until the camera lens rode above the wispy sea oats. I attached a small shotgun mic to the camera, cabling both to the computer, and plugged in a pair of ear buds. I booted up the computer, and once that process was completed, an image of the house appeared on the screen.

Nicole handed me a glass of wine. Not a plastic cup, a crystal goblet. She did have a certain flair. Actually, lots of flairs.

"What's all this?" she asked.

"Best way to watch the house without crawling around in the grass. We can stay off the radar, so to speak, and still see and hear everything. Record it, too. Watch this." Using the up and down, right and left, and plus and minus keys, I changed the camera's alignment and zoomed in and out.

"Very cool."

"Ray does have some fun toys. This is standard lighting." I tapped the "2" key. "This is low light." The image immediately brightened, revealing the house in greater detail. I tapped the "3" key. The image took on a hazy green glow. "This is night vision."

"Wow."

"Not done yet." I tapped the "4" key. Now the image went darker. "Nothing to see right now. This is infrared. Picks up body heat. If someone was up there, either in or around the house, they'd show up."

"What's that?" She pointed to the screen.

A small yellow-orange form moved across the rear patio. I zoomed in, revealing an unmistakable feline shape. "A cat." I returned the image to the low light mode. The cat's silhouette faded into the shadows.

"Your spy bag is much cooler than mine," she said.

"But not edible."

"There is that. Cheese?"

"Sure. Seems like dinner was a long time ago."

She laughed. "See, my spy bag has its uses."

We ate and drank, finishing the first bottle of wine in no time. I placed the laptop on my now empty canvas bag, next to the blanket, and stretched out on my back. "Now we wait."

Nicole sat next to me, cross-legged, munching on a strawberry. In the moonlight, the strawberry juice glistened on her lips. She then sucked the juice off each finger. Slowly. One at a time. Staring directly at me.

"Are you being naughty?" I asked.

"Of course."

"Thought so."

"Roll over," she said.

I did. She straddled my hips and began massaging my neck and upper back.

"Best stakeout ever," I said.

She continued her massage and then leaned forward and nibbled one ear.

"Definitely the best stakeout ever."

"Bet you say that to all your beach bunnies."

"Beach bunnies? Me?"

"Shut up." She kneaded my shoulders. "You're all tight."

"Wonder why?"

"Stress." Her efforts moved to my mid back, her fingers digging into the muscles along my spine.

"That must be it," I said. "I'm sure you sitting on me has nothing to do with it."

"Are you complaining?"

"Not a chance."

She slid off and stretched out next to me on her back. A soft, warm breeze tickled the sea oats, and I could hear the gentle lapping of the water against the sand. Nicole rolled on her side, snuggling up against me, one arm over my back. Doesn't get much better.

After a few silent minutes, she said, "Tell me about your dad."

"Ray? He's a tough dude. In many ways."

"How so?"

"Ray and I don't often see eye to eye."

"Yet you work for him?"

"No, I'm doing him a favor. He and Pancake are stacked up with cases right now so he asked me to do this little bit of surveillance work." She didn't say anything, so I went on. "Except for my base-ball career, he thinks I'm somewhat of a slacker."

"Are you?"

I twisted my head toward her. "More or less."

"I don't buy that. I mean, you own a business. You had a pro base-ball career. Not exactly underachievement."

"Tell that to Ray. When baseball disappeared, Ray wanted me to join him. Do the PI stuff. Not exactly my thing." I smiled. "Though you make it a little more palatable."

"Palatable? Never been called that."

I raised an eyebrow. "I think I'll let that one slide."

"And your mother? What about her?"

"We lost her when I was in college. Cancer."

"I'm sorry."

"Wasn't easy, but that was a long time ago."

She started to say something, but I stopped her with a raise of my hand. The computer screen had flickered to life.

"Here she is," I said.

We sat up, side by side. Car lights flared, flashed across the screen, and then disappeared into the garage. A minute later an in-terior light popped on. I zoomed in as Barbara Plummer entered her kitchen. She was slim and attractive in a silver dress that ap-peared to be silk. She opened a bottle of wine, poured a glass, and headed upstairs. An upper light snapped on. I tapped the keyboard, adjusting the camera angle. Bedroom. The curtains were open, but sheers covered the French doors. Barbara's silhouette moved in and out of view.

"Looks like she's headed to bed," Nicole said.

"Or prepping for a visitor."

"Let's hope."

"You're quite the voyeur," I said.

"You're the one with the camera."

She had a point.

Barbara came back down to the kitchen, refilled her wine glass, and then flowed into the den. I settled one earbud in place, Nicole the other one. After adjusting the filters to dampen the noise of the breeze, soft jazz filled my ear.

"The trap is set," Nicole said.

"Trap? You women are all alike."

"Poor baby." She mussed my hair. "Helpless and vulnerable. Adrift in a world of wanton women."

"My favorite kind."

"You and the others of your ilk."

"Ilk?"

"The half of the planet's population with dicks."

Hard to argue with that logic.

For the next fifteen minutes little happened. Barbara refilled her wine glass once more, but mostly sat on the sofa, head back against the cushions, apparently enjoying the music.

Then a shadow moved across the screen. I adjusted the zoom and lightened the image. A man. Maybe six feet, slightly overweight. Shorts, golf-type shirt. He climbed onto the broad deck that faced the beach and extended the length of the house. As he reached the back door, Barbara opened it for him. They embraced.

"Showtime," I said.

"Now who's the voyeur?"

"Strictly business."

"Right."

They entered the kitchen where Barbara poured a glass of wine for her visitor. His back was toward us so I couldn't see his face. Barbara laughed at something he said. Adjusting the gain on the shotgun mic, I honed in on their conversation.

"Any trouble getting out?" Barbara asked.

"None. She drank a bottle of wine with dinner. She's zonked out."

"How long do we have?"

"A couple of hours, anyway."

"What if she wakes up?"

"The usual. Couldn't sleep. Went for a walk on the beach."

They embraced again. He spun her around and they kissed. When the kiss broke, he stepped back and looked at her. Now I could see his face.

"Oh, Jesus."

"What is it?" Nicole asked.

"It's Walter. My ex's husband."

"No way. He's her secret lover?"

"Sure looks that way," I said.

"Not who you were expecting, huh?"

"Not even close. Walter's mostly a wimp."

"Even wimps have erections," Nicole said. "And those always lead to trouble."

"Sounds like the voice of experience."

"I've raised a couple in my life."

"Only a couple?"

"I'll take the Fifth."

"I'll let you in on a little secret," I said. "You raise more than a couple simply walking across the street."

"That's good to know."

Like she didn't know it. Get real.

Back to work. We watched Walter and Barbara climb the stairs to her bedroom. Barbara slid back the sheers and opened two of the French doors that looked out over the deck and the beach. The lights went out.

For the next two hours there was little to see, but the shotgun mic picked up a few unintelligible murmurs, soft laughter, and several "Oh, Gods," but mostly a rustling of the sheets and heavy breathing. They surely made the most of their two hours together.

To say it was a bit uncomfortable listening to my ex-wife's husband doing the dirty with his lover didn't quite cover what I was feeling. I kept telling myself it was a job, nothing more, but mostly I felt dirty and intrusive. Nicole apparently felt my discomfort. And didn't pass on the opportunity to tweak me.

"He's an animal," she said.

"Not exactly my image of dear old Walter."

"The evidence is what it is."

Finally, thankfully, they fell silent and a few minutes later Walter came back down stairs. He flicked off the kitchen and den lights, stepped out the back door, looked up and down the beach, and hurried back up the sand toward home.

We waited a few minutes but saw no further movement and heard nothing else from the Plummer residence.

"After a workout like that she's going to sleep like a log," Nicole said.

"You aren't going to let it go, are you?"

"Of course not."

I stood. "I think our work here is done. Let's pack up and get out of here."

Back at Nicole's we finished the second bottle of wine, while sitting on the sofa. After a few kisses and some handsy explorations, Nicole asked, "Hot tub?"

"I didn't bring a swim suit."

"Me either." She stood and pulled me to my feet. "Come on. You won't rust."

The hot tub, a redwood rectangle that could hold an entire football team, sat in one corner of the deck, beneath a canopy. She peeled off her tank top, revealing a pair of small firm breasts. Then her tights, leaving behind black thong panties. Those disappeared, too. No tan lines. Guess the point of The Point was perfect for nude sunbathing. She eased into the bubbling water, cool blue from the underwater lighting.

"Don't be bashful," she said.

I had to admit that the past twenty-four hours hadn't turned out as expected. Not even close. Sleeping on her sofa last night and now this. Was this a dream? Seemed to me that exchanging a couple of broken car windows for this was a pretty good deal. Maybe I should thank Tammy. After all, it was her insanity, her bashing my car, that lit Nicole's curiosity.

I stripped and settled in the tub, across from where she sat on one of the underwater benches. Still not sure exactly where this was going.

She glided through the water, climbed into my lap, straddling my legs. Her lips settled over mine. When the kiss broke, I asked, "Is this a good idea?"

"You seem to think so." She reached down and grasped my already full erection.

"I hate it when he does that."

"No you don't."

Her lovemaking could only be described as aggressive. She rode like a rodeo star. Water sloshed over us. The deck, too. Little I could do but hold on and try to make it last.

I failed.

Later, after another round of bumping in her super king bed, we were both frosted with sweet sweat. She pulled open the drawer of the bedside table, retrieved a joint and a purple gas station lighter, and fired it up. She took a long hit. "Want some?"

I did.

After we each took a couple of hits, she balanced the remainder of the blunt on the edge of the nightstand and slid into the crook of my arm, her head resting against my chest.

"You aren't the shy type, are you?" I asked.

"I'm a California girl. Hookups are in our nature."

"Nice to be a hookup."

"Better than being off the hook," she said.

"Shut up and come here."

"Hmmm. Bossy."

Round three. Afterwards we lay in each other's arms, catching our breath.

"You're kind of fun," she said.

"More than your bartender boyfriend?"

"Much more."

"I *know* he wouldn't want to hear that."

She laughed. "He's in the archives now, anyway."

"Archives?"

"You know—history. Out of here. Past tense."

"Cold."

"Honest."

"At the risk of examining something that might be better unexamined," I said, "why did you go out with him?"

"He was funny. Witty and charming. Great in a crowd. Not so much one on one."

"So, what do I have? Maybe a week before I'm in the archives, too?"

"We'll see." She pinched me. "But so far, you're okay."

"Just okay?"

"Let's say very okay."

I was smart enough to let that lay. Or is it lie? Never could keep those straight.

# CHAPTER SIX

THE NEXT MORNING, I opened my eyes at exactly 8:11. According to the bedside clock. I rolled over. No Nicole. The aroma of coffee filled the air. I found my sweatpants wadded on the floor, stepped into them, and staggered to the kitchen. Too much wine last night. Maybe too much Nicole.

She stood over the marble cooktop island, spatula in hand. She wore an oversized t-shirt, black, AC/DC logo on the front. Her perfectly tanned, perfect legs bare. Feet, too.

On second thought there was no way to have too much Nicole.

"Guess you worked up an appetite last night," I said.

"Proud of yourself, are you?"

"Something like that."

A tongue of steam rose from the skillet before her. "You do deserve an 'atta boy.'"

"That's what I strive for."

She pointed the spatula at me. "Actually, you were magnificent."

"As were you."

"Thank God. I'd hate to think I was merely adequate." She smiled. "Or is it palatable?"

"Definitely the latter." I pulled out one of the island stools and sat down. "What are you making?"

"Pancakes. That okay?"

"Love a woman with an appetite."

"That's me."

She slid a large pancake from the skillet onto a plate and sat it on the counter before me. "Now shut up and eat." She handed me a squeeze bottle of syrup.

"Yes, ma'am." I sloshed on a dose of syrup and took a bite. "Perfect," I said around the mouthful.

"Me, or the food?" She poured more batter into the skillet.

"These are great, but I think I like you better."

"All of me?" She grinned.

"Some parts are better than others, but I can't say I found any faults."

"You obviously haven't looked hard enough."

"Really? I thought I looked everywhere."

She laughed. "That you did."

"You're beautiful, smart, funny, and you can cook. The whole package."

"Pancakes aren't exactly gourmet fare."

"Works for me."

"But you're easy," she said.

"You noticed. I'm flattered."

My cell phone chimed. I could barely hear it since it was still inside my "spy bag" over by the French doors where I had left it last night. By the time I retrieved it, the call had jumped to voice mail. The screen said I'd missed three calls and two text messages. All in the last hour. All from Ray.

Ray answered after a single ring. "You don't answer your phone anymore?" No "hello" or "how are you?" So Ray.

"Sorry. Didn't have the phone nearby."

"Where are you?" he asked.

"At a friend's place."

"That explains it."

"What's up?" I asked.

"I was fixing to ask you that same question. You got anything to tell me about last night?"

"Actually, I do. Barbara had a visitor. You'll never guess who."

"Don't have time for games." Also so Ray.

"Walter Horton."

There was a brief hesitation as Ray processed that little tidbit. Then, "You sure?"

"Yep. Got it all recorded."

"Not who I expected."

"Me either. Tammy will go nuclear."

"That's what she does best. Anything else you got to say?"

Did I? Was I forgetting something? No, Walter being Barbara's lover about covered all the news I had. "Like what?"

"Like why cops are crawling all over her place."

"Tammy's?"

"No, Barbara Plummer's."

"What?"

Nicole stood against the island, coffee cup in hand, looking at me. She started to say something, but I held up a finger.

"Did I stutter?" Ray asked.

"That makes no sense."

"Apparently it does to the local PD."

"Why are they there?"

"Don't know yet," Ray said. "Got a call in to Bob Morgan."

"Homicide Bob Morgan?"

"All I know is that he's on the scene. And he wouldn't be there unless he had to be."

This was getting weird. Or weirder. First Walter humping Barbara. Now a homicide detective at her house. I felt the hair on my neck rise. I hate that feeling. The one that said things were likely even worse than they seemed. And they seemed bad. Did Walter kill Barbara? Right in front of Nicole and me? While we sat in the sand watching and listening to the entire affair? Affair being the operative word. I hadn't heard anything that sounded like a struggle or a gunshot or yelling or anything. Of course smothering and strangulation didn't make much noise.

*Slow down. Don't assume anything.*

"I've left him a couple of messages," Ray said, "but it seems no one is returning my calls."

"I did."

"Eventually."

"Funny," I said. "I'm just up the street. I'll venture down that way and see what's going on."

"Be cool."

Be cool. Ray speak. He didn't mean hip or with it or any of that type of cool. Be cool was Ray's code for giving nothing away. More than simply keeping your mouth shut, your face flat, expressionless, giving away nothing. But also never look away, never smile, never express surprise or anger or any emotion, never give a clue as to what you're thinking. Be cool.

"You mean like don't give them what I recorded last night?" I asked.

"Especially what you recorded last night."

"Isn't that withholding evidence or something?"

"It's called protecting a client's privacy," Ray said.

"Is that legal in a homicide?"

Nicole's eyes widened. I shook my head and again raised a finger.

"If this is a homicide," Ray said.

"Must be if Morgan's there."

"I guess it depends on who did what to who and why. But I'll handle all that. Just stay cool." He sighed. "Something doesn't feel right here."

*Ain't it so.*

"Just see what the story is," Ray said. "Don't dig around. Not yet. Not until we know more. Then we'll sit down and decide how to handle the video."

"Will do."

"And do not engage Morgan. Play dumb. I'm sure you can do that." Ray, my father. "In fact, avoid him completely if possible."

"Got it."

# CHAPTER SEVEN

ONE OF THE many tricks I had co-opted from Ray was to always have several outfits on hand. For Ray, that and a few disguises were part of the job, part of staying below the radar. Whatever he might need to "be invisible" or "be someone else" as he put it. For me, it was a bit different. Whether at my own bar, or trolling the other local watering holes, I often ended up crashing somewhere other than home and having extra clothes and toiletries in my car saved a lot of shuffling. One night stands being what one night stands are. I know, I know, piggish at best, but at least I was always prepared. Like an Eagle Scout.

Another sore point between Ray and me. For some reason he didn't accept running a bar and chasing bikinis as a real job. Seemed to work for me, so what the hell. Ray felt I only had two options: hurling fastballs or working for him. The former was a previous life and the latter not really an option. For me, anyway.

I stepped outside, snatched my gym bag from the rear seat floor-board of Ray's pickup where I had dropped it, and carried it inside.

"When are you going to tell me what's going on?" Nicole asked.

"As soon as I know."

She jammed her fists against her hips. "And when exactly will that be?"

"As soon as we wander down the street and have a chat with the cops."

"What cops?"

"The ones that are snooping around Barbara Plummer's place."

"You're kidding? Is it the homicide cop you were talking to Ray about?"

"I suspect so."

"Someone was murdered? At her house?" Her eyes widened. "Was it Barbara?"

"I guess we'll see."

"Then quit fooling around and let's go."

"Give me a sec." I began sorting through the items inside my bag: workout togs, sweats, jeans, tees, windbreaker, a suit, shirt, and tie rolled inside a plastic garment bag, and an assortment of shoes and caps.

"What's that stuff?" Nicole asked.

"Clothes."

"You carry a closet around with you?"

"Never know what you'll need."

"You're a regular Boy Scout," she said.

"Eagle Scout."

"Of course you are."

I think she was being sarcastic but I chose to let it slide.

I selected a pair of jeans and a blue polo. Plain, vanilla, functional. Nicole, on the other hand, wore painted-on jeans and a silky black long-sleeved pullover that hugged everything, sleeves pushed up to her elbows, hair combed out and scrunchied into a long ponytail, no makeup. She looked stunning.

We jumped into her SL and she fired it down the street, covering the half mile at warp factor four. She slid to a stop across from the Plummer home. Three uniforms stood in the front yard. They looked up, irritation etching their faces. Probably deciding whether or not to hand out a speeding ticket. Their collective expressions changed to ones of awe as Nicole stepped out. She had that effect on all of us with XY chromosomes. Probably on most with an XX pattern, too. I think she just racked up three more erections. She was on a roll.

We crossed the street and approached the gathered officers.

"What's going on?" I asked.

"Who are you?" one of the officers asked.

"Longly. Jake Longly. This is Nicole Jamison."

He heard me, I think, but he wasn't really paying attention to me. Instead his gaze devoured Nicole. Finally, he said, "You know the folks who live here?"

"Not really."

Now he looked my way, his head cocked to one side. "That sounds like a qualified no. Do you or don't you?"

"Never met them."

"Then what's your interest here?"

"Just curious. All this activity looks like something big."

This activity consisted of the three officers, four patrol units, two unmarked cars, and the ME's van, which squatted in the driveway.

"Just curious?" the uniform asked. "You know anything about this?"

"This what?"

"Jake Longly?" The voice boomed from the front door where another uniformed officer stood. I recognized him immediately. The no-nonsense Blake Cooper. Just great.

"What the hell are you doing here?" Cooper asked as he walked toward us.

"Says he's curious," the first officer said.

Cooper ignored him and asked me, "You know anything about this?"

"Like I told Officer . . ." I nodded toward him.

"Coffman. Charlie Coffman."

"Like I told Officer Coffman, we saw all the activity and stopped to see what the story was."

"The story is there's a woman inside. Mrs. Henry Plummer. She's been murdered."

"Really?"

"No, I'm making it up. Of course, really."

His attitude was a shade less friendly than it had been the night Tammy five-ironed my car windows. Maybe several shades.

"We didn't know," I said.

Cooper fixed his glare on me, holding it, and then said, "Do you see my problem? The other night I have to run you off. Lurking just up the street. In a neighborhood that isn't yours. And now like magic here you are again."

"Last time I was working. This morning we were just heading out for breakfast."

"And exactly where were you last night?"

"With me," Nicole said.

Cooper's face gathered an expression that said, "Yeah, right." I understood his confusion. I still hadn't figured out how I ended up hanging with a woman like Nicole. Some things defy explanation.

Cooper then gave Nicole an up and down, pausing here and there, taking her in. "All night?"

"Not that it's any of your business, but yes, he was. And he was magnificent."

She was good. Very good. Seemed to knock some of the wind out of Cooper's sails.

"Look, Ms . . ."

"Nicole. I live just up the street."

"And just happened by?"

"Like Jake said, we were going out for breakfast and saw all this."

"And you're his alibi?"

"Not that he needs one, but sure." She propped her fists on her hips. "And he's mine." She smiled. "In case I'm a suspect, too."

Did I say she was good? Very good? No hesitation, no nervousness. She jumped right into the lie and took off with it. Pretty good acting job.

"Didn't say either of you were suspects," Cooper said.

"Sounded like it to me," Nicole said.

Cooper shoved his hands in his pockets, rocked back on his heels, and looked back at me. Mostly. His gaze kept bouncing in Nicole's direction. "See, the part that bugs me is that this is one hell of a coincidence. Bumping into you here the other night. And now this. At a murder scene."

"Don't know what to tell you," I said.

Cooper rattled what sounded like keys in his pocket. "I don't believe in coincidences. Mainly because they never are. Seems they usually end up connected."

"Can't argue with that."

"So, tell me again. Why were you here the other night?"

"Doing surveillance."

"For Longly Investigations, right? Your dad's firm?"

I nodded. "That's right."

"Staking out who?"

"Can't say."

"Wasn't Mrs. Plummer, was it?" Cooper asked.

"Still can't say."

"I could run you in. Bright lights. Hard interrogation. All that crap."

"My answer would still be the same. I don't know anything about a murder and can't talk about a client."

"So she—the dead woman—Mrs. Plummer—she wasn't your target?"

I chose not to respond. Or smile. Or look away from Cooper's firm gaze. Be cool. The silence that followed was thick. And uncomfortable.

Cooper nodded as if saying, "So that's the way it's going to be?" Then he spoke. "Detective Morgan's inside. Bet he has a few questions for you."

Ray's admonition to avoid Morgan echoed in my head. The plan was to chat with someone lower down the food chain. Like Cooper, or Coffman. Grab a few details and hit the road. Of course, running into Morgan was always a possibility. After all it was his crime scene. But Morgan wasn't Cooper. Not even close. He was tough and didn't take *no* well. A bulldog and not above bending the rules. I'd heard that hard interrogations under Morgan could be harmful to your health. Since we had what we needed, that a murder had occurred and that Barbara was the victim, I decided it was time to vacate the premises.

"Sure," I said. "Tell him to call me any time."

Cooper nodded to one of the uniforms who headed toward the front door. "He'll be out here in a minute."

"Wish I had time, but we have to run."

Cooper straightened his spine, tried to appear authoritative and in control. "Breakfast can wait."

"Not really. You see, Nicole has hypoglycemia and she's sinking fast." I didn't wait for a response. I grabbed Nicole's arm and directed her toward her SL.

"I'd suggest you wait," Cooper said. "Morgan won't be happy if he has to track you down."

"I'm easy to find." I tossed a wave over my shoulder.

"Some folks just can't get out of their own way," Cooper said.

As we climbed into Nicole's car, I saw Morgan. Coming out the front door, talking with a crime scene tech.

"Move it," I said. "Let's get out of here."

She fired up the SL, hung a U, tires chirping, and raced back up the street.

"What was that about?" Nicole asked.

"Morgan. Tough SOB. I'd rather let Ray deal with him. They're about equal on the tough SOB scale."

"And you're not? Poor baby."

"Now you're a comedian?"

"I have my moments," she said. "Where now?"

"Go up around the bend and pull over."

She did.

I called Ray. "The victim's Barbara Plummer."

"I figured," Ray sighed.

"I managed to dodge Morgan but I'm sure he'll be pointed our way soon enough."

"No doubt. Head on back over here and we'll come up with a game plan."

"I think I'll stop by and have a chat with Walter first."

"Good idea," Ray said.

Me? Good idea? Was this really Ray?

Ray continued. "Get a feel for his stress level. See what he does and doesn't know."

"Before Morgan even knows he's on the radar?"

"Exactly."

"I know Walter," I said. "He's a great attorney but a shitty poker player. Never can hide what he's thinking. If Barbara's murder is news to him, I'll know."

"And if it's not?"

"I'll know that, too." Ray didn't respond so I continued. "Should I tell him we know about the affair? About the video we made?"

"Better if it comes from you than from the police." I heard Ray sigh. "And it wouldn't hurt to let him know that we'll have to give Morgan the video. I'm sure he'd appreciate the heads up."

"When will that happen?"

"As soon as he asks for it. Which will be as soon as he knows we were watching Barbara Plummer. Hate to do that to Walter, but we can't withhold that. Besides, he's not our client. Henry Plummer is."

"Okay. I'll be over there soon."

"Be cool."

"Always." I disconnected the call.

"What now?" Nicole asked.

"Wait a few minutes. Then we'll ease back down to Walter and Tammy's. I want to see if Walter's home."

"Why not just call him?"

"Need to see his face when I talk to him. Gauge where his head's at."

"Makes sense."

"If you can creep this German rocket ship and not drive like Speed Racer."

She stuck her tongue out at me. It was a nice tongue. Pink and perfect. Like everything else Nicole.

# CHAPTER EIGHT

"WHAT DO YOU want, Jake?" the ever-pleasant Tammy said when she answered my knock.

Nicole had managed to control her lead foot long enough to ease back down the street and turn into Tammy's drive, snugging up close to the garage door where a thick shrub partially hid the car. It wasn't easy for her, being a Danica Patrick clone. I complimented her. Another tongue directed in my direction.

When I suggested she stay in the car, Nicole said, "No problem. I've seen what the woman can do with a golf club."

Smart move. Tammy wasn't thrilled to see me at her door and Nicole would probably have caused her DNA to unravel. Tammy had both fists jammed on her hips, head to one side, a plush white towel around her neck. Soft music drifted out the door. She wore sweat-stained gray tights and a pink tee, her face flushed and moist. Home Pilates no doubt. Tammy was big on Pilates. And about every other fad that swept through her world. What else did she have to do now that she had married all the money she'd ever need?

"Is Walter here?" I asked.

"Why?"

"Need to talk to him."

Her eyes narrowed. "About what?"

"I'll save that for him."

She looked past me toward the car. "Who's that?"

"A friend."

She squinted, shielding the morning sun from her eyes with one hand. "Is that who I think it is?"

"Depends on who you think it is." Did Tammy know Nicole? They lived in the same neighborhood after all.

"You know the one I'm talking about. Little blond, big tits."

Several possibilities ran through my mind. "You're going to have to help me here."

She slugged my shoulder. She always liked to do that. Sometimes a rib shot. Those hurt more. Sometimes taking my breath away.

"Asshole," she said.

"We aren't married anymore. You can't hit me."

She cocked her fist. "Try me."

"Look, you're trying to make a point. I'm trying to help you here."

She shook her head. "The point is you're a pig."

"So you've said."

"The girl. She was the golf pro over at the country club. Liked to screw on the seventh green."

"Sarah Jane. She liked some of the others, too. But, yes, I think the seventh was her favorite."

"How good for you."

"No, that's not her."

She looked past my shoulder again. "Then who's the new bimbo?"

"She's not a bimbo."

"If she's with you, she's a bimbo."

"She's actually a nun. Or a supermodel. Or a neurosurgeon. I forget which."

"Jake, I'm busy." A patrol car slid by. She stepped out on the porch and her gaze followed it. Then she saw all the other police cars. "What's going on?"

"Don't know. Probably an alarm went off by accident."

"All those cars? I don't think so."

"Maybe a burglary."

"In this neighborhood?"

"Is Walter here or not?" I asked.

"No. He's doing a deposition later today so he's at his office prepping."

"I'll catch him there." I turned and headed toward the drive.

"Jake, you need an appointment."

I waved and climbed in the car. Tammy walked off the porch into her yard and stared down toward the Plummers' house. I knew she'd go check it out. It was in her nature to nose into everything and this would be too much to pass up. Then she'd call Walter. Not good. I wanted to talk with him before she had a chance to tell him what was going on. Of course, if he did indeed kill Barbara, he already knew. The evidence at least suggested he just might have been the last person to see her alive.

Was that why Barbara hadn't walked him to the door last night? Locked up after he left? Last night I had assumed she was too tired to get up, after a couple of hours of horizontal dancing with, as Nicole put it, the "Animal." But maybe she'd been too dead to get up. Things didn't look good for old Walter.

"Where to?" Nicole asked when I climbed back in the SL.

"Walter's office."

"Where's that?"

"Orange Beach. The Wharf."

"Got it."

"And step on it," I said.

"Music to my ears."

The tires spun and squealed and we were off. Should have taken fifteen minutes. Took about seven.

# CHAPTER NINE

TAMMY WATCHED THE red SL slide around the corner and out of sight. Jake and his goddamn girl toys. She was absolutely sure it was that golf-course-loving bitch in the car. Her hair seemed a little longer and a little straighter but it was just as blond. Had to be her. She was also sure he had brought her along just to rub it in her face. All those years of him hiding his escapades and now this? He was such an insufferable prick.

She couldn't deal with that right now. She had other fish to fry. She turned her attention toward the Plummers'. What the hell was going on? Was it a burglary? Something worse? Whatever it was, this many police meant it was juicy. And she was damn sure going to find out before Betsy Friedman did. Then a disturbing thought— What if Betsy already knew? She did live directly across the street from Barbara and Henry. And her nose could sniff out a story in a nanosecond. Gossip was high-value currency in this neighborhood and one-upping Betsy was Tammy's top priority. Tammy would be the one to dig up the facts. She would be the one everyone invited over for coffee, the one they relied on for information. Not that bitch.

She stepped back inside and inspected herself in the mirror that filled one wall of the entry alcove. Her face was flushed, her hair a mess, sweat stains on her clothes, no makeup. Maybe a shower and a change of clothes first. But that might be just the delay Betsy needed. Screw it. They were just cops after all. Not really important. Well, maybe important when you needed them, but right now she didn't. Except for whatever tidbits of information she could weasel out of them.

She gave her reflection a closer look. Did she really want to go out in public looking like this? What if someone took a photo and posted it online? Of course, the cops wouldn't, but Betsy sure as hell would. She'd done it before. Last summer. On the beach. Said she only posted it so her grandkids up in Minnesota could see the sun-drenched beach. Sorry that Tammy's butt protruded into the picture. Lower right corner. Hanging out of her bathing suit at just the right angle to appear saggy. And that was one thing she did not have. She worked hard at keeping it high and tight.

She turned sideways, inspecting her rear. Perfect, even if she did say so herself. So to hell with Betsy and off she went.

As she neared the Plummers', two uniformed officers climbed into one of the squad cars and raced up the street. A third walked up the sidewalk toward the front door.

"Excuse me?" Tammy said.

The officer stopped and turned toward her. She recognized him. Couldn't remember his name but he was the guy from the other night.

"Mrs. Horton," he said. "What can I do for you?"

Now she saw his name tag: Officer B. Cooper.

"What's going on?" Tammy asked.

"I take it you know the Plummers." Cooper said. It was sort of a question but more a statement the way he said it.

"Yes. They're very close friends."

"I'm sorry."

She didn't like the sound of that.

Cooper continued. "Mrs. Plummer was murdered last night."

Her breath literally left her body. She felt dizzy and staggered a step.

He grabbed her arm, steadying her. "Whoa. You okay?"

"Murdered? When? How? Who?" The questions in her head went to war, each trampling the other in an effort to get out.

"Can't tell you any more than that. Just that Barbara Plummer was murdered."

A man in jeans, a white golf shirt, and a gray jacket came down the front steps toward them. "What's going on here, Cooper?" he asked as he drew near.

"Lives up the street," Cooper said, as if that explained anything.

"I'm Tammy Horton," Tammy said. "I live right there." She pointed toward her house.

The man didn't bother to look that way but rather kept his eyes focused on her. His gaze seemed overly intense. As if she were a suspect or something.

"I'm Detective Bob Morgan," he said. Then, "You related to Walter Horton?"

"My husband." She couldn't resist a glance toward Betsy's house, half expecting to see her charging across the street. Trying to steal her gossip before she even had it. No Betsy. She looked back at Morgan. "What happened?"

"Can't say."

"But Barbara was murdered?"

Morgan now leveled a harsh glare at Cooper, but when his gaze came back to her it seemed to soften. He gave her a slight nod. "That's correct."

"Who would have done such a thing? Here in this neighborhood?"

"That's what we're trying to uncover," Morgan said. "Did you see anything unusual last night?"

"Like what?"

"Anything out of the ordinary. Maybe someone driving by? Or walking around the area? Anyone who shouldn't be here?"

Tammy shook her head. "Not last night."

"Not just last night. Any time lately."

"Just Jake. My ex. Snooping around my house."

Morgan glanced at Cooper. "That the incident you told me about?"

"Yep."

Then to Tammy, Morgan said, "You know anyone who might have issues with Barbara Plummer?"

"No. She was a lovely woman."

He shrugged. "What about her and Henry? Any troubles in paradise?"

"Lord, no. They were a perfect couple. Loved each other very much. You don't think Henry did this, do you?"

"Do you?"

"Of course not. Henry's a sweet man. He would never . . . " She couldn't even finish her thought. Henry? Kill Barbara? Not possible. How could this detective guy stand here and ask such questions? She wasn't stupid. She knew that's what cops do. Suspect everyone. Especially the spouse. Even the cops on TV did that. But here? On The Point? Maybe up in Birmingham or over in Atlanta such things happened but not here.

"Heard that before." Morgan shrugged. "But Henry has a pretty good alibi. He's in New York."

"That's right. I forgot." She looked at the house, its image blurring as tears collected in her eyes. "Does he know?"

"Yeah. I called him. He's scrambling for a flight home right now."

She sniffed and wiped a hand across her nose. "This will kill him."

He nodded. "I might have more questions for you later." He handed her a card. "If you think of anything, let me know."

She didn't look at the card, her gaze fixed on Barbara and Henry's front door. What had happened in there? As images from movies, from all those *Forensic Files* shows she watched, began to form she yanked her thoughts back.

"I've got to call Walter," she said more to herself than to Morgan. She turned toward her home but stood there for a minute. Her feet seemed frozen as if she had forgotten how to walk. "I've got to call Walter," she repeated.

# CHAPTER TEN

THE WHARF WAS one of those mixed-use areas that had a marina, popular with fishermen and recreational boaters, both sailors and powerboaters; a coffee shop that also served pastries, salads, sandwiches, and free Wi-Fi; three busy restaurants; a bank of expensive condominiums; and a two-story professional building that housed the offices of Horton, Levine, and Steen; Walter Horton being the founder and senior partner.

Nicole and I took the stairs to the second floor, pushed through double glass doors, and entered Walter's world. Classy. Top drawer all the way. Soft colors, deep sofas, and smooth jazz that seemed to ooze from the walls. Two people occupied the waiting area: a young woman working on a laptop; an older, well-dressed man thumbing through a copy of *Field and Stream*, the cover showing a slick green largemouth bass arching from the water, a red-feathered lure hooked in its lip. A middle-aged, stern-faced woman looked up from her anchorage behind the reception desk. The name plate identified her as Constance Streelman, Executive Assistant. She wore a white blouse beneath a gray jacket, glasses hanging from a gold chain around her neck, and a frown that suggested she wasn't having a good day. When she looked up she did manage a smile. Sort of. Seemed a bit forced.

"Can I help you?" she asked.

"Need to talk with Walter," I said.

"And you are?"

"Jake Longly."

Her gaze shifted to Nicole, a disapproving look, and then back to me. "You don't have an appointment."

"I know. But I think he'll want to talk to me."

"About?"

"It's private."

"I'm sorry. He's very busy."

"Let him know I'm here. I think he'll find the time."

She hesitated as if deciding exactly how far to push this and then snatched up the phone. After buzzing through to Walter, explaining that Jake Longly "desired a minute," her exact words, she hung up and stood. "Follow me." She was not happy.

Walter's office was spacious, also classy, and definitely expensive. He sat behind his massive desk, top littered with stacks of paper, a thick binder open before him. He stood. His eyes traveled to Nicole.

I dropped in one of the chairs that faced Walter's desk, Nicole in the other.

"This is Nicole," I said.

"Nice to meet you." Then to me, "What can I do for you, Jake?"

"Barbara Plummer. You know her?"

The look on his face suggested that that's not exactly what he expected. Tension lines formed at the corners of his eyes. Not a good reveal for a poker player. Or a trial lawyer, for that matter. But that was Walter. One of those faces that was an open book.

"Sure," Walter said. "She and Henry live near us. Why?"

"How well?"

Now he was full-on flustered. "How well do I know her?"

I nodded.

"They're friends. Why?"

"That's it? Just friends?"

He settled back into his chair. "What's this about?"

"When did you see her last?"

"I don't understand."

"It's a simple question." I opened my hands toward him. "When was the last time you saw Barbara Plummer?"

He shuffled some pages on his desk, buying time. The tension lines in his face deepened. "I'm not sure. A few days." He couldn't look at either of us, keeping his attention on the papers.

As a lawyer, Walter was accustomed to asking questions, not answering them. So I guess I could cut him a dab of slack for being out of practice. Or was it fear that I detected in the creases around his slightly narrowed eyes? If so, my next question would likely cause him to implode.

"Not last night?" I asked.

His gaze snapped up to me. "No. Why?"

"She was murdered last night."

He paled and wavered in his chair as if blown off-balance by a strong wind. His pupils expanded, gobbling up the blue of his eyes. Was this news to him or was he surprised things were moving so fast? I couldn't be sure which.

"Barbara? Murdered?" He swallowed hard.

I didn't respond. Waited him out. *Be cool.*

"When? Where?"

"Her home. Where you were last night?"

"I'm afraid you're mistaken."

"I could show you the video."

"Video?" A slight patina of sweat now frosted his forehead. "What are you talking about?"

"Nicole and I filmed you visiting the late Barbara Plummer. You left a little after midnight."

He looked at Nicole. She nodded. "It's true. The video is amazingly clear. So is the audio recording."

"Jesus." His head fell forward and he stared at his desktop.

"Tell me, Walter."

The intercom buzzed. A jerk of surprise and then he punched the button.

"Your wife is on line two."

Tammy. That didn't take long. Not that I thought it would. I was sure she had ventured down the street to see what all the action was about. And that had given us just enough time to reach Walter, see his reaction to the news firsthand, before Tammy could scurry back home and call. Nicole's NASCAR mentality did have certain advantages.

"Thanks, Connie." He took a deep breath and picked up the phone but said nothing, listening. Tammy's voice spilled from the handset. I couldn't make out what she was saying, but the timbre was high, almost hysterical, and the words came out rapidly. It sounded like Minnie raying at Mickey. The half of the conversation I could hear went like this:

"I know. Jake's here."

"He was?" He looked at me.

"I know. I can't believe it either."

"Calm down. I'll see what I can find out."

"I have that deposition."

"No, I can't cancel it. It's already been rescheduled twice."

"I'll be home early."

He hung up.

More paper shuffling. Buying time again. Collecting thoughts, I figured. Finally he looked up. "Why were you two outside Barbara's last night?"

"Can't say. You know that."

"Henry? Did he hire you?"

I stared at him.

Walter loosened his tie. I noticed his fingers trembled and his face seemed even paler, the patina of fear-sweat even more pronounced.

"Look, Barbara and I've been seeing each other," Walter said, his voice weak and hoarse. "A few months." He hesitated. "Actually nearly a year."

"And last night was another conjugal visit?" I asked.

Walter's eyes narrowed in a brief flash of anger but then relaxed. "Yes."

"Let me guess. She was alive and well when you left her?"

"Asleep actually."

That could explain why she didn't see him out last night. Again, I waited. Better to let him stew a bit.

"I swear," he said.

"Doesn't look good, Walter. You sneaking in and out. Her turning up dead."

"Do the police know? About Barbara and me? About the video?"

I shook my head. "Not yet. But they will."

Walter sighed and massaged his temples. "This is a goddamn nightmare."

I stood. "We'll leave you to your work."

Before we could reach the door, Walter said, "Jake? A word?" He glanced at Nicole. "In private."

"I'll wait outside," Nicole said.

After she left, he said, "Two things. First of all, can't you keep this under wraps?"

"Can I? You're the lawyer. What would you advise a client under such circumstances?"

Walter's face collapsed. "To turn everything over."

"Then there you go."

"When will you give them this video?"

"When they ask. And I suspect that'll be soon."

"Why?"

"Because I was in the neighborhood night before last. On a case for Ray. Your always-charming wife hammered my car with a golf club. A cop showed up. Then I saw him again this morning when I stopped by the Plummers' to see what was going on. So, he definitely knows who I am, and I'll definitely be one of those infamous persons of interest."

Walter nodded. "And when they do, you'll have to tell them everything."

"I suspect so. But if and when will be up to Ray. I work for him."

Walter now massaged his neck. "This is unbelievable."

"Did you kill her, Walter?"

"God, no. I . . . "

"You what?"

His eyes glistened. "I loved her."

That was definitely not the answer I expected. Maybe that Barbara was a distraction. One of those things that just seem to happen. A mistake. But this? This was not even in the ballpark. This wasn't even the same sport.

"Oh boy," I said. "Does Tammy know anything? Or suspect anything?"

"No."

"I don't envy you that ordeal. Been there. It ain't pretty."

Walter nodded, his gaze focused on nothing. The thousand-yard stare. Sometimes the light in the tunnel was indeed a train. Guilty or not, Walter was about to be trampled by the system. I almost felt sorry for him. Almost. Didn't quite make up for the hammering old Walter had laid on me during the divorce. Old story. Common story. Woman files for divorce, guts the soon-to-be ex, and then ends up running off with her attorney.

"And the other thing?" I asked.

"That girl." He nodded toward the door.

"Nicole. Her name's Nicole."

"Yeah. I don't appreciate your airing this in front of her."

"It's okay. She's cool. And she was there. Remember?"

"I know what she is. She's another one of your playmates. You don't seem to be able to hold on to them so I see her getting pissed at you and taking it out on me."

"Walter, I don't think you should point fingers considering the current situation. Not to mention dumping a ration of shit on the guy with the film that could make your life a living hell."

"But . . . "

"But nothing. You need all the friends you can rally about now."

"Are you, Jake? A friend?"

"Walter, I'm not sure you and I could ever be friends. Past history and all. But I wouldn't want to see you jammed up for something you didn't do."

"I didn't."

"Believe it or not, but I do believe you."

I thought he might cry, so I left. Nothing worse than seeing a guy tear up. Especially one you'd spent years fantasizing about punching his face purple.

# CHAPTER ELEVEN

I KNEW TROUBLE was brewing as soon as Nicole dropped out of warp speed and crunched into the shell parking area at Ray's. Trouble in the form of an unmarked police car. No doubt Detective Bob Morgan's ride. I knew Ray and I'd eventually have to talk with him, but I'd hoped to sit down with Ray first. Make a game plan. Decide what to do with the video of Walter's comings and goings. No pun intended.

I considered telling Nicole to turn around, head back to her place, somewhere Morgan wouldn't find me. Cowardly, I know, but Ray could handle him without me. But I also knew I was the topic of whatever conversation was going on inside—what other topic could it be?—so I decided it was best to get this over and done. At least here I'd have Ray running point.

The office was empty; kitchen, too. Then I heard voices. Coming through the open glass sliders that led to the deck. I grabbed Nicole's arm, stopping her short.

I recognized Morgan's voice. I also recognized that I was indeed the topic under discussion.

Morgan: One of our guys had a face to face with him the other night. Near the crime scene.

Ray: Actually he was in front of Tammy Horton's place.

Morgan: Which is a lob wedge from the scene.

Ray: So?

Then another voice jumped in. Male, harsh, slightly nasal. Jeremy Starks, Morgan's partner. I had met him a couple times, the reason I knew his distinctive voice.

Starks: Then he shows up again this morning.

Ray: So?

Starks: So why was he there?

Ray: Working a case.

Starks: What case?

Ray: Can't say.

Morgan: We know all about client privilege.

Ray: Doesn't sound like it.

Morgan: Ray, don't you think a little cooperation might be in order here? Or are you going to be your usual jackass self?

Ray: Jackass works for me.

Time to show up. I walked out on the deck. Nicole followed. Ray occupied his usual spot, laptop and papers on the table before him, a Dew at the ready. Morgan sat across from him. Starks stood against the rail, back to the view, arms folded over his chest. Tall, lanky, with a thin face and prominent nose, Starks had been a star wide receiver in high school. Up in Foley. Same area that spawned Alabama All-Americans Kenny Stabler and DJ Fluker. Starks was a prick, though less so than Morgan.

Starks' gaze lifted to me and his eyes lit up. "Here he is."

I introduced Nicole. The three men nodded, each, including Ray, looking her up and down.

"What's happening?" I asked, playing all innocent.

"You," Morgan said. "Got a few questions for you."

Ray stood, scraping back his chair. He looked at me. "A word first." He jerked his head toward the kitchen.

"Not a good idea, Ray. Wouldn't want to file obstruction charges against you."

"You won't."

Morgan's eyes narrowed and his jaw tightened.

Ray stared back, giving not an inch. "So unless you have an arrest warrant for me, or Jake, I'm going to have a chat with my son."

Morgan shrugged and waved a go-ahead hand.

Once in the kitchen, Ray asked, "You two together last night?"

Nicole smiled. "All night."

Ray rolled his eyes. "Morgan will ask. Just want to be clear on that point."

"We didn't make a video or anything like that," Nicole said. "Well, not of us, anyway."

"Don't take this the wrong way," Ray nodded to Nicole before locking his glare on me, "but I don't think taking a date on a stakeout is good business."

"She was actually a big help," I said.

Ray shook his head. "Story of your life."

"We got the video though," I said.

"And breached confidentiality. How do you know you can trust her?"

"Hey," Nicole said, the edge in her voice grabbing Ray. "Don't talk about me. Talk to me."

"Okay, how do I know you can be trusted with what you now know?"

Nicole squared her shoulders and raised her chin. "You don't."

"My point exactly."

"And I don't know if I can trust you guys either," Nicole said. "That's not exactly true." She looked at me. "I think I can trust Jake. Though I'm not sure why I think that."

Ray huffed out a snort. "Because he's charming. At least to those of your persuasion."

"Persuasion?" Nicole asked. A frown crinkled her forehead.

"Young, pretty, female."

"That supposed to be a compliment?"

Ray shrugged.

"Look," Nicole said, "Jake drug me into this so here I am. Deal with it."

Ray hesitated, and then laughed. "Jake, I like this girl. She doesn't seem to be the usual airhead you cull from the herd."

"The herd?" Nicole asked.

"Maybe not the best turn of phrase," Ray said. "But I'll say this, you got spunk."

Nicole offered another perfect smile. "I feel so loved. All warm inside."

"That was last night," Jake said.

She looked at Ray. "Didn't you teach him not to kiss and tell?"

"Lord knows I tried to teach him a bunch of stuff. Jake doesn't always listen, though."

"So I noticed."

How did I become the target of all this? Time to change the topic. "So, what's the play here?"

"Been thinking on that," Ray said. "Don't see any way to keep the video from him. Not that I wouldn't love to twist his tit a bit." To Nicole, "Sorry."

"Gee. Never heard that word before."

Ray actually smiled. It evaporated when he looked at me. "Withholding the video would be obstruction. Could cost me my license. Not worth the risk. Especially to protect Walter the creep."

Ray's dislike of Tammy had long ago spilled over to Walter. Not to mention he and Walter had locked horns in court on many occasions. No love lost there.

Ray continued. "No doubt the guy you filmed was Walter?"

"None. You'll see. Besides, he admitted it."

Ray raised an eyebrow.

"But he denied having anything to do with Barbara Plummer's death," I said.

"You believe him?"

"Actually, I do. He seemed shocked at the news."

Nicole nodded her agreement. "Unless he's a very good actor."

"Attorneys usually are," Ray said.

"Not Walter," I said. "He'd make a lousy poker player. Hell, he couldn't beat a five-year-old at Go Fish."

Ray hesitated. "Okay, let's get this done."

While I set up my laptop, connecting it to the 60-inch flat screen that hung on the living room wall, Ray brought Morgan and Starks inside. They settled on the sofa facing the screen.

"This video was taken last night," I said. "We set up on the beach, maybe a hundred and fifty feet from the Plummers' place."

"So she was the target of your investigation?" Morgan asked.

"She was," Ray said.

"Who's the client? The husband? Henry?"

Ray shrugged. Not exactly an admission, but Morgan got the message.

"Play the video," Morgan said.

We watched Walter enter the house. He and Barbara embracing. Wine in the kitchen. I paused it briefly at a frame that clearly showed Walter's face over Barbara's shoulder. As if he were looking directly at the camera. Then their climb up the stairs. The shadowy movements behind the sheers followed by the bedroom going dark. Then the second video showed Walter leaving, scurrying back up the beach.

"I have an audio file I can give you, too," I said.

Morgan leaned forward, pinching the bridge of his nose as if a headache was making its appearance. "I was hoping this would be some miscreant pulling a B and E that went wrong. Walter Horton is another thing altogether."

True. Walter was a big deal. Well respected. Friends all the way to Montgomery. Handled about every important case in the county.

"The media will eat this up," Starks said.

"We had a chat with Walter," I said. "Just before we got here."

"And?"

"Admitted he was having an affair with Barbara. Said he loved her."

"Tammy will skewer him," Ray said.

"She's pretty good with a golf club," Nicole said.

"Misplaced love is always a motive for murder," Morgan said.

"He denied killing her," I said. "Told us he knew nothing about it."

Starks gave me a "get real" look. "What would you expect him to say?"

"True. But I believe him."

"Walter better have his own video," Morgan said. "One that shows Barbara Plummer alive and well when he left her." He stood. "Guess we better go have a chat with him."

"One more thing," I said. "What was the cause of death?"

"Why is that important to you?" Morgan asked.

"Because we didn't hear anything. No struggle, no screaming, no gunshots or anything like that."

Morgan hesitated and then said, "This doesn't leave the room. Got it?"

"We understand," Ray said.

He looked at Nicole. "This applies to you, too, young lady."

Nicole made a zipping motion across her lips. Those wonderfully perfect lips. "I don't know any of the players here. Except for the ex and she's crazy."

Morgan almost smiled. More a slight twitch at the corner of his mouth. "Barbara Plummer was killed in her bed. Single gunshot to the forehead. Looks like she never saw it coming."

"You thinking this was a pro?" Ray asked.

Morgan shrugged. "Or, in spite of Jake's opinion, Walter."

"So he screws the woman he's supposedly in love with and then shoots her in the head?" I asked. "Does that make sense?"

"Murder never makes sense," Morgan said. "Besides, I've seen that exact scenario before."

"But Walter? He doesn't have the *cojones*. I can't imagine Walter-the-wimp doing that."

"It's often the wimps that do this domestic violence stuff," Starks said.

I shook my head. "Not Walter."

"Regardless," Ray said, "from your description of the scene it surely sounds like a hit."

Morgan scratched an ear. "Could be. Looks like a small caliber. Shot was dead center. Nothing out of place. Like he just walked in, popped her, and left. So yeah, I'd say this smells like a hit. Not domestic. Not a quarrel or a fight, just a cold killing."

"So if not Walter, who?" I asked.

"Maybe the two of you?"

I gave him my best smile. "We were busy making a video."

"Just giving you some shit," Morgan said. "I take it you two didn't see anyone else out there?"

I shook my head. "No one."

"How long were you there?"

I glanced at Nicole. "Three hours, max. Got there a little before ten. Walter left just after midnight. Since we had what we needed, we packed up and left shortly after that."

"Any idea what the time of death was?" Ray asked.

"Based on the core temps the techs took, sometime between ten and two. Best guess, anyway."

"Who found her?" Ray asked.

"Cleaning lady."

"Someone had to have come along after Walter left," I said. "After we left."

"Maybe." Morgan stood. He shoved his hands in his pockets and rocked on his heels slightly. "Which opens up all sorts of possibilities."

"Like murder for hire?" Ray asked.

Morgan's expression remained flat, empty. "Did Henry know about the affair?"

Ray gave him his own blank stare.

"You don't have to tell me," Morgan said. "He's your client. Nothing else fits. Isn't it always some wayward spouse that drags you into these things?"

"Sometimes."

"Henry hires someone. Guy drops by while Henry's out of town. A thousand miles away. Wife gets popped. Couldn't be him. Right? Read this story before."

"If that were the case," Ray said, "why would Henry hire me to surveil her? It'd be like supplying your own witness to the crime." When Morgan didn't respond, Ray continued. "If the shooter was identified, and then squeezed by you guys, he just might roll over on Henry. So hiring me would have been a stupid move. And what I know of Henry Plummer, stupidity isn't part of the picture."

"So, we're back to a B and E gone wrong," Starks said.

"The back door was unlocked," I said.

"And you know that how?" Starks asked.

"Walter left through that door. Barbara didn't come down and see him off or lock up or anything like that. At least not that we saw."

Morgan nodded. "It was unlocked. No signs of forcible entry. And the alarm wasn't set."

Ray crossed his arms over his chest. "What about Tammy?"

I looked at him. "Tammy kill Barbara? Not a chance."

"Not herself," Starks said. "Hired someone."

"Did she know about the affair?" Morgan asked.

No one had an answer for that, but I said, "I doubt it."

"Based on?" Morgan asked.

"I would've heard."

"Why? You're the ex?"

"Tammy calls and vents her problems to me all the time. I have no idea why, but she feels the need to talk things out and I'm . . . what's the word? . . . safe."

"Safe?"

"Weird, I know. But I think it's because I know she's crazy. When she talks crazy or rants, I've seen it all before. She doesn't feel exposed."

"Weird is right," Morgan said.

I smiled. "Weirdness is her most endearing quality."

"Still . . ."

I shook my head. "Tammy wouldn't do it and she wouldn't hire it done. The truth is she actually loves Walter. She'd forgive him even if he did step out of line."

Morgan nodded. "Voice of experience?"

I shrugged. "You might say that."

Everyone fell silent, as if absorbing the possibilities, trying to shake out which one made the most sense.

"What if Walter was the target?" Nicole asked.

Everyone looked at her.

"I mean, not directly. Maybe someone wanted to frame him for her murder. Someone who had a beef with him. Someone who knew about the affair. Someone who knew he'd be there that night and what time he usually came and went."

"Came and went?" Morgan raised an eyebrow.

"Okay. Poor turn of phrase," Nicole said, smiling. "But Walter's an attorney. Attorneys make enemies. Criminal enemies. Ones who wouldn't hesitate to kill or frame someone for a murder. And Walter's rich. Rich folks make rich enemies. Ones who can easily afford to hire a pro."

Morgan's forehead creased and his gaze dropped as if considering what she had said.

"Henry was into software, wasn't he?" Nicole asked.

Morgan nodded. "Made his first fortune in that world. Now making a second one in real estate."

"So maybe Henry was the target," Nicole said. "He just wasn't home. Or maybe someone was trying to frame him. I mean, some of those software geeks are like gangsta rappers. Long on cash but short on walking-around sense. Could be a competitor hired the guy to either kill Henry or frame him for the murder, but he didn't know Henry was away. It's hard to kill a guy who isn't there and just as hard to frame someone who's a thousand miles away."

I looked at her in awe. The more I saw of her the more impressed I was. Beauty and brains. I was in way over my head here.

"Came up with that on your own, did you?" Morgan asked.

She squared her shoulders, and gave him a glare that could melt steel. "Some blonds aren't stupid."

Morgan raised defensive hands. "Sorry. Actually I'm impressed. Good thoughts."

"But I didn't come up with it on my own," Nicole said. "A couple of years ago, out in California, Orange County, same thing happened. Some computer geek offed his rival's wife. Tried to frame hubby for it. They were bashing each other in court over some patent infringement allegation. Big money involved. Couple of hundred million, if I remember correctly. One geek lost and hired a pro to frame the other geek. So it's not an original idea."

"Still a good one," Starks said.

"She's a screenwriter," I said, as if this explained Nicole's insight. Which in many ways it did.

"That's relevant how?" Morgan asked.

"She makes up stories," I said. "Writes screenplays."

Nicole rolled her eyes. "But that one wouldn't fly in Hollywood. Too mundane. A business competitor hiring a killer's been done a thousand times." She shrugged. "Now if it were space aliens or killer artichokes, Hollywood would eat it up."

"I don't think we'll be dealing with homicidal vegetables here." Morgan smiled and then looked at each of us in turn. "Any other story ideas come to mind?"

No one responded.

Then to Nicole and me, Morgan said, "We'll need to take a statement from you two."

"No problem," I said.

"And we'll need your laptop."

"Not without a warrant," Ray said. "But we'll burn you a DVD of the video and audio files."

"That'll work. For now."

While I copied the files, my thoughts turned to Tammy. On one hand, I felt for her. Husband cheating, maybe facing murder charges, police showing up with search warrants, which would surely happen at some point, trashing her home, her world spinning out of control. Tammy the control freak wouldn't handle all that well. Sure she was a crazy bitch, but did she deserve all that?

On the other hand, I felt sorry for myself. Once Walter was arrested, or was at least named as a suspect, and the news hounds camped out on her street, Tammy would jump into full meltdown mode. And when she discovered it was my video that spun the wheel of misfortune in Walter's direction, all her heat would come my way. A full-on China Syndrome.

I felt a headache coming on. Or a tumor. Maybe an aneurysm.

# CHAPTER TWELVE

DETECTIVE BOB MORGAN was anxious. Wanted to talk to Walter as soon as possible. Before he could create a believable story. If there was one. But if anyone could conjure up a story, it would be a skilled attorney like Walter. So as Starks drove away from Ray's place, Morgan called Walter's office only to find that he was mired in a deposition. Secretary said he'd be done in about a half hour. He considered going on in, shutting it down, but decided a scene, in front of some client and a handful of other attorneys, probably wasn't the best course of action. Could be negative PR for the department. Hadn't they had enough with that officer-involved shooting three weeks ago? The fact that the miscreant pumped three rounds through the patrol car's windshield before he took a pair in the chest himself, didn't seem to mitigate squat with the local media.

Besides, he didn't want to raise Walter's hackles. He wanted Walter at least partially receptive to being questioned.

So now, he and Starks leaned on the wooden railing that embraced The Wharf's marina, and munched on snow cones. His cherry; Starks' pineapple.

Morgan watched a good-sized Chris Craft, thirty-eight feet, thereabouts, slide up to the dock. A charter back from a morning fishing run. Two couples with bright pink skin, suggesting a need for more sunscreen, stepped over the gunwale and then stood by

while the three-man crew off-loaded several large, silvery fish, plac-
ing them in an orange plastic cooler, dumping ice on top.

"What do you think?" Starks asked.

"I think Walter is screwed twelve ways from Sunday."

"He might be innocent."

"He's still screwed," Morgan said. "This kind of deal is like dog
shit on your shoes. You can scrape it off but the odor lingers." He
finished the snow cone and tossed the paper container into a blue
barrel trash can.

"He'll deny it one way or the other," Starks said.

"Don't they all?"

In his twenty years on the job how many times had Morgan heard
such denials? Like maybe a thousand. Even the most guilty deflected
involvement. Of course, he didn't trouble himself with that. Not his
job to decide who was guilty and who wasn't. He only needed to dig
for the facts. And grind a suspect down to the point that confession
seemed the only option. Deep down he didn't buy into all the innocent until proven guilty crap either. He started with guilty and worked
back from there. After all, if they weren't guilty, or at least possibly
guilty, they wouldn't have popped up on his radar in the first place.

But he had to admit that Walter as a cold-blooded killer didn't
fit. He was too—what was the word?—soft. Not all macho and tes-
tosterone infused. But then again, neither was Gladys McComber.
Two years ago. A substitute teacher and volunteer at the library.
Small, frail, mousy, quiet, she had shattered her husband's skull with
a baseball bat. While he slept. Then tried to dissolve his corpse with
acid in a metal tub in the backyard. Didn't work. The acid ate the
tub and the fumes alerted a neighbor. Best laid plans being what
they are. So could Walter have whacked Barbara? You bet.

"You think Henry might've set all this up?" Starks asked. He
continued working on his snow cone.

"Possible. Some folks can't spell divorce. Remember the Petersen case? Out in California? Or the other Petersen up in Chicago? Anyway, if Henry knew about Walter and his wife, and he must've at least had a suspicion if he'd hired Ray, he could take care of both."

"You mean like the killers might've missed Walter? Got there late? Something like that?"

Morgan gave a slow nod. "Or killing Barbara and framing Walter would accomplish the same thing."

"Like that Nicole girl said?"

Morgan nodded. "Seen stranger scenarios."

"Diabolical."

"You got that right."

"But we don't know Henry hired Ray," Starks said.

"He did. Nothing else fits."

Morgan watched the two sunburned men struggle up the ramp, the fish-filled cooler between them, making walking awkward. The wives followed, both talking at the same time with lots of hand movements. The men loaded the cooler into the back of a blue Chevy SUV with Missouri plates and a Kansas City Chiefs decal on the rear window.

"Any news on when Henry's getting back?" Starks asked.

"Still trying to get a flight out of New York, last I heard. I suspect later tonight. Tomorrow morning at the latest. He said he'd call as soon as he knew."

Starks finished his snow cone and tossed the paper in the trash. He pulled a couple of napkins from his jacket pocket and wiped his hands.

"She's a real beauty," Starks said.

"Who?"

"Nicole."

Morgan nodded. "Yes, she is."

"That's Jake Longly. Always gets the best tail. Seems the good-looking guys always end up with chicks like that."

That was true. Jake was maybe six-two, lean and fit. Looked like he could still play in the bigs. Had that confident athletic air about him. Sort of pissed Morgan off.

Morgan grunted. "His looks aren't his problem. Getting led around by his dick is."

"A girl like that could lead me around any time."

"My point, exactly." Morgan glanced at his watch. "Let's go see if Walter's done."

# CHAPTER THIRTEEN

ONCE THE OTHER attorneys packed up their papers and snapped the locks on their briefcases, and the court reporter stored her equipment in a small rolling case, Walter showed them out. Closing the door, he turned to the empty waiting room. Was this his future? If he wasn't in jail, that is. His innocence aside, even a whiff of guilt, or scandal, could evaporate his practice as quickly as water sprayed on hot asphalt. He had canceled his afternoon appointments, not in the mood to listen to others' problems right now. He had enough of his own.

"Detective Morgan called," Connie said.

Walter sighed. "What'd he want?"

"To talk with you. I told him you were in a meeting. He said he'd stop by."

And so it begins.

Walter nodded and headed into his office where he collapsed in his two-thousand-dollar leather chair. His life was a goddamn mess. The deposition had been a goddamn mess. He couldn't focus. Could barely speak. His brain felt like pâté, and his throat felt as if it were choked with soot. The stenographer had said, "Can you repeat that?" maybe a dozen times. He'd have to read the transcript later to see what questions he had asked, much less the answers.

At one point, when his questions seemed to drift like an unanchored boat, opposing counsel had asked if he wanted to reschedule.

No, he didn't want to reschedule. He wanted to get this over with. He wanted to deal with his own case. His own defense.

His own defense? Those words seemed so foreign. How could this happen? Him a suspect? He had no illusions about that. And even if by some creation-level miracle he wasn't, he soon would be. If Morgan was already snooping around, it could only mean that he had talked with Jake Longly. Probably seen that damn video. Fucking Longly was going to hang him. Maybe he shouldn't have stolen his wife. But that wasn't really true. Jake had lost Tammy long before Walter entered the picture. Of course Jake might not see it that way. Walter had skewered him pretty good in the divorce.

Walter's head hurt, his stomach churned. What was he going to do? Barbara murdered. Morgan pointed in his direction. Like he was some low-rent criminal. Like many of Walter's clients. But he wasn't like them. He was a respected professional. The best god-damn attorney in the county. Ask anyone. So why did his chest feel so tight? Why were his hands shaking? Why did he feel so ... guilty?

Because he was. Of betraying Tammy, anyway. Of giving in to his needs. Was that all it was with Barbara? A need? And if so, why did he need such a distraction? What did that say about him? About Tammy? About their marriage?

He jumped when the intercom buzzed.

"Yeah, Connie," he said.

"Detectives Morgan and Starks are here."

"Give me a couple of minutes and then send them in."

"Will do."

Just great. The circus was beginning and he hadn't even begun to figure out how to handle it. He walked to his private bath on unsteady legs. The mirror reflected an image he barely recognized. He looked ill, pale, scared, sweat beading on his forehead and upper lip. Not the courtroom warrior image he always tried to project. He splashed cold water on his face. Didn't help. He decided vomiting wouldn't either, even though he felt as if he might.

He was settling in his chair when the door opened.

Morgan sat, facing him across his desk. Starks remained standing, his lanky, six-four frame adding more than a hint of intimidation. Walter had hoped Morgan would come in friendly. Casual. But one look at his stone face told Walter that Morgan and Starks were not going for the good-cop bad-cop approach. More like bad-cop badder-cop. He also sensed that the two detectives knew everything. About him and Barbara. The video. Off-balance didn't quite cover it.

*Get your game face on, Walter.*

A dozen lawyerly tricks rattled around in his head. Dodges, head fakes, spin moves, all the usual courtroom maneuvers. Things that were second nature to him. He'd used them against Morgan before. Morgan was tough, smart, and always prepared, but Walter had managed on a couple of occasions to twist him around pretty good. In court. Where he had home field advantage. Seemed his own office should afford him the same upper hand, but sitting right here, right now, he knew all the cards were on Morgan's side of the table.

"Tell me," Morgan said.

Walter attempted to paste on his most innocent face. "Tell you what?"

"Walter, we're far beyond the BS game here. Okay? We saw the video. Saw you skulking away from a murder scene. So tell me."

"I didn't kill her. I swear."

Rather than responding to Walter's protestation of innocence, Morgan stared at him, flat-faced. Walter recognized the cop trick. Morgan simply letting the pressure build. And it was. In Walter's head, his chest.

Finally, Walter sighed. "Yes, we've been seeing each other. Yes, I was with her last night. But when I left, she was fine."

"How long you two been an item?"

"A while. Nearly a year. It wasn't planned. It just happened."

"As those things usually do," Starks said.

Walter massaged his temples. "I know this looks bad. I know I have to be suspect number one. But I didn't harm her." A quick sob escaped. "I couldn't. I wouldn't."

"Know how many times I've heard that?" Morgan asked. "A bunch."

"I know," Walter said. "Me, too. But, I swear, I didn't kill her. I loved her."

And there it was. The truth. Not to mention one of the oldest motives for murder. Love, hate, powerful sides of the same coin.

"If not you, then who?" Morgan asked.

Walter hadn't expected that question. He should have, but right now his mind wasn't exactly running on all cylinders. In fact, it was vapor locked.

"I have no idea."

"Henry? You think he could be involved?" Morgan asked.

"He's out of town."

Morgan leaned forward, elbows on knees, and looked directly at Walter. Walter could see the butt of Morgan's service weapon peeking past the lapel his jacket.

"Not what I asked," Morgan said. "Do you think he could have hired someone?"

"No way. Not Henry."

"But he knew about the affair. Right?" Starks said.

"No. I'm sure he didn't."

"But he hired Ray Longly," Morgan said.

Walter's shoulders suddenly felt leadened. He slumped forward. "I don't know anything right now." He looked up at Morgan. "None of this makes any sense."

"Murders often don't. There are always other ways to fix problems, settle things, but for some reason killers rarely see that. Until it's too late to unwind bad judgement."

Walter felt tears pushing against his eyes. Damned if he would let them out. Not here in front of Morgan.

"Do you own a gun?" Morgan asked.

"Three. I have one here in the office and two at home. Actually, one of them is Tammy's."

"I'll need all three."

"No problem." Walter pulled open his desk drawer and lifted out a holstered .38. He handed it to Morgan. "I have a permit. Even a concealed carry one. But I rarely take it with me."

"Walter, I'm not going to waste your time or mine with all the usual questions. I know what time you visited her and what time you left. I know that the time frame more or less matches the time of death. I know you had means and opportunity. What I don't know is if you had a motive."

Walter started to say that he would never kill Barbara or anyone else and that all this didn't make him guilty but before he could organize his thoughts and speak, Morgan raised a hand, stopping him.

"And I also know that if you had a motive you wouldn't tell me," Morgan said. "But the evidence suggests that either you did it or someone knew your schedule or it was just dumb bad luck coincidence. Any of those work for me."

"I didn't do it. I swear. And I don't believe Henry would. It had to be someone else."

Morgan stood. "Walter, none of this bodes well for you."

"Am I under arrest?"

"Not yet. Not if you consent to a search of your office and residence. If you refuse, I'll need to pull warrants, and if I do, I'll snag one for your arrest."

"Sure." He stood, clutching the corner of his desk for balance. "I don't have anything to hide."

Morgan raised an eyebrow.

"About the murder. The affair? Sure. But I guess that charade is over."

Morgan nodded. "True."

"What are you searching for?"

"Papers, computer stuff, phone records, weapons, that kind of thing. So what's it gonna be? Consent from you or a warrant from a judge?"

"You can search." He picked up the phone. "I'll call Tammy and let her know."

Morgan shook his head. "No. I would then have to assume she destroyed any evidence before we got there."

"Of course." Walter settled the phone back into its cradle knowing Tammy would go ballistic when they showed up without warning. "Maybe I should go with you."

"You stay here. One team will be here soon. You'll need to help them avoid anything that might be protected by attorney-client privilege."

Walter nodded. "I understand."

"Any of that stuff at your home? Client papers?"

"No. That's kept here in the office."

"And the guns? The ones at home? Where do I tell my guys to find them?"

"Either side of our bed. In the top drawer."

Nausea crept upward in Walter's stomach. He swallowed hard. "How . . ." his voice broke. His throat felt as if it were filled with concrete. "I don't even know how she died?" When Morgan didn't respond Walter continued. "She must have been shot."

"Why do you think that?"

"Why else would you want my guns?"

"You know I can't share that kind of information with you."

Walter sighed. "Because I'm the number one suspect."

Morgan shrugged. "For now."

# CHAPTER FOURTEEN

TAMMY HORTON DID not suffer unexpected interruptions well. Not ever, not from anyone. Shouldn't a seven-figure home in an exclusive neighborhood protect her from intrusions? Even from the occasional solicitor who somehow found his way into the community? How did these nuisances get past the guard gate, anyway? Nuisances like kids selling candy for new basketball uniforms, local charities scratching around for donations, and don't even get her started on the Jehovah's Witnesses and Mormons. Didn't they have enough money, anyway?

So when the doorbell buzzed, she ignored it. When it buzzed again, she glared in the direction of the hand-carved oak double doors and took a sip of her wine. Sure, it wasn't anywhere near happy hour, but she was watching a cooking show after all. How could she get into viewing all that food preparation without a glass of wine? Didn't seem right.

With the third buzz, she placed the wine glass on the coffee table, a copy of *Southern Living* magazine protecting the expensive wood. The fourth irritating doorbell scream brought her to her feet.

She had been smack in the middle of the final round of The Great Gulf Coast Chef Challenge on local station 16. She had faithfully watched every episode as twenty local chefs were whittled down to two for the grand finale, which pitted Claudell Pulver and her Mile-High Strawberry Shortcake, featuring four layers of rectangular buttery pound cake, Sauterne-soaked strawberries, and sweet cream ganache, against Georgette McClure's Kicked-Up Key Lime Pie, the kick coming from its cayenne pepper-tinged, crushed-pecan crust and rum-infused whipped cream topping. The three judges were in the middle of their tasting when she snatched up the controller, paused the DVR, and marched toward the front door, prepping her tirade en route.

"This better be good," she said as she swung the door open.

"I don't think it will be."

It was Detective Bob Morgan. Behind him stood two geeky dudes in jeans, white shirts, and blue windbreakers with some sort of official-looking gold emblem on the left breast area. Not what Tammy expected. Surprise and curiosity tamped down her anger a notch.

"Detective? What can I do for you?"

She glanced back inside. Had she paused the DVR?

Morgan thrust a piece of paper at her. "We need to search your home."

"What?"

"Your husband consented." He waved the page at her. "Got his signature right here."

She glanced at it but didn't really see it. "Well, I sure as hell don't consent."

Morgan gave a slow nod. "Well, that presents a problem."

"It sure as hell does." She jammed one fist against her hip.

"We don't really need your permission since Walter, the homeowner of record, has given us the green light."

She waved a hand. "Do you see him? I don't. And if he isn't here, you aren't coming in."

Morgan folded the page and slipped it into his jacket pocket. "I can grab an official warrant in no time. If that's the way you want to play it."

"What's this about?" Now she propped a second fist against the other hip. "What are you looking for?"

"It's an ongoing investigation. Can't really say more than that just yet."

"You sound like a TV cop."

"Thanks," Morgan said. "That's what I was going for."

"Come back when you can tell me what this is about." She started to push the door closed. Morgan's hand stopped its progress.

"Mrs. Horton, I'm afraid you'll have to step outside until we get this sorted out."

"The hell I will."

"Ma'am, if I even suspect you might be destroying evidence, I can come in. Warrant or no warrant. Such circumstances override the Fourth Amendment."

Was that true? Tammy had no way of knowing. But she was sure Morgan and every other cop on the planet would lie if need be. It was in their nature. At least that's what happened on all the true crime shows she watched on *Discovery ID*. And didn't they do the same on *Law & Order*? Even Monk fibbed.

"So," Morgan asked, "can we get started?"

"You still haven't told me what you're looking for. Or why."

"Maybe you should ask Walter."

"I told you, he isn't here."

"I know. He's at his office. We've got some guys searching his office right now."

"I don't understand."

"Call Walter."

"Wait here."

Again she tried to close the door and again Morgan stopped her.

"Leave it open and stay where I can see you. As I said before, it's an evidence issue."

"Walter will skewer you."

"Maybe, but for now, let's do this my way. It'll be easier on everyone."

She huffed out a breath, spun, and marched across the foyer and into the media room. The big screen displayed the frozen image of one of the judges with a forkful of shortcake hanging before his widely opened mouth. She snatched her cell phone from the coffee table, punched in Walter's speed dial number, and brought it to her ear.

Tammy waited through three rings. "Let me talk to Walter, Connie."

"He's busy right now," Connie said.

"He isn't that busy. Get his ass on the phone."

Connie did.

Walter wouldn't tell her anything. Just that he'd explain later but to let Morgan do his search.

"Look," Walter said, "they're going to do it one way or the other so just get it over with."

"Does this have anything to do with Barbara's murder?"

He sighed. "Yes."

"I don't understand." She glanced toward the door where Morgan and the two officers stood staring at her.

"Let him do his job," Walter said. "We'll talk later. But right now I'm a bit busy. Okay?"

He disconnected the call. She stared at the phone, then dropped it next to her wine glass. She returned to the door.

"Okay, Andy, Barney, and Floyd, have at it."

Morgan nodded. He and the geeks stepped inside. "I'll have to ask you to vacate the premises while we do the search."

"You're throwing me out of my own house?"

"Just until we finish."

"How long will that take?"

"Not sure. Maybe an hour."

"You guys would've made good Stormtroopers."

"Ma'am." He waved a hand toward the door.

"Five minutes," Tammy said. "Can you give me five minutes?"

"Ma'am?"

She jerked her head toward the TV. "They're doing the final judging. I've been waiting for weeks."

"Ma'am?"

This guy was a broken record. "The Gulf Coast Chef Challenge. I'm sure the key lime pie's going to win."

"Don't you think that can wait?"

Tammy felt frustration tears collect in her eyes. "Why are you doing this to me?"

"Ask Walter."

# CHAPTER FIFTEEN

AT THAT MOMENT the search of Walter's office was winding down. Walter stood against the wall in his office—the wall that displayed all his degrees and honors and photos with various politicians and celebrities—as an officer lugged his computer out the door, followed by another rolling a dolly stacked with three boxes of papers. He followed them into the hallway and watched as they trundled toward the elevators.

"Walter, what's going on?" Connie asked as he closed the door.

"Connie, I can't talk about it right now."

"But . . ."

"I'll tell you later. But right now I need to talk with Howard and Anthony. Are they here?"

She looked hurt. He wanted to hug her and tell her not to worry, but if he did he feared he'd break down. Right now he had more pressing issues.

"They're down in the conference room. Working on their opening statements for tomorrow's trial."

Walter hesitated, not relishing this conversation, then turned and headed down the hall.

He found his two partners, Howard Levine and Anthony Steen, leaning over the massive conference table, its surface littered with papers. They looked up when he entered. After apologizing for the interruption, Walter sat across from them and told them everything. They slowly settled in chairs as he spoke, disbelief on their faces. But he held nothing back. The affair. Barbara's murder. The whole story. Their shock was only outweighed by the fear that wound around his gut.

"Looks like you guys are now my defense council," Walter said.

Levine raised an eyebrow. "Might be better if you got someone outside the firm, don't you think?"

Walter shook his head. "I don't trust anyone else."

"Walter, I'm afraid I agree with Howard here," Steen said. "It would be like you defending yourself."

"So?"

"Only a fool represents himself. You know that."

"But this story needs to be contained. The fewer people who know, the better it will be. For the firm. For me."

Levine leaned forward, resting his elbows on his knees. "Don't you think this story will hit the news? Big time?"

"But we can delay it until Morgan realizes I didn't do it. That way, when it does break, I'll no longer be in the suspect pool."

"You think the cops can do that before the six o'clock news?" Steen asked.

Levine nodded his agreement. "A murder on The Point? Henry Plummer's wife? Big news."

"The cops'll keep a lid on suspects, on me, for as long as they can. You know that. All that ongoing investigation crap. Morgan won't give the media shit. He never does until he has to."

"I hope you're right." Levine shrugged.

Steen glanced at Levine and then said, "I still don't think it's a good idea, but you know we'll do it. If that's what you want."

"I do." Walter looked at Levine, and then Steen. "I didn't do this. Sure, I was seeing her. Sure, I was there last night. But she was alive and very well when I left."

"We believe you," Steen said.

"Thanks," Walter said. "I need that about now."

Walter wanted to believe he could clap a lid on this. Really believe it. But he knew otherwise. He didn't trust Morgan or think he would do a speedy job. Not speedy enough to save him from being ravaged in the media. Morgan never rushed anything. He was a plodder. Looked under every rock. Rarely made a mistake. Took his own sweet time. Right now Walter needed time. A day, even a few hours, could make all the difference. Besides, Walter had another plan.

Ray Longly.

Walter's next stop.

# CHAPTER SIXTEEN

I TURNED THE pickup into the lot at Ray's and parked next to a gleaming silver S63 Mercedes. Big V12, polished chrome wheels, deeply blacked-out windows, and a license plate that read: HRTN LAW. Walter's ride.

*Interesting.*

I had left Nicole at her place so she could work on her screenplay. The murder of Barbara Plummer had given her several new ideas for plot twists. She had given me the thumbnail on the ride over to her place. The story focused on the murder of a business executive, a Silicon Valley mogul, who crossed a business partner and ended up floating in the San Francisco Bay, head missing.

Woman had a dark side.

She also said I'd better be back by eight to take her to dinner. Woman had a bossy streak, too. No argument from me, though. Dinner with Nicole was one thing, nice and pleasant, but the après-dinner activities were a whole other story.

I found Ray and Walter huddled at the deck table. The late-day sun cast the western sky orange and bent long shadows from the beach umbrellas below. Many of the beachgoers were packing up to head home. Others remained stretched out on towels, grabbing the day's last bit of UV radiation.

I settled in an empty chair. "What's going on?"

Ray nodded toward Walter.

"I didn't kill Barbara."

"And, as I told you," I said, "I'm inclined to believe you."

"For the record, I do, too," Ray added.

Walter puffed out his cheeks, exhaling slowly. "I'm not sure anyone else does. Certainly not Detective Morgan."

Walter had had a terrible day. No doubt about that. One of those that make you question everything. I mean, an affair exposed, his lover murdered, his marriage likely damaged, his career in jeopardy, even his freedom at stake. Doesn't get much worse than that. And it showed on his face. Pale, drawn, and with sad droopy eyes. Walter looked a lot older about now.

"That's his job," I said. "To suspect everyone."

"Particularly those filmed leaving the scene?" Walter looked out toward the Gulf, his unfocused eyes almost glassy. "I can't believe this."

"Have you told Tammy?" I asked. "About you and Barbara?"

"Not yet. Haven't been home. Not sure I want to." He sighed. "This isn't something you discuss on the phone." He looked down at his hands, clasped together before him. "She will go ballistic."

"And then some." I rested my elbows on the table. "So why are you here?"

"I want to hire Ray. To find the real killer."

Not what I'd expected. Nor was I sure how I felt about it. Definitely fuel on the fire. When Tammy found out Walter was humping Barbara, and I had made a video that put him in the crosshairs of a murder investigation, and then old Walter hired Ray, well, she would go apeshit. Big time. And I would hear about it. Bigger time. A throbbing pain blossomed in my left temple.

"Isn't that Morgan's job?" I asked. "To track down killers?"

"Don't trust the cops. They'll take the easy way."

There was truth to that. "So why us?"

"Because you believe me. Because you already know everything. I want as few people as possible to know about this. That's best for Tammy. For me. For the firm."

Walter was in la-la land. If he thought this would stay under wraps, he was delusional. I told him as much.

"I know. But if I can just slow it down. Just until I'm cleared."

Walter looked like a drowning man, reaching for an imaginary life preserver. As though his rudder wasn't engaged and he was motoring around in circles. I could only guess at all the chaos rattling around in his brain. Yesterday, everything was good, smooth, life on an upward trajectory, and then bam. Maxwell's silver hammer. Like a massive eighteen wheeler T-boning his big Mercedes.

"There might be a bit of a conflict here," Ray said. "Henry hired us to shadow Barbara. Find out what she was up to."

"And now you know," Walter said. "Seems like that wraps up your deal with him."

"Maybe. Let me talk with Henry first. See what he says."

Walter leaned forward, burying his face in his hands. "This will never end."

"Tell you what," Ray said. "You think about it overnight. Be sure we're the ones you want to hire. I'll have a chat with Henry. Then we'll go from there."

Walter looked up, then nodded. "Okay." He stood. "What now?"

"Go home," I said. "Talk to your wife."

# CHAPTER SEVENTEEN

RAY DROPPED ME at Alberto's Exotic and Vintage Cars, saying he had computer stuff to do but would meet Pancake and me at Captain Rocky's around eight. When Alberto led me into the garage area, I saw that he had again worked his magic. Said he found the windows I needed at a salvage yard up near Fairhope. Apparently the only two windows remaining intact in another '65 Mustang that reached end of life in a head-on collision on I-10 over near Tillman's Corner. Lucky for me, less so for the owner.

Alberto's guys had washed, waxed, and detailed the Mustang so that now as I sped down Highway 182, Perdido Beach Boulevard, toward The Point, the low-hanging, red-orange sun deepened the burgundy of the car's hood. And the car seemed to run better. A wash, a wax, and a couple of new windows will do that. I knew I was an hour earlier than Nicole and I had planned, but I had nothing else to do, so why not?

"You're early," Nicole said when she opened her front door. She wore white jogging shorts and an orange cropped tee. Sweat covered her face and flat belly, her feet bare. She had great feet. Better legs.

"What are you up to?" I asked.

"Went for a beach run."

"Sorry to barge in, but I'm starving."

"For me?" She smiled.

"That, too."

"Anxious. I like that in a man." She stepped back and I entered. "Pour us a drink. There's some Patrón in the freezer. I'll jump in the shower."

"Need your back washed?"

She raised an eyebrow. "That might delay dinner."

I smiled. "I'll survive."

She laughed. "Bring the drinks with you."

She turned, lifting the t-shirt over her head as she headed toward her room. Lord, she was something else.

Thirty minutes later, I toweled off, dressed, and then sat on the edge of the bed, strapping on my sandals. Nicole, in jeans and a dark-green pullover, brushed out her still damp hair, pulled it back into a ponytail, and secured it with a black scrunchy.

"Now I'm hungry," she said.

"Great sex will do that."

"Who said it was great?"

"You did," I said. "Several times, if I remember correctly."

She playfully punched my arm. "Smart-ass."

"Just keeping the record straight."

We walked outside.

She eyed my Mustang. "I see you got your car back." She held out a hand. "I'll drive."

"Not sure that's a good idea. This car's fifty years old. Doesn't handle like your Millennium Falcon."

Palm up, fingers curling, "Gimme."

I did. No point in arguing with her. I mean, she had all those girly parts that make guys, even a stud like me, do stupid stuff. Like handing over car keys. Which I did.

Once we were buckled in, and I made damn sure my seat belt was snug, she reversed from the drive, yanked the shifter back to D, and with a sharp chirp from the rear tires, launched down the street. After a couple of hair-raising turns, she climbed onto 182, and the race was on. She didn't share the road well. The other motorists never had a chance.

"Seems to handle just fine," she said as she swerved around an SUV and then slid through a nearly nonexistent gap between a pickup and an eighteen wheeler into the far left lane, the air pushed aside by the big rig wobbling the Mustang. She didn't seem to notice as she accelerated past a white Corvette.

I offered no response since my heart clogged my throat, rendering speech impossible.

Finally I unfolded from the car amid the cloud of shell dust she kicked up when she slid to a stop in Captain Rocky's front lot. My cell buzzed. Caller ID read: *Tammy*.

"Go ahead," I said. "I'd better get this."

I answered, watching Nicole's jean-clad hips sway toward the entrance. My, my. Tammy's voice yanked me back to reality.

No hello or how are you or any other pleasantries, she simply said, "What the hell is wrong with you?"

"Nothing. I'm fine actually. But thanks for caring."

"You asshole. You put Walter in the middle of all this."

"I think Walter put himself in the box. No pun intended."

"Fuck you, Jake." She was working up a head of steam now.

"Nicole beat you to it."

"God, you're such an ass."

"I work at it."

"Why did you take a video, for Christ's sake?"

"That's what we were hired to do."

"But you gave it to the cops. Are you insane?"

"I sort of had to. Withholding evidence being what it is."

She scoffed. "And we both know how much you and your dickwad father care about the law."

"What do you want, Tammy?"

"The truth."

"Ask Walter." I disconnected the call.

One thing you can say about Tammy is that she's relentless. Took one minute, two minutes, and three minutes for her to call back three more times. All before I could reach the deck table where Nicole, Ray, and Pancake sat. Each time I bounced the call over to voice mail. I had nothing to say, and she wouldn't listen anyway, so why waste time and breath?

I slipped into the vacant chair next to Nicole. The Gulf was calm, moonlight silvering the crests of what waves there were, the evening breeze light and warm.

"I ordered you tequila," Nicole said. "Thought you'd need it after a chat with Tammy."

"How'd you know it was her?"

"Intuition."

Ray raised an eyebrow.

"Tammy wasn't exactly thrilled with us dragging Walter into this," I said.

"Walter drug himself into this shit," Pancake said.

"Somehow Tammy doesn't think that absolves us of our sins."

Ray chuckled. "No surprise there."

The drinks arrived.

I took a sip of the chilled tequila. Nicole was right. I needed it. "What now?" I asked.

"Henry called from the plane," Ray said. "Wanted an update."

"And?"

"I told him the guy seeing Barbara was Walter. Figured why wait."

"What'd he say?" I asked.

"You mean after he regurgitated his tongue?"

"Can't say I blame him," I said. "Lucky he didn't have a stroke. I mean, finding out your wife is murdered and the last guy to see her was a friend."

"This is definitely a screenplay in the making," Nicole said.

"Probably common out there on the left coast," Pancake said. He rested his elbows on the table. The long-necked Pabst Blue Ribbon he held seemed downright Lilliputian in his massive hands.

"Except for the motive part." Nicole draped her hair over one shoulder. "In LA screwing around is the norm. Part of doing business. Not worth whacking someone over. Money and power and good scripts, on the other hand, are worth killing for."

Ray smiled at that, tipping his own PBR in her direction. Ray's way of saying, "Good one."

"Anyway," Ray said, "I told Henry that Walter admitted to the affair but denied he harmed Barbara."

"He believe that?" I asked.

"Actually, he did." Ray drained his beer.

"Really?"

"He knows Walter's a wuss. Couldn't kill a garter snake."

That was true. Walter was a wuss.

Ray continued. "I also told him that Walter wanted to hire us to find the real killer. He said he did, too."

"What are we going to do?" Pancake asked.

Ray shrugged. "I guess we're working for both of them."

"Can we do that?" I asked. "I mean talk about conflict of interest."

"If they both agree, I don't see why not."

"This is now *like* totally LA," Nicole said in a mock Valley girl accent.

"The screenwriter at work," I said.

"Plots are where you find them."

"Pancake's started sniffing around in Henry and Barbara's world," Ray said. "See if Henry had any troubles. Or maybe a motive of his own."

"You mean like his wife humping a neighbor?" I asked.

Ray nodded. "Or maybe some business dealings that went sideways. Pissed someone off. That sort of thing. Meanwhile I'm rolling into Walter's world. We should have something by tomorrow."

"What do you want us to do?" I asked.

"Us?" Ray looked at Nicole. "You part of this now?"

"If you let me," she said. "After all, I was there from the beginning. So to speak."

Ray shook his head. "No can do. I think we've already compromised client integrity enough by allowing you to know what you already know." He hesitated and then said, "Unless you're on the payroll."

"Then hire me," Nicole said. "I think I like this PI stuff."

Ray hesitated and then said, "I suspect we could do that. Mainly to keep an eye on Jake. Don't let him screw up."

"That would definitely be full-time employment," Nicole said.

"Funny," I said.

Ray shrugged. "Probably won't work anyway." He looked back at Nicole. "Legally, if you're going to be inside these investigations we need to protect the company. Confidentiality issues. If you're an employee those aren't a concern."

"Cool." She clapped her hands. "I've always wanted to play PI. Do I get a code name? Or a badge and gun?"

"You're dangerous enough with a car," I said.

She mussed my hair. "Wimp."

Ray smiled. "No badge. No gun. No code name. But you'll get a shiny little plastic ID. Pancake'll make it up for you."

A camera appeared from Pancake's canvas bag. He aimed it at Nicole. "Smile."

"My hair's a mess," she said.

"The way you drive your convertible, I'm amazed you have any left," I said.

She gave me a "get real" look. "Major wimp."

"Don't matter," Pancake said. "All gnarled like that makes you look badass. Now hold still."

She did and he snapped a couple of pictures. "I'll print it up and laminate it as soon as we're done here."

"What's my salary?"

Ray shrugged. "Whatever Jake says it is. Since you're his sidekick, he'll be paying you."

"I always wanted to be Tonto." She looked at me. "So how much?"

"Didn't I just pay you? In your shower."

"Not much of a payment." She flashed a wicked smile.

"The claw marks on my back would indicate otherwise."

She laughed. "But, I'm more of a cash girl."

I raised an eyebrow. "I'll let that slide."

She rolled her eyes. "So how much?"

"A dollar a day," I said.

She gave me a mock pout. "I feel so cheap."

"Okay. Make it five."

"Daddy Freakin' Warbucks here," Nicole said, yanking a thumb toward me.

I smiled. "Or we could work out something else."

"And I'll let that slide," Ray said. "Anyway, Henry's plane gets in at ten-thirty. Your first duty will be to go with Jake to pick him up."

"Seems the police would meet his plane," I said.

"Henry arranged for a sit-down with Morgan tomorrow." Ray waved his empty bottle toward Carla Martinez who nodded back from her station behind the bar.

"Where are we taking him?" I asked. "To a hotel?"

"Home."

"The police are finished there?"

Ray nodded.

"I'm not sure I'd want to go home just yet," I said. "I mean after what happened. Seems weird to me."

"It's Henry's choice," Ray said. "So pick him up and deposit him there."

"Will do."

"And be cool."

"Always."

Carla handed Ray a fresh beer. "You guys want any food? Or are you drinking dinner tonight?"

# CHAPTER EIGHTEEN

THE TRIP TO the airport in Mobile should have taken thirty minutes. Took fifteen with Nicole as pilot. She treated the highway like it was part of the NASCAR circuit. Door handle to door handle and triple digit speeds. Several screaming horns, friendly fingers, and flashes of high beams fell in her wake. She seemed not to notice.

"Do you have a wall somewhere decorated with speeding tickets?" I asked.

"If I did it'd be empty."

"You've never been pulled over?"

"Sure. Just never got a ticket."

"I see."

"A smile and a little cleavage works wonders."

"I'll remember that."

She maneuvered past a delivery truck and then whipped around an SUV, alternating the brake pedal with the accelerator. "Not sure you qualify."

"What's wrong with my smile?"

"I don't think that's the important part."

Hard to argue with logic.

My body ached with tension from the death grip I had on the dash and door handle by the time she wheeled into the parking deck, snatched a ticket from the automatic dispenser, and spun up to the third level. She parked along a low concrete wall, facing the airport runways. An American Airlines flight lifted into view, engines whining.

"There were plenty of spaces on the lower levels," I said.

"More people, too. Up here, we're alone."

"So?"

"So, we have thirty minutes."

"At the risk of being redundant, so?"

"Get out of the car."

I did. I looked around. The third floor was poorly lit and sparsely populated. A dozen cars, only one parked nearby. A jacked-up red pickup, its sides and oversized wheels splattered with dried mud, "Crossroads Off-Roading" stenciled on its doors in white lettering.

"Now what?"

She stood next to the wall and watched as a United flight hit the air. "Isn't this great?"

It was. The plane elevated slowly, turned away from us, its engines bright red dots that shrank and finally winked out.

"Cool."

"Want to do something really cool?" she asked.

"Like what?"

I heard a zipper.

She wiggled from her jeans and bright red thong, letting them bunch at her ankles. She leaned, straight-armed on the edge of the wall. "I think you can figure it out from here."

"Is this a good idea?" I looked around sure that someone was watching from the shadows.

"We're down to twenty-five minutes. Get over here and do your thing."

"My thing?"

"Okay, my thing."

I did.

Another plane, Delta this time, rose, the sound of its engines mingling with Nicole's soft moaning and my own raspy breathing. The night suddenly seemed much warmer. Four more flights departed before we reached the finish line. I zipped up. Nicole tugged her thong and jeans up.

"Feel better?" she asked.

"I was just fixing to ask you the same thing."

She smiled. "A lot better."

"Me, too," I said. "You give picking someone up at the airport a whole new meaning."

"Let's go meet Henry."

We found Henry at baggage claim. He stood near the carousel, cell phone to his ear. He looked, well, normal. I expected him to be pale and drawn and red-eyed and exhausted. Henry was none of that. His suit and shirt were crisp, his tie snugged. He looked as if he was heading to a business meeting. He nodded as we approached but continued his conversation.

What I heard went like this:

"Get the partnership agreements and the other papers together and meet me in the office at ten."

"No, I should be finished with the police by then."

"Yes, the attorneys should be present."

"No, that'll have to wait until the death certificate's finalized."

"Why? Because she's not legally dead until she's legally dead."

He disconnected the call and slipped the phone into his jacket pocket.

I shook his hand, introduced him to Nicole, and then asked, "Everything okay?"

"Barbara was a partner in the company. Her death will create a mountain of paperwork and BS."

Really? That's his concern right now? I felt a little off-balance. "Sorry for your loss."

Henry nodded. "Thanks."

This was odd and not what I expected. Henry seemed distracted. Definitely not torn up over Barbara's death. Seemed all business as usual. Was he in shock or did he simply not care? Did he have her whacked?

He seemed to sense my confusion. He sighed. "I'm sorry. I guess that sounded cold. Or uncaring. Or whatever." He shook his head. "Truth is that we have a lot of deals in the works. Things that could unwind very quickly if investors felt the company was wobbly or in any kind of trouble." He looked at me. "The business world never takes a day off. Hell, it never even takes a nap."

I nodded. "I understand." Though I'm not sure I really did.

"Howard Hughes died on a Monday," Henry said. "He was on a plane flying from Acapulco to the medical center in Houston. I have a friend, a doctor, who was there in training at the time. He and the staff knew Hughes was on the way. They also knew he was dead. But the world didn't know. From what I understand, the powers to be in the Summa Corporation, Hughes Company, and maybe even the Feds, squashed the news until after the New York Stock Exchange closed that day. They feared his death would ripple, maybe even crash, the markets. He was that big. The delay gave the Summa folks until Tuesday morning to reach out to investors and assure them that business as usual would continue." He shrugged. "Not that my little businesses are in that league, but the principle's the same. Nervous investors make poor decisions. We can't afford to let that happen."

"I guess that's true," I said.

After collecting Henry's luggage, we packed into the car. I drove. Nicole protested, but I countered that her driving might give Henry a heart attack.

"You survived," she said.

"I got lucky."

I wound down the deck, paid the gate attendant, and headed toward the airport exit. I studied Henry in the rearview mirror. He looked calm and relaxed. I had a million questions I wanted to ask, but Henry beat me to it.

"Any new leads on who did this?" he said.

"How much did Ray tell you?"

"He told me about Walter. Said you made a video. Walter leaving around midnight."

"That's right."

He looked out the side window as if watching the scenery go by. "I must say it's not what I expected."

"What did you expect?"

"I don't know. But not Walter." He sighed and then turned his gaze to the rearview mirror, where our eyes locked. He looked down. "This might sound strange, but I'm actually relieved it was Walter."

This guy was full of surprises. "Why?"

"I'm not sure. I guess because Walter is a friend. He and Barbara were always close. I didn't know they were this close but close nonetheless."

"I guess that makes sense," Nicole said. "On some level."

"A friends with benefits situation I can understand. I was afraid it was some young beach stud."

"Any reason to suspect that?" I asked.

"Let's just say Barbara was a very friendly person."

Nicole twisted in her seat and looked back at Henry. "What do you mean?"

Again he sighed. "This isn't her first indiscretion. There were three others that I knew of. Last one was a few years ago. I thought she was beyond all that now." He looked out the window again, unfocused. "Guess that wasn't the case."

"Do you think Walter killed her?" Nicole asked.

"Anything's possible, but that would surprise me. Walter doesn't seem the type."

"Killers often don't," I said.

"True. But Walter would be a stretch."

"He was the last one to see her alive."

"Maybe," Henry said. "Unless someone came along later. Did you see anyone else around? When you were there making the video?"

"No."

"The beach was very quiet that night," Nicole said.

"You were there?"

"We had sort of a spy date."

"Spy date?"

Nicole shrugged. "Didn't want Jake to be lonely on his stakeout."

"You work for Ray?"

"Sure do. Sort of. Mostly just hanging with Jake."

Henry nodded. "Still, I don't see Walter as a killer."

"Just an adulterer?" I asked.

"That's a long way from murder."

"Passion can be a motive. Maybe an argument? Maybe she was going to break it off? Some guys don't handle that well. Maybe things simply escalated? That sort of thing."

"I suppose."

"What about you, Henry?"

"Me? I was in New York."

"A man of your means would have no problem hiring someone."

Henry's gaze snapped to mine in the rearview mirror again. His eyes narrowed. "I don't like where this is going. You accusing me?"

"Just asking the questions that have to be asked. You can bet Morgan will."

"I'm sure." His narrowed eyes relaxed. "And I'll tell him like I'm telling you now—no way. Barbara and I had our differences. She had her affairs. I worked too much. Wasn't the most attentive. But in the end we loved each other."

"And she was part of your company?"

He nodded. "From the beginning."

"What happens to her ownership shares?" I asked.

"They go to me."

"Could be a motive," I said.

"Jake, get real. They were mine anyway. We were married."

That made sense. And if the profits, dividends, whatever went into the family pot, Henry had no reason to off Barbara. At least not a financial one. Unless a divorce was in the offing.

"Anyone with a grudge against you?" Nicole asked. "Or your wife?"

"Definitely not Barbara. She was easygoing. Most of the time. I mean she had her flare-ups. Could be a perfectionist at times. But nothing that would bring this her way. Me? I've stepped on a few toes. Bested some folks in business deals. Software is big business. Real estate, too. Lots of money involved. Very competitive. It can be . . . what's the word? . . . confrontational at times."

"My point," Nicole said. "Money and competition can lead down some dark alleys."

"And be a strong motive for murder," I added.

"Why would such a person, if such a person exists, kill Barbara?" Henry asked.

"Maybe you were the target," I said. "Maybe they thought you were home."

"God, I hope not. I couldn't live with that. The thought that something I did led to her murder."

"So, back to the original question. Anyone you can think of that might want to harm you?"

"Not really. "

"But?"

"A couple of guys. One worked for my software development group. A guy named Ely Thompson. We caught him stealing sensitive documents. Had designs on going out on his own. I fired him. But that was years ago."

"Could have percolated," I said. "Some folks can hold on to a grudge."

"Can't argue with you there. But I heard he wasn't well. Had some heart issues or something. I know he moved. Orlando, last I heard."

"And the other one?" Nicole asked.

"Jason Hughes. Young kid. Early twenties. Sued us. Maybe two years ago. Claimed a copyright infringement. A program we developed that tracks medical records and payments. Better than anything out there."

"And?"

"He developed something similar. Independently. We showed the court all our R and D documentation. Showed we had been working on it for a couple of years. The judge tossed his case. He wasn't happy." Henry massaged a temple. "The irony is that he was a very bright kid. The kind we would have hired."

"We'll need to talk with both of them."

"I'll have all their info for you tomorrow."

I pulled into Henry's drive and then helped him carry his luggage to the front door.

"God, I dread this," Henry said. "The house will seem so empty."

"Sure you want to stay here? I can take you to a hotel."

"And then I'd have to face it tomorrow. I'd rather be home right now." He unlocked the door and then looked at me. "I had nothing to do with all this. Nothing." I nodded so he went on. "Fact is, I want to keep you guys on the clock. To find whoever did this."

"Isn't that what the police are doing?"

"Sure, but I know Ray can do things the police can't." He pushed open the door. "I'll call him tomorrow."

Back in the car, I headed toward The Point.

"I feel sorry for him," Nicole said. "He seems so sad. Almost lost."

"Didn't seem too broken up to me."

"You have to look around the edges. His eyes, his voice. He's hurting."

"Unless he hired someone to whack his wife."

"He didn't," she said.

"Okay, Sherlock, how do you know that?"

"Intuition."

*Lord, help me.*

Back at Nicole's, I called Ray, bringing him up to date on what Henry said, giving him the two names Henry had offered, and telling him Henry wanted to keep Ray on the case.

"I figured he would."

"What are we going to do?"

"I'll give Henry a call and then talk with Walter in the morning," Ray said. "See how it all shakes out."

"I'll see you at the office in the morning."

"What are you up to now?" Ray asked.

"Watching a very beautiful young lady with a bottle of tequila prance naked around her living room."

That was true. Nicole had gone to her room and returned sans clothing, towels in one hand, a bottle of Patrón and two glasses in the other. She pushed open the door and stepped out on to the deck. A warm breeze came off the Gulf.

"Lucky you."

"Yes, lucky me. Looks like it's hot tub time."

"Don't want to interfere with that."

"Wouldn't want you to. See you around eight."

# CHAPTER NINETEEN

THE WILBANKS BROTHERS were as different as two people could be. Not in appearance, mind you. Both tall, pushing six-one, rail thin, with brown hair that could use a good washing, pulled back into ponytails. Many thought they were twins, but in truth, Darrell had two years on Darnell, Darnell a bunch of IQ points on Darrell.

Their biggest differences resided in their personalities. Darrell, twenty-four, acted more like fourteen. Mind and body always in overdrive. Jumpy. No focus. His life one party after another, happy hour beginning around ten in the morning most days. Not to mention his love of meth. Probably a big reason he could never sit still, never carry on a real conversation, thoughts and words flitting this way and that. He never finished high school, not even a GED, and slid from job to job, always leaving after a few weeks because of some insult or slight, real or imagined. Darrell simply didn't play well with others.

He was the same with women, snagging and shedding them with a disturbing regularity, as if he feared that if any stayed around too long they'd take root. Darrell rarely showed fear of anything, probably because he rarely grasped the true nature of any situation. Always bragged that he never walked away from a fight. Often preferring that to dialogue. Darrell believed that everything would always work out well. For him, anyway. And, indeed, things usually did. One of those guys with a golden umbrella hanging over his head that protected him from all the chaos he stirred up.

Darnell was a different thing altogether. Twenty-two, yet seemed ten years older. Actually had a couple of responsible bones in his body. Quiet and soft-spoken, he endlessly tried to rein in his brother, an impossible task that he went about with a calm and thoughtful demeanor.

After snagging a legitimate high school degree, Darnell signed on with a local AT&T store at eighteen and never left. Actually liked the job. He dated some, no one steady, and drank only after sunset and on weekends. His meth use was a fraction of his brother's. Yet even Darnell had to admit his brother's golden umbrella had saved him more than a few times. He hoped it would be unfurled in their current situation but he had a bad feeling about this one. Darrell had led him further out on the plank than he'd ever been and Darnell couldn't shake the feeling that their life was on the verge of unraveling.

"What time is it?" Darrell asked.

"Five after four," Darnell said.

Darnell's six-year-old Honda Accord, gray with a primered left front fender, was parked just off Highway 180, a hundred yards or so short of where Fort Morgan Road splintered off, the fort itself sitting near the tip of the sandy spit where it had since its construction just after the War of 1812. Dauphine Island, across the way, guarding the other side of the entrance to Mobile Bay, wasn't visible at this time of the morning. Nudged up behind Darnell's Honda was a yellow VW bug that belonged to Darrell's latest squeeze. Heather Macomb, a seventeen-year-old high school senior, who had snuck out of her house to "see Darrell off." The trio stood on one of the many low sand dunes that flanked the road and faced the beach that angled down to the dark waters of the bay.

"They should be here soon," Darrell said.

"I don't understand any of this," Heather said.

Darrell gave her a glance. "You don't have to."

"Don't be pissy. I mean, what kind of person has you meet him out here? In the middle of the night?"

"The big man don't like attention. He says meet him here, we meet him here."

Heather shook her head, her long dark hair swaying behind her. "Who is this guy, anyway?"

"I told you. He's the big boss. He ain't got no name."

Heather kicked at the sand. "That's just silly. Everybody's got a name."

"This one you don't want to know."

"How do you know?" she said, more than a sliver of defiance in her voice. "You've never met him."

Darrell picked up a loose rock and threw it across the beach. It almost reached the water. "Don't have to. Raul knows him. Raul got us this job. That's all I need to know."

"Okay, what's his name?"

Darrell looked at her. "Better if you don't know."

"Bet you don't know, either." She pointed her chin at him.

"Oh, we know. Don't we, little brother?" Darnell didn't say anything so he continued. "But you have no reason to know, and he likes to keep a low profile."

Heather apparently wasn't finished challenging him. "So why does this mysterious boss dude want to meet you out here in the middle of the night?"

Darrell brushed sand from his hands. "Because he's a careful guy. That's why he's the boss."

"I don't like this." She grabbed his arm. "You're going out on a boat for a business meeting? Who conducts meetings on a boat? All secretive like this?"

"The kind that's going to make us rich." He hugged her to him. "Don't worry none. We'll be back tomorrow morning with enough money for that trip down to Disney World we talked about."

She stepped back. "I still don't like it." Her lower lip descended into a pout.

Darrell laughed. "You miss me already?"

"It's just that my parents are going away for a couple of days, and I wanted to spend them with you."

"You will. Starting tomorrow."

"That'll leave us only one night. With my curfew, we never get to spend an entire night together."

"I know. But me and little brother got business to attend to. Ain't that right?"

Darnell shrugged.

The three turned toward the water as the sound of a powerboat broke the silence. Still far out, around the point, the thick seaside air carrying the vibrations.

"That'll be them now," Darrell said.

"Sounds like a fishing boat," Heather said. "How are you going to do business on that?"

Darrell laughed. "That's just our taxi. The boss man has a big yacht. Probably around the point and out in the Gulf."

"Oh."

"Supposed to be a floating palace."

"Really?" Heather's eyes lit up. "I'd like to see that."

"You can't. Fact is, you ain't supposed to be here. No one's to know where we are."

The sound of the powerboat increased second by second as it seemed to near the point. They'd be able to see it soon.

"You better scoot," Darrell said.

"Something isn't right about all this," Heather said.

"You'll see. We'll be down at Disney before you know it. Now get going."

"What about Darnell's car?" Heather nodded toward the Honda. "You just going to leave it here?"

"One of the boss man's crew is going to pick it up. Needs it for some job."

"What job?"

"Don't know. Don't care." He stretched and gave a half yawn. "We do as we're told."

"That makes no sense."

"Ain't supposed to. Now scoot." He patted her jean-clad butt.

"So, how're you going to get back home? When you get off the boat tomorrow?"

"You're going to pick us up at the marina." He smiled.

"What if I'm busy?"

Darrell rolled his eyes. "Yeah, right."

She set her jaw and her eyes narrowed as she glared at him. "I have stuff to do. Important stuff. Just like you."

"You mean like pick us up tomorrow morning?"

She sighed, her shoulders relaxing in resignation. "Okay. What time?"

"I suspect early. Seven or eight."

"I'll be there."

He hugged her, giving her a kiss on the forehead. "You're the best."

"But you'll owe me." Now she gave a fake pout.

"Disney World, here we come."

He walked her to her car. "And don't tell no one about this."

"I won't. You know that." She climbed in her car, lowering her window. "Be careful."

"Nothing to be careful about." He tapped the roof of her car. "See you tomorrow."

She backed up, pulled a U-turn, and drove away.

"That wasn't smart," Darnell said as her taillights faded in the distance. "Bringing her here."

"She's cool. She won't tell nobody. Besides, she's one of the best fucks I've ever had."

"You and your pecker. You need to rein it in."

"Cut me some slack. Just because you ain't gettin' any."

"And you ain't gettin' nothing legal."

"Trust me on this," Darrell said, "that girl's all woman."

Darnell shook his head. "That ain't it, anyway. Raul said don't tell no one. I'm sure that included your seventeen-year-old bimbo."

Darrell produced a small glass vial from his pocket. "You need a little tune-up." Using a tiny metal spoon he dipped out a dose of meth, snorting it loudly. He extended the vial toward his brother.

"I'll pass. Clear thinking might be best here."

"Suit yourself." Darrell filled his other nostril, sniffing and shaking his head, then rubbing his nose with the heel of one hand. "Man, this is some good shit. Sure you don't want some?"

"I'm sure."

Darrell returned the vial to his pocket as the boat appeared, a faint white smudge in the darkness. It turned toward the beach. They grabbed their duffels and walked down the sandy slope to the water's edge.

"She's right, you know," Darnell said. "I don't like this either."

"You worry too much."

"We don't even know this guy."

"Don't need to. All we need to know is he's the guy paying. And Raul vouches for him. Says he'll have more jobs for us. Big money jobs."

"Maybe," Darnell said. "But he better not find out Heather was here."

"He'll never know. How could he?"

"I think he can find out most anything he needs to."

The boat was now a hundred yards out, closing.

"That's true. He found us. Hired us. This is going to be our gravy train."

Darnell snorted. "According to who?"

"Raul."

"I don't trust him, neither."

"Jesus, little brother." Darrell clapped him on the back. "You can screw up anything."

"What the hell does that mean?"

"It means we have a good gig here. We did good work for him. Time to reap the rewards."

The boat's engine dropped a few notches as it began a slow slide toward the beach.

Darrell shook his head. "You worry when there's nothing to worry about. Same way Mom was when she was still with us."

"Don't go there."

"I'm just saying, she worried about everything. Even worried about worrying."

That was true. She had been a natural-born worrier. Of course her meth habit, which finally took her, added to her innate paranoia.

The boat slid up against the beach with a soft scrape. Three men stepped off.

"Howdy," Darrell said.

Brief introductions followed.

Joe Zuma, short, thick, dark, Hispanic, greased back hair, muscular tattooed arms hanging from a blue University of Florida sweatshirt, sleeves ripped off at the shoulder.

Frank Boyd, tall, thin, shaggy blond hair, jeans, black t-shirt.

Carlos, no last name given, Hispanic, stood apart, head down, no eye contact, as if he wanted to remain invisible.

"Where's your car?" Zuma asked.

"Up there," Darnell said. "On the road."

Zuma's dark gaze fell on him. "And the other car? Who was that?"

"Other car?"

"The one that just drove away."

"Oh," Darrell said, laughing. "Some chick was lost. Asked for directions."

"This time of night?"

Darrell looked at him but said nothing.

"You know her?" Zuma asked.

Darnell didn't like where this was going.

Darrell didn't seem to be bothered in the slightest. "Nope. Never seen her before."

Zuma nodded and glanced at Boyd. He said, "Let's have the keys." Darnell handed them to him and he tossed them to Carlos. "You got everything you need?"

Carlos nodded.

"Get going."

Carlos climbed the slope from the beach to the road while the four men settled into the boat, Boyd at the wheel. He backed away from the beach, fired a "hold on" over his shoulder. The big Evinrude spun to life and the boat jerked forward.

# CHAPTER TWENTY

I WAS STILL nursing a hangover brought on by too little sleep, too much tequila, and way too much Nicole when I climbed into her SL. I had said we could take my Mustang, which sat in her garage right next to her red Mercedes, but she insisted on driving, saying that riding with me was "boring" and "like going to church with a little old lady." I started to launch a defense of my manhood but though better of it. A losing battle, for sure. Besides, I could console myself with the fact that Nicole probably thought the F-22s the top guns flew out of Pensacola were boring. Head throbbing, I held on as Nicole launched from her driveway, spun around The Point, and in a whirl of wind climbed to warp factor four. Definitely not boring.

First stop—Ray's. It was just shy of eight a.m.

Ray and Pancake sat on the deck, papers strewn before them, coffee cups nearly empty, a Dew next to Ray. I poured coffee for Nicole and me and refilled Ray's and Pancake's cups. I sat at the table, Nicole next to me.

Pancake rummaged inside his canvas bag and pulled out Nicole's laminated ID card. He handed it to her.

"I'm official," she said. She looked at the photo. "Hmm. Not a bad picture considering it was a bad hair day."

Get real, I thought. Nicole didn't have bad hair days. Or really bad anything days.

"You look mighty fine," Pancake said. "Bad hair and all."

"Thanks." She smiled at him. "Maybe you should consider photography."

He shrugged. "One of my many talents." His red eyebrows gave her a couple of bounces.

"And the others?" she asked.

"Too many to enumerate."

"Are you guys finished?" I asked.

"Probably not," Nicole said.

I looked at Ray. "What's the latest?"

Ray nodded to Pancake.

Pancake flipped open a red folder. "Walter has accumulated a long list of folks who might think he's Satan. He does about every kind of law. Contracts, divorce, liability, criminal defense. Boy's a regular jack of all trades." He handed me a stack of papers. "These would be the most likely possibilities."

I scanned them, Nicole scooting her chair closer to see them better. There were eight pages, each with a name in bold print on top, several paragraphs of info below. Three had red Xs scratched next to the name.

"The ones marked are the ones I think top the list," Pancake added. "George Rose. Big player in Mobile real estate. Has a big boat. Apparently a young lady went overboard during a party. Very intoxicated. Very drowned. Her father sued for wrongful death. Walter took Rose for just north of twelve million."

"Ouch," Nicole said. "That's adult money."

"Indeed." Pancake nodded his massive head. "Rose made a bunch of threats. Walter's practice, Walter's house, Walter's life, the usual."

I flipped to the next red X'ed page. "Santiago Gomez?"

"An illegal who blew away two guys in a parking lot. Drug deal. Santiago walked away with the money and the drugs. Got popped trying to sell the drugs to some undercover dude. Still had the murder weapon stuffed beneath his belt. Real genius. Walter put together some bullshit defense that didn't work. Big shock, Santiago got life without. Santiago's brother Raul, apparently one of the cartel's bad boys, threatened Walter. Walter called in ICE, the FBI, everyone he could think of. Each told him to pack sand. Said Raul had rights. Hadn't broken any laws. He'd be my number one. Violence being part of his basic personality and all."

"Sounds like he could use a little anger management," Nicole said.

"I think old Raul is way beyond all that. I'm just saying." Pancake drained his coffee cup in two gulps. "The last one is Satinder Singh. Walter gutted him in a divorce. Couple of years ago. Planted a bomb in Walter's car. Lucky for Walter it was a dud. Didn't explode but flared into white-hot fire that reduced Walter's Mercedes to a mass of twisted metal."

"I remember that," I said. "Tammy went all nuclear. Bent my ear about it for a month. Didn't Singh go to jail?"

Pancake nodded. "Besides having to cough up a hundred grand to pay for Walter's car, he got three years. Out after fifteen months. Just a couple of months ago."

"And all these others?" I asked, waving the pages toward Pancake.

"Second tier," Ray said. "We'll concentrate on them later if none of those pan out."

"Anything on the names Henry gave us?"

"One was easy," Ray said. "Ely Thompson did have some heart trouble. Had surgery down at Tampa General. Didn't make it. The other one, the young kid, Jason Hughes, has a condo over in Destin. Developed a start-up he called Media Magic. Mostly gaming stuff."

I nodded. "So what's the plan?"

"You and Nicole check out Hughes and Singh," Ray said. "Pancake and I'll chat with Rose and Raul."

# CHAPTER TWENTY-ONE

WALTER DREADED THIS talk. Didn't see any way to avoid it, had to be, but the pressure in his chest and the tightness he sensed in his scalp screamed "run away." Avoid this at all cost. But he couldn't. He had screwed up. Big time. Now he had to do the right thing. To pay for his sins.

He stood at the front door of Henry Plummer's home, finger hovering near the doorbell, frozen. As if he had suddenly been paralyzed. He had rehearsed what he would say, how he would apologize, guessed at Henry's possible responses. Had laid awake most of the night going through multiple scenarios. Over coffee and eggs this morning he did the same, Tammy asking where his head was, why he was so quiet. He brushed her aside saying that he had a lot on his mind.

You think?

I mean the affair with Barbara aside, he had to be the main suspect. He had read that in Morgan's eyes yesterday.

He had called his office, saying he'd be in late, telling Connie to cancel a couple of clients. He rarely did that but now he'd done it two days in a row. The last thing he wanted to do was sit and listen to some other poor bastard's legal woes. Right now his own troubles trumped even paying clients.

Connie had told him that some newspaper guy had been there bright and early. Actually waiting for her when she unlocked the office, saying he wanted to talk with Walter. He even said he'd wait.

She had dismissed him in no uncertain terms. She didn't remember his name or even who he worked for, only wanting to send him away before Walter showed up and got caught unawares.

Connie was worth every penny he paid her.

His finger touched the button, but he couldn't push it. He glanced up the street toward his own home. His refuge. Maybe he should go back to bed. Worry about this later. But, procrastination wasn't in his nature. Before he could fret over this any longer he pressed the button. Chimes sounded, followed by footsteps. The door swung open.

The shock on Henry's face was real. He even took a step back.

"Sorry to bother you, Henry," Walter said. "But we should talk."

Henry wore slacks and an untucked golf shirt, his hair still damp from a morning shower. He hesitated, and then took another step back. "Come in."

They sat at the kitchen table after Henry poured them each a cup of coffee.

"I'm so sorry," Walter said. "For everything."

Henry nodded, cradling his cup in both hands. His gaze stayed on the table as if he couldn't look at Walter.

"I want you to know I had nothing to do with what happened. To Barbara."

Again, Henry nodded.

"I wouldn't. I couldn't."

Finally Henry looked at him. "I know."

Walter felt as if he could exhale for the first time. As if the bubble in his chest deflated with an almost audible whoosh.

Henry continued. "I told the police that, too. That I didn't see how you could be involved." He sighed. "In her murder, anyway."

"And the other, the affair, I'm sorry for that, too. It was a betrayal. Pure and simple."

"It is that."

"I don't know how it happened. It wasn't intended and it certainly wasn't meant to hurt you. I know Barbara felt the same way. She loved you."

"Odd way to show it, don't you think?"

"I do. And if she were here, she'd feel as badly as I do."

"You going to tell me how my wife felt? Like you know her better than I did?" Henry took in a deep breath and let it out slowly. "I'm sorry. That wasn't called for."

"Sure it was. You have every right to be angry."

"I'm not angry, Walter. Not with you. Not with her. I'm just disappointed."

"I'm sure."

"Truth is, I understand. I wasn't the best husband. I worked too much and I traveled too much. I never gave her the attention she deserved."

"Don't do this. It wasn't your fault. Barbara told me as much. She was happy with you."

"Apparently."

"She was. She loved you. What we had, what we did, was . . . I don't know what it was. It just happened."

Henry drained his cup. "Walter, I'll tell you like I told Ray Longly, part of me was relieved it was you."

Not what Walter expected. "Really?"

"Yes, really. You might or might not know, but Barbara had done this before. She had had other affairs."

"I didn't know."

"She did. Three times, actually. I was afraid it was some young beach dude or something like that. With you, I understand on some level. You and she were always close."

"We were friends. It sort of evolved from there."

"As things like that do." Henry stood, refilled his coffee, waving the pot toward Walter, who declined. He returned to the table. "So, we're good, Walter. I don't blame you."

"You should. It was not my best decision."

"But it's done. You can't un-ring that bell."

"I have to ask, Henry, did you have anything to do with this? With Barbara?"

Henry's eyes narrowed. "You know I didn't."

"I do, but I had to ask." He sighed. "Any idea who might have?"

"None."

Walter clasped his hands together, resting them on the table. "What now?"

"Find out who did. And why?"

"Morgan's all over that," Walter said.

"As is Ray."

"I know. Do you have any problems with him working for both of us?"

"I don't really give a damn about all that. I just want answers."

"Me, too."

Walter stared at his coffee cup, the coffee now cold. It was time to leave, but he couldn't move. As if something else needed to be said. But he came up empty. Further apologies or recriminations didn't seem right. Didn't even seem necessary with Henry so accepting of his and Barbara's failures. But he still felt he should do more.

Henry broke the thick silence. "Got a call from some newspaper guy this morning. At the office. My staff deflected him, but I suspect I'll have to talk with them sooner or later."

"Probably the same guy who stopped by my office this morning."

"You? Why you?"

"I guess they already know about Barbara and me."

"How could they?" Henry asked.

"Some of these reporters have sources deep inside the local PD. Always have. I suspect that's the source."

Henry let out a heavy sigh. "This nightmare has a lot of tentacles, doesn't it?" He looked up at Walter.

Walter nodded, thinking, boy does it ever.

# CHAPTER TWENTY-TWO

"DON'T YOU THINK torching his car was a bit excessive?" I asked.

Nicole and I had intercepted Satinder Singh in the parking lot of his real estate office near the beach in Gulf Shores. Singh was a slight man, wrapped in a gray suit, white shirt, burgundy tie, and matching turban. He had led us into his office where we now sat.

"It surely does now." Singh spoke perfect English with a slight British accent. "At the time I was filled with anger. I mean that bastard lied in court. My ex-wife did, too. Cost me a small fortune."

"Looks like you recovered," I said. The office had all the trappings of success. Expensive leather furniture, art on the wall, the whole deal.

"So it might appear," Singh said. "But with me locked up for fifteen months my business suffered greatly. I'm just now getting it back on track."

"And?"

"And what?" Singh asked.

"Any residual animosity toward Walter?"

"Of course. I'll hate that son of a bitch forever."

"Enough to want harm to come his way?"

Singh's forehead creased and a note of caution crept into his voice. "What is this about?"

"You watch the news?"

"No." He shook his head. "Too depressing."

"So you don't know about the murder out on The Point the other night?"

Singh looked confused. "Sure. I heard about that. What does that have to do with Walter? Or with me?"

"Maybe nothing. But the lady lived right down the street from Walter."

"You think Walter had something to do with it?"

"Or maybe someone wanted it to seem that way."

Singh's eyes widened. "You mean someone like me?"

I shrugged.

Singh jumped from his chair. "Are you insane? Me? I could never . . ."

"What?" I asked. "Torch someone's car? Kill someone? Hire someone to kill another person? Frame someone you had *issues* with?"

Singh leaned on his desk. His dark eyes stabbed at me. "How dare you come into my office and ask such questions. Make such accusations. I think you should both leave."

I didn't move. Neither did Nicole.

"I'm simply asking the questions the police will," I said.

"The police?"

I nodded. "They know what I know. Or soon will. I think they'll look into this angle. The possibility that someone was trying to frame Walter. And when they do, they'll come knocking on your door."

Singh collapsed into his chair as if he were a deflating balloon. "Of course." He folded his hands before him, almost as if in prayer. He looked like he might cry.

"Look," he said. "I had issues with Walter. I handled them badly. I paid for my poor judgement and my despicable actions." He swallowed hard. "But this? I had nothing to do with this."

I believed him. And since I couldn't think of anything else to ask, we left.

By the time we reached Nicole's car, my cell chimed. It was Tammy. My reflex was to send it over the voice mail but decided I'd better see what she had to say. Maybe some news on Walter. I punched the answer button.

"What the hell is wrong with you?" she screamed.

Tammy can sometimes be a broken record. Seemed to ask me that same question at the beginning every conversation we'd had for years. Most of them, anyway.

"Nothing. Thanks for asking." My standard response.

"You called the newspapers? Sent them out here?"

"I did not."

"Then why are they here asking questions about Walter and Barbara?"

"Because stories like this sell newspapers."

"Listen, numbnuts," she said, almost a hiss, "I know what they do. I know they're bottom feeding scum. But what I don't know is how they got that information. How they even knew to come here looking for Walter. Riddle me that, loser."

Now I wish I had sent the media her way. I mean, if you have to do the time you might as well do the crime. I started to say just that but instead I said, "Most reporters have contacts inside the police department. You think that might be it?"

Silence. Guess she hadn't thought if that. Much easier to simply blame me.

"Look," I said, "I haven't told anyone except the police."

"So, what do I do?"

"Tell them 'no comment' and close the door in their face."

I heard a heavy, frustrated sigh. "Can't you come over and run them off?"

"No, I can't."

"Can't or won't?"

"Same thing."

"But—"

"But nothing. Call Walter." I disconnected the call.

Nicole raised an eyebrow at me.

"You don't want to know."

"I think I have a pretty good idea."

We climbed in the SL and were off. Next stop: Jason Hughes' place.

Which turned out to be on the fifth floor of an upscale condo building on the sand in Destin. Jason was the prototypical nerd. Thin and pale, as if, even though he lived on the beach, he never really ventured outside. Apparently a night owl since our knock on his door seemed to have roused him from bed. He greeted us in gray cotton drawstring pants, a dark blue t-shirt, bare feet, and serious bedhead, his longish hair a cluster of cowlicks. We apologized but he was gracious, saying he always worked until around four in the morning and usually slept until ten or so.

He offered juice or coffee, but we declined, so after he made himself a cup of instant coffee, we sat at his dining table. He answered our questions without hesitation, though he couldn't keep his gaze from straying to Nicole, over and over. He said he held no grudge against Henry Plummer and that he'd actually learned a lot from the lawsuit process, that it had cost him very little as an attorney friend did the work in exchange for Jason setting up his home and office computer systems. He had now moved on to gaming and his new company, Media Magic, was on the verge of popping—his word. He had heard nothing of Barbara's murder as he never watched TV or read a newspaper. And no he wasn't involved in any way.

I believed him, too.

Two dead ends.

# CHAPTER TWENTY-THREE

RAY WASN'T HAPPY. He hated hot weather. Of course, living on the Gulf Coast meant he had to deal with it on a regular basis, but still, he hated it. And today, the temp was already on the climb. No clouds, no Gulf breeze, no relief in sight. Didn't bode well for his mood. Supposed to reach the 90s, according to the local weather gurus. But Ray knew they batted five hundred at best. Pancake, for all his size and padding, was the exact opposite. The hotter the better for him. Said it reminded him of his August two-a-day practices. Hittin' weather, he called it. So now as Ray sped down Highway 180, Pancake rode shotgun, window down, playing airplane with his hand.

That was one of the many things Ray liked about the big guy. Sure he was smart, and tough as a bag of nails, but inside Pancake was still a boy. Always seemed to grab life by the handful and enjoyed every minute of it. Ray often wished he had a dose of Pancake's playfulness and bit less of his own deeply rooted cynicism. But it was an empty wish. He was too old, too set in his ways to change, so he simply enjoyed Pancake's enjoyment of life.

The house Raul Gomez rented, like the entire neighborhood, was in every respect modest. Tan stucco, worn green tile roof, grass mowed but scattered with spiky tufts of crabgrass. Ray walked up the cracked walkway toward the front stoop, Pancake following behind. His knock got no response.

"He isn't home."

The voice came from his left. When he looked he saw a stooped, thin, elderly woman, gray hair pulled up into a topknot bun, a single loose strand hanging over her left eye. She wore rolled-up jeans, sockless tennis shoes, and an oversized, dirt-stained, white t-shirt. She carried a black plastic flat of flowers. Mostly red and white.

"Any idea when he'll be back?" Ray asked.

She settled the flowers near her own walkway. Ray now saw that dark strips of turned dirt edged each side.

"Who are you?" the woman asked, wiping her hands on a frayed pale-blue towel she then tossed on the ground next to the flowers.

"Ray."

"That don't tell me nothing." She waited for his response but when he said nothing she went on. "Name's Hattie. Hattie Shaw."

Ray smiled. "I'm Ray Longly. This is Pancake."

"Pancake? Never heard that name before."

Pancake nodded. "Me neither."

"Your mama must've liked breakfast." She brushed dirt from the knees of her pants.

"Something like that," Pancake replied.

"We're looking for Raul," Ray said. "Need to ask him a couple of questions."

"You a friend?"

"No."

"A cop?" She propped one fist on her hip and parked the wayward strand behind her ear. Her face glistened with sweat.

"No, ma'am."

"Wouldn't surprise me none with that brother of his."

"Santiago?"

"That's the one."

"He's in jail," Ray said.

"Where he belongs. That young man was nothing but trouble. Loud music. That rap crap. Always a bunch of trouble hanging around with him. Frightfully annoying is how I see it."

Ray couldn't suppress his smile. He liked Hattie Shaw. No nonsense. The same way Ray saw most things in life.

"I don't think Santiago will be out of jail for a long time," Ray said.

"That's good." She stretched out her back, bending to one side and then the other. "Getting too old for all this."

"What about Raul? He any trouble?"

"Nope. Nice young man as far as I can tell. Quiet, anyway. And polite."

Ray stepped off Raul's front stoop and walked toward her, stopping at the edge of the yard. Pancake followed.

"What about visitors?" Ray asked. "He get many?"

"Not that I know. Not many, anyway. Least not like his brother."

"Any idea where I might find him?"

"Right here if you wait a bit."

"Oh?"

"Every morning he goes down to the beach. One of those coffee shops where he can hook into the Wi-Fi. Saw him head out half hour ago with his laptop."

"Any particular coffee shop?"

"Can't say. I think he finds the one that ain't that busy. Leastwise that's what he said one day."

Ray glanced at his watch. "We have another appointment. We'll drop back by later."

"Suit yourself."

"I'd appreciate it if you didn't tell him we came by."

"Is he in some kind of trouble?"

"No, ma'am. Like I said, just a few questions."

"While ago it was a couple. Now we're up a few."

Ray smiled. She was a pistol and then some. "Simply don't want to worry him."

She shrugged. "I don't stick my nose in other folks' business." She knelt next the flowers, picking up a trowel, stabbing at the loose dirt. "Besides, I might not see him. Once I get this bunch in the ground I'm gonna get me some sweet tea and take a nap. Get to the rest of it later when it cools off."

Ray left it at that.

Next stop, the tallest building in downtown Mobile where the office of George Rose occupied what Ray estimated was about a third of the top floor. Lots of glass, clear views out over the bay.

The visit was brief and to Ray's mind more or less cleared Rose of any involvement in Barbara Plummer's murder, or any plan to tweak Walter. According to Rose, the twelve-million-dollar wrongful death settlement Walter won against him was later reduced to just under seven, his insurance taking the big hit, costing him only in the low seven figures. From the look of his plush office, something Rose could handle.

According to Rose, the young lady had indeed fallen off his boat and drowned, during a drunken party. An accident that could have been prevented by "a dash of common sense." Seems Rose was away and wasn't on the boat that night. His twenty-year-old son Kyle had taken the eighty-foot vessel out. Without permission but with a bunch of his "reprobate" friends. After that, the boat was off-limits. Rose even sold it, downsizing to only fifty feet. Kyle then saw the "wisdom of a stint in the military." Seemed to be doing fine "getting the shit shook out of his brain."

Back to Raul's.

Hattie Shaw was nowhere to be seen. Probably into her sweet tea and nap.

Raul's place now showed signs of life. The front door stood open, the entry covered by a screen door. A box fan churned in an adjacent window, drawing in the cooler air that gathered beneath a large hackberry tree. Ray rapped on the screen door frame. No response so he rapped again. The sound of a toilet flushing, down a hallway that led straightaway, and then Raul appeared, heading their way, zipping his fly.

"Can I help you?" he asked, his English clear, despite his thick accent.

"I'm Ray. This is Pancake."

"Pancake? What kind of name's that?"

"Mine," Pancake said.

Raul apparently didn't have a comeback for that.

"Need to ask a couple of questions," Ray said. "About Walter Horton."

His eyes narrowed and his body seemed to slide back a bit. "You a cop?"

Ray shook his head. "No."

"Then I don't have to talk to you."

"No, you don't." Ray smiled. "But it'd probably help both of us if you did."

"That was a long time ago. I talked to the cops then. I told them I was just angry about him not getting my brother off."

"Houdini couldn't have gotten your brother off, Raul. He did blow away a dude in broad daylight in front of a bunch of witnesses."

"So? Don't mean nothing. That shit-for-brains attorney gets people off all the time. White people, anyway."

"So you still have a hard-on for Walter?"

"*Es verdad.*"

"You know anything about a murder out on The Point the other night?"

Now his shoulders squared and his chin came up. "What murder?"

"Woman killed. Near Walter's place."

He shook his head. "I don't know nothing about that."

"I see."

Raul adopted a defiant stance, eyes leveled at Ray, fists balled at his side. "What's some white woman getting killed have to do with me?"

"How'd you know it was a white woman?"

His gaze darted right and then left and then back to Ray. "You said The Point. That's the only kind of woman that lives out there."

True. More or less.

"So you don't know anything about it?" Ray asked.

"Just what was on television."

"Where were you Tuesday night? Say around midnight or so?"

"Don't remember."

"You with anyone that night? Someone who can alibi for you?"

"I don't need an alibi." He looked at Pancake. "But if I did I could round up all the alibis I needed." He twisted his neck one way and then the other. "But I don't need none and I don't know anything about what goes on out there in that neighborhood."

Ray stared at him but said nothing. Be cool. Let the pressure rise.

"Maybe Walter killed her," Raul said. "You say he lives out there. Wouldn't surprise me if he did."

"Maybe he did. But I'd suspect you'll need an alibi anyway."

"*Por qué?*"

"I'm sure the cops will pay you a visit."

"Why would they want to talk to me?"

Ray sensed a rising note of tension in his voice.

"They're investigating a homicide. Talking to suspects is what they do."

# CHAPTER TWENTY-FOUR

CARLOS FERNANDEZ WATCHED the drama unfold while squatting behind the bank of rhododendrons that insulated Raul's yard from his neighbors. He had cruised by earlier, just as two men walked up Raul's walkway. One lean and fit with short grayish hair, the other a massive dude with bright red hair. Not knowing who they were, and more importantly not wanting to be seen, he had parked Darnell's Honda on a side street a half block away. He then scurried through the shadows of the hackberries, Palmettos, and pines that flanked the rear alley and shaded the neighbor's property before settling behind the shrubs.

He couldn't hear what was said, but since Raul left them on the porch, not inviting them in, he knew they weren't friends. And from the looks of the two guys, they were all business. Especially the older one. Definitely the one in charge.

He pulled the Smith & Wesson .357 from his back pocket, and held it tightly against his haunch as he watched. Last thing he needed right now was a pair of civilians mucking this up. He had a job to do. Borkov expected it. He needed to tie up a loose end as Borkov had put it. Raul was definitely a loose end. And a screwup. And Borkov wouldn't tolerate any more screwups. It was not in his nature.

Carlos also knew that leaving and coming back later wasn't an option. He was on a short time leash. He only had thirty minutes until his ride met him at the Chevron three blocks from where he squatted. How long could he wait?

"I'm not a suspect." Raul's eyes grew dark and angry. "I didn't do anything."

Ray shrugged.

Raul again flicked his gaze right and then left and finally back to Ray. "Okay. I was at Pedro's. With about a hundred other people."

Pedro's Surfside Bar was a dingy dive a couple of miles up the beach. The clientele decidedly blue collar. Construction workers, yardmen, day laborers, mostly Hispanic. The kind of place where the beer was cold and fights common. Easy to pick up a knife wound or two if you said the wrong thing or looked the wrong way or hit on the wrong woman.

"We'll check it out," Pancake said.

"You do that. Now I suggest you guys leave or I'll call the cops myself."

"Go ahead."

Raul looked as if he'd been slapped in the face. Obviously not the answer he expected. Of course, Ray knew calling the cops wasn't an option for Raul.

Raul, apparently out of words, slammed the door. The lock clicked.

Ray and Pancake retreated to the car and cranked it up, the blast from the AC welcome.

"He knows something," Pancake said.

"Sure does. The question is what?"

He considered moving up behind the two. Take them out, deal with Raul, and run like hell. But that would be messy at best. Not to mention the distinct possibility of attracting unwanted attention in such a cramped neighborhood.

A decision he didn't have to make as the door slammed, leaving the two men standing on the porch. They climbed in their car and sat talking for a couple of minutes while examining the house. The car cranked to life and they drove away.

Raul's back door was unlocked. Carlos stepped into the kitchen, gun in hand. Raul entered from the dining area and jerked to a stop.

"Jesus, Carlos," he said. "You scared the shit out of me."

"Sorry, man."

Now Raul focused on the gun. "What's that for?"

"Thought those two dudes might be trouble."

"I got rid of them."

Carlos stuffed the gun into his belt. "Who were they?"

"I don't know. They weren't cops, if that's what you're thinking. At least they said they weren't."

"And cops never lie? Right?"

"All I know is that they asked about the woman out on The Point."

"And you said what?"

"That I didn't know nothing about it."

Carlos nodded. "How'd they find out about you?"

"All that crap with Walter Horton and my brother. They said Walter lives near that lady. The one out on The Point."

"And you threatened Walter." Carlos shook his head. "That was a bad move, man."

"I know, but Walter fucked over my brother. I had to do something."

"But that wasn't cool," Carlos said. "And the boss isn't happy about it."

"I bet he's happy I took care of the woman for him, though?"

Carlos shrugged. "Actually, you got someone else to do it."

Raul laughed. "Why get my hands bloody when I don't have to?"

"Should've done it yourself."

"I'm just trying to build my own crew. Get me some guys I can depend on. Guys who have blood on their hands and can't turn on me."

"And you think those two were a wise choice?"

"Why are you coming on all aggro, dude? I got the job done." When Carlos didn't respond, he continued. "Besides, I'm paying them out of my cut, so no problem."

"The boss doesn't like folks altering the setup without him knowing."

"I'll smooth it. You got my money?"

"In the car."

"What's the plan?"

"Get you out of here."

"Let's go."

"Pack your shit and let's hit it." Carlos looked around. "You got any weapons or drugs here?"

"My gun's in the back. And I got a little meth. Want to tune up before we hit the road?"

"No time. Grab your shit."

Carlos could hear Raul opening and closing drawers, talking to himself. He walked that way, finding Raul in the front bedroom. Raul had packed his entire life in a small rolling suitcase and a canvas tote, his laptop jutting at an angle from the unzipped top.

"That's it," Raul said. "Let's get going."

"One more thing."

"What?" Raul asked.

"This."

Raul's eyes widened and he raised his hands as Carlos leveled his .357 at him.

The bullet punched a small round hole in Raul's forehead and carried blood and brain and skull bits out of a gaping wound in the back, splattering the bed and wall. Raul dropped like the sack of shit he was.

Carlos quickly searched the house, looking for anything that shouldn't be found. Closets, drawers, even the fridge turned up nothing. He slid Raul's wallet from his back pocket and stuffed that and the handgun that lay on the bedside table into the tote. He grabbed the suitcase and the bag and eased out the back door.

Loose end tied.

# CHAPTER TWENTY-FIVE

THE *SEA WITCH* was beyond magnificent. Darnell had never seen anything like it. Huge, plush, including the side-by-side staterooms where Joe Zuma had settled him and Darrell. Better than any hotel Darnell had ever seen. And he'd actually stayed at the Ritz Carlton down in Naples. Talk about plush. But it couldn't hold a candle to this. Maybe, just maybe, Darrell was right. Could this really be what their new life would be like? More perks than the phone store for sure.

Since the launch ride from the beach out to the *Sea Witch* only took twenty minutes, they had reached the yacht well before sunup. During the trip, Darrell had tried to engage Joe Zuma and Frank Boyd, find out what was what, but neither of the men had much to say. Which of course led Darrell to press them for answers. He asked why everything was some big secret. Why they had to meet on a beach and sneak out to the boss man's yacht in the middle of the night. Don't tell no one about it. Why was that, Darrell wanted to know.

Sometimes Darnell didn't understand his brother. Make that most times. Darrell's brain seemed to run off the tracks with disturbing regularity. He never saw the obvious, living inside his own little screwed-up world. Not that Darnell didn't have the same questions, he simply didn't think asking these two was the wisest move.

These two dudes weren't going to say shit about shit. Darnell was sure of that. He suspected the boss man didn't have people around who talked, or who told secrets. But Darrell kept quizzing them until Zuma finally said, "You ask too many questions."

Darrell apparently missed the irritation building in Zuma's voice and went on with his BS. "That's how you find out stuff. Asking questions. Everybody knows that."

Darrell also missed the look that Zuma and Boyd exchanged, Zuma finally saying, "Chill out. Mr. Borkov'll tell you everything later."

Thankfully, that shut Darrell up for the final leg of the trip.

Once they climbed from the launch onto the deck of the *Sea Witch*, Zuma hadn't shown them around or anything. Like he wanted to be rid of them. Didn't want to babysit. Merely took them down some stairs, along a hallway lined with rich wood and even richer works of art, to their staterooms, telling them to settle in and meet in the dining area around eight for breakfast. And not to leave their rooms, not to wander around, not to do shit until then.

Breakfast took place around a large, oval, burled table that sat at one end of an expansive living/dining area. Encased in dark, rich wood, thick cut carpeting, curtained windows, and even more art work, it was all class. Juice in wine glasses; bacon and cheese frittata, fruit, and croissants on china; aromatic coffee in matching cups. Better than the Ritz was Darrell's take on it, and he said so.

The brothers ate alone, a single crew member dressed in a crisp white uniform serving them, ferrying away dirty dishes, and constantly refilling their coffee cups. He said little, answering Darrell's questions simply, and vaguely. Darnell figured everyone in Borkov's world was tight-lipped.

By ten, Darnell and Darrell sat in lounge chairs on the aft main deck, protected from the sun by the overhanging roof, where a long-bladed white ceiling fan stirred the air. Zuma and Boyd were nowhere to be seen.

"Want some?" Darrell asked, pulling his meth vial and the stub of a plastic straw from his pocket.

"You think that's a good idea? Here?"

"I think it's a perfect idea." He carefully tapped out two fuzzy rails on the teakwood table between the two chairs, bent over, and snorted one line. He rubbed his nose with the heel of one hand and then looked at Darnell. "You sure?"

"I'm sure."

He shrugged, did the other line, and returned the vial and straw to his pocket.

A woman walked out on the deck. And what a woman. Young, tight, long dark hair, long legs, white bikini beneath a dark blue hooded jacket, open to reveal a flat, tanned belly. Darnell was speechless. Darrell wasn't. He never was.

"And who are you?" Darrell asked.

"Grace." She curled on another lounge chair across from them and removed her designer sunglasses, settling them on the teak table next to her. "You guys must be the new guests I heard about."

Darrell and Darnell introduced themselves.

One of the staff appeared. The same young man who had earlier served them breakfast. He carried a coffee mug, which he sat on the table next to Grace's sunglasses, and filled it from a silver coffeepot.

"Thanks, Robbie," Grace said.

"The usual, ma'am?"

She smiled. "That would be great."

He gave a short bow and left.

"So you're the boss's girlfriend?" Darrell asked.

She laughed. An easy laugh. "Seems so."

"You're very pretty."

She lowered her eyes slightly. "Thanks."

Darrell fidgeted, rubbed his nose again. Darnell wasn't sure what he feared most—that his brother would offer her some meth or say something incredibly stupid. Turned out to be the latter.

"I guess if I could afford a boat like this, I could get a girl like you."

She frowned. "I didn't come with the boat."

"But you sure add to it."

Whatever insult she might have felt seemed to evaporate in another laugh. "Well, thank you."

Darrell was the only person Darnell had ever known who could say stupid stuff and get away with it. That golden umbrella preventing the shit from raining down. Hadn't he basically called her a whore? Like she could be bought like a yacht? But then again, wasn't that the case? Probably, but only Darrell could get away with saying it.

The young man returned, bowl in hand, and passed it and a spoon to Grace. "Anything else, ma'am?"

"Not right now. Thanks."

Again he nodded and disappeared.

"What's that?" Darrell asked.

"Yogurt, flax, granola, and strawberries." She took a spoonful, speaking around it. "And it's very good. I can have them bring you some if you want."

"We had breakfast," Darnell said.

She pointed her spoon at him. "Frittata? Right?"

"Yeah."

"I smelled it." Another spoonful of the yogurt mixture. "I can't eat that heavy stuff. Puts the weight on." She patted her belly. "And Victor doesn't like it if I gain weight."

"You don't look like you could gain an ounce if you wanted to," Darrell said.

"I wish that was true. Eat the stuff they make around here and you will definitely pack on the pounds."

"Where is Mr. Borkov?" Darrell asked.

"In our stateroom. He's got some business to deal with. He'll be up shortly."

Shortly turned out to be a half hour, most of the time Darrell peppering Grace with questions:

How old was she? Twenty-two.

Where did she grow up? Naples.

Go to school? Naples High.

College? No.

How did she meet Borkov? She was a waitress and met Victor at a restaurant.

On and on. Darnell couldn't take it so he strolled to the stern of the ship and sat in the sun, watching the Gulf's gentle rise and fall and the foamy wake that churned behind the vessel. No land in sight.

Finally, Darnell saw who could only be Victor Borkov walk onto the deck. He was tall, fit, tanned, with short dark hair and wore white slacks, pink shirt, and sandals. Darnell returned to the shade and sat next to his brother again.

"Welcome to the *Sea Witch*," Borkov said as he dropped onto a lounge chair next to Grace.

"Thanks for inviting us," Darrell said. "We've wanted to meet you for some time."

"And I you."

"That's my cue," Grace said. "You guys want to talk business. Boring business." She settled her sunglasses in place, stood, and gave Victor a kiss on the cheek. "I'm going up top to get some sun." She left.

"So tell me," Borkov said. "How'd it all go down the other night?"

"Smooth," Darrell said. "Easy. Piece of cake."

"Raul set it all up well, then?"

"He sure did," Darrell said. He rubbed his nose again, leaning forward, elbows on his knees. "Of course, it turned out there wasn't much for him to do."

"That right?"

"I mean, he was going to jack the alarm system for us, but when he flipped open the box, it wasn't even on. And the back door was unlocked. So he took off and left us to do our thing."

"Your thing?"

Darrell smiled and shrugged. "You know. Take care of it for you."

Victor nodded. "The woman give you any problems?"

"Never saw us. She was out when we got there. Sound asleep. Pop. Done deal."

"Good. See anyone around?"

Darrell shook his head. "Nope."

"There was a couple," Darnell said. "On the beach."

"That's right," Darrell said. "I forgot about them."

Victor nodded. "What about them?"

"I think they were screwing," Darrell said. "Had a blanket and a small cooler or something like that."

"They see you?"

"No way. We were up on the slope, looking down. They never knew we were there. I thought they might screw everything up, but after a few minutes they packed up their stuff and walked up the beach."

"See anyone else?"

"No. It was very quiet that night."

"Good. Good."

"Mr. Borkov," Darrell said, "we really appreciate you hiring us. Letting us work with you."

"I didn't hire you. Raul did."

"Yeah, but I'm sure he wouldn't've come to us without your okay."

Borkov shrugged but said nothing.

"Where is Raul? Will he be here?"

Borkov smiled. "No. He's a bit detained."

"So, do we get our money from him later? Maybe tomorrow after we get back?"

"I have your money here. I'll take care of it."

"You already paid Raul his cut? Or do we have to?"

"Relax. All is taken care of. Raul will get his share, and you'll get yours."

"That's great." Darrell looked at Darnell. "Ain't it, brother?"

Darnell nodded but said nothing, keeping his gaze down. Something wasn't right here. Why would Borkov bring them out here just to give them some cash? Why wouldn't he have Raul pay them? Or Zuma or Boyd? Why expose himself to the hired help? Darnell felt a tightness gather in his scalp. When he looked up, Borkov was staring at him.

"You're probably wondering why I brought you here." Borkov waved a hand. "I do much of my business on the yacht. Away from prying eyes and ears."

"That's smart," Darrell said.

"I'm glad you approve," Borkov said.

"Mr. Borkov. He didn't mean . . ." Darnell began.

Borkov cut him off with a wave. "Just pimping you." He smiled. "Truth is, I wanted to meet you both. Thank you properly for your work."

Darrell punched his brother's leg. "See, little brother. I told you we did good."

Borkov folded his hands before him on the table. "And your work will not go unrewarded."

"We're glad to be on board," Darrell said. He giggled, rubbed his nose again. "That was funny. No pun intended."

Borkov didn't smile. He lifted the lid of a burled cigar box, selecting a large Cohiba Maduro. He clipped the end, lit it, and took a few puffs, the smoke swirling skyward.

Darrell wasn't finished. "We want to tell you that's it's an honor to work for you. And if you need anything from us, just ask. We'll do it. No questions."

Borkov nodded. "That's good to know."

Darrell rubbed his hands together. "This is going to be fun. The kind of thing we've been looking for."

Another pair of puffs, Borkov waving away the smoke with one hand. "Today is for fun. Enjoy yourselves. Go fishing if you want. The boys will take the boat out later. Who knows, you might even catch dinner."

# CHAPTER TWENTY-SIX

HENRY PLUMMER'S HIGH-DOLLAR home had a high-dollar view from a high-dollar deck. Twenty feet deep, forty wide, and nothing but sand and water between it and the Yucatan. Detective Bob Morgan stood near the deck's railing, facing the water. It was eleven, the day already heating up. To his left an undulating sandy slope, pocked with clusters of sea oats, angled down toward the Gulf. He knew that somewhere among those sandy bumps was where Jake Longly and his latest squeeze Nicole had camped while filming Walter.

The Gulf was flat today. Almost no wind. A smattering of people gathered on towels soaking up the sun. A few strollers hugged the lapping water, leaving faint footprints in the water-firmed sand. Two kids on Boogie boards splashed in the shore break, a foot high at most, their giggles rising up to him. He knew the beaches of The Point didn't get much traffic, most people hanging near the resorts that lined the sand to the east.

Henry stepped out, two cups of fresh coffee in hand. They sat at a round teak table shaded by a yellow umbrella.

"Sorry for your loss," Morgan said.

Henry sighed. "It's hard. Not something you expect to happen." He looked out toward the beach. "Especially here in this neighborhood."

"Unfortunately, no one's immune to these things."

Henry dragged his gaze back to Morgan. "Anything new?"

"Not really."

"Have you talked with Walter?" Henry asked.

Morgan nodded.

"Did he have anything to do with it?"

"He was here. He was, as far as we know, the last person to see Barbara alive."

Henry shook his head. "I don't see any way Walter would do something like this."

"You're probably right, but I've seen less likely candidates up to their ears in murder. In my experience, people do what people do and often there are no clues ahead of time. Least not any that anyone sees."

Henry nodded. "I suppose that's true."

"And you weren't aware of the affair? No clues at all?"

"None. Not with Walter, anyway." He hesitated. "Look, Barbara had had affairs before. Last time a couple of years ago. In the past few months I saw some of the same signs. That's why I suspected something and why I hired Ray Longly."

"What signs?"

"Withdrawn. Less sex. A few phone calls quickly ending when I came in the room. That sort of thing."

Morgan took a sip of coffee, and then cradling the cup in both hands, looked at Henry over the rim. "Did you suspect anyone in particular?"

"No. That's what I was hoping Longly would find out."

"Let's put Walter aside for a minute," Morgan said. "Any business competitors that might have had a grudge against you?"

"Nothing they'd do this over."

"But something?"

"Look, I'm into software and real estate. Both are very competitive. Both can make you an enemy or two. But this?" He shook his head. "I can't imagine."

"How'd you get from software to real estate development?"

"Business software has about had its run. For us smaller players, anyway. Can't keep up with the Apples, Microsofts, and Googles of the world. They each seem to have unending capital. Hard to level the playing field. Also, much of the software business is now devoted to the gaming world, and I have no interest in that. So back eight or so years ago, I decided it might be prudent to diversify. Here along the Gulf, real estate is a big-dollar game. So I used some of the capital I had accumulated and jumped in."

"Quite successfully, I understand."

Henry gave a half shrug. "I do all right."

Morgan guessed his all right and Henry's all right were birds of different species. He knew Henry's property portfolio included two golf courses, a resort hotel in Panama City, a pair of high-rises, one in Mobile, the other in Pensacola, and a handful of strip malls. That's about as all right as it gets.

"So, back to the original question," Morgan said, "you can't think of anyone who might want to do you harm?"

"Not really."

"Not really? That's a qualified no."

"There were a couple of guys I had legal problems with. One stealing materials from my software company. Another sued, saying we stole his concepts." He told Morgan about Ely Thompson and Jason Hughes.

"You think either of them could be involved?"

Henry shook his head. "That would be a stretch."

"Anyone else? Maybe in the real estate world?"

Henry shook his head, then hesitated, his gaze out toward the water. "Maybe one. Guy named Victor Borkov. You know him?"

"Heard of him."

Truth was everyone in law enforcement knew that name. Victor Borkov. Ukrainian. Suspected to be into drugs. Meth, cocaine, marijuana. Believed to be hooked up with the cartels, but nothing that could ever be proven.

"I think he's some criminal type," Henry said. "Drugs, I think. But lately he's been trying to go more legit. Buying up property and things like that." He drained his coffee cup and placed it on the table. "I'd bet it's a scam to launder dirty money. At least that's what it smells like to me."

"Why do you think that?"

"He's got the bucks but he's not really a real estate guy. Doesn't seem to know much about it. Buys some risky stuff. I understand he loses as much as he makes. Hard to be successful if the bottom line isn't positive."

Now Morgan drank the last of his coffee, settling the empty cup on the table. "Unless it's free money?"

"Maybe not free, but easy."

"What's your connection with Borkov?" Morgan asked.

"For the last year we've been bidding on a prime piece of land in Panama City. Adjacent to the resort I own down there. My group had it pretty well locked up until he entered the picture. He's been a major headache since then. He started a bidding war, and I believe he's contaminated a couple of my investors."

"Contaminated?"

"Run off. Threatened. It's what folks like Borkov do."

"You have proof of that or is it merely a hunch?"

Henry opened his hands, palms up. "More a hunch. But I'd say it's a good hunch."

Morgan nodded. He understood that. His entire life was following a series of hunches. It's what homicide detectives do. Of
course, hunches more often than not turned into facts once you
dug around.

"I take it you've met him?" Morgan asked.

"Our paths crossed a couple of times."

"And?"

"Victor Borkov is a scary guy. The kind you don't cross. Comes
on nice, smiles a lot, says little. But you know, you just know, there's
a lot going on beneath the surface. Like he might cut your liver out
and smile while doing it."

That's more or less what Morgan had heard about Borkov. Fact
was, many felt he was moving into competing with the cartels.
Something you didn't do unless you had a lot of muscle in the wings.

"Scary enough to engineer this?"

Henry's brow furrowed. "Maybe. I've heard he might've ordered
a couple of murders in the past."

Morgan believed that was true. A judge in Coral Gables for one.
He was presiding over a criminal case that involved one of Borkov's
people. The judge suddenly disappeared, and the case miraculously
evaporated. Rumor was he grabbed the judge and dumped him in
the Atlantic. No body was found and nothing was ever proven, but
there had been a lot of smoke surrounding Borkov.

"Those are the rumors," Morgan said.

"But why Barbara? If he had a beef with me?"

"Maybe he thought you were home?"

Henry took a deep breath and let it out slowly. "If that's the case,
do you think he'll send them back? For me?"

Morgan shrugged. "We've got to at least consider that."

Henry leaned forward, burying his face in his hands. "This is a
nightmare."

"I'll make sure a couple of extra patrols hang around here, but maybe you should consider staying somewhere else for a while."

Henry looked up. "Where?"

"Another city. Another state."

"No." Henry shook his head emphatically. "I'm not leaving my home. I've never shied from anything in my life."

"But—"

"But nothing. If I run now I'll be running forever. If Borkov had anything to do with this, that is."

"I understand." Morgan sighed. "This is a bit convoluted, but what if the target was Walter?"

"You mean the killers might've followed him here?" Henry's brow furrowed. "Why here? Why not at his place?"

"Maybe he knew about Walter and Barbara. Wanted to frame him for her murder?"

Henry took a deep breath, held it, and then exhaled loudly. "Oh, Jesus."

"What?"

"Walter was involved in this deal. He was doing all the legal work for me on the Panama City property."

"Are you kidding?"

Henry stood, walked to the railing, braced stiff arms on it, and stared out at the water. His breath came deep and raspy. He turned back to Morgan. "If this was Borkov and he planned to kill Barbara and me, and blame Walter, he'd clear the decks. The property would go to him by default."

"This puts an entirely different spin on things."

"I can't believe it. A piece of sand? Barbara dead over a real estate dispute?" His eyes glistened.

"Money makes folks do some pretty nasty things," Morgan said. "Particularly big money. Like this. But that might not be it. Could be something else entirely. I mean, Walter does have some pretty sordid clients."

"That's true. I've even talked to him about that before. Asked him why he does that criminal defense stuff. He surely doesn't have to."

"What did Walter say to that?"

"He agreed. In fact, just a few months ago he said he was considering giving up that part of his practice. I think that guy that fire bombed his car got his attention."

"That was a divorce case, though."

"True. Still it knocked him off-balance for a while." Henry wiped his moist eyes.

"I need to ask you about your alarm system," Morgan began. "Do you use it?"

"Sure. All the time."

"Barbara, too?"

"Especially her."

Morgan nodded. "Looks like it was off that night. And the back door was unlocked."

"That doesn't sound like Barbara. She was overly cautious, if anything."

"Maybe a bit distracted that night? With Walter being there?"

"I suppose that's possible." Henry's eyes screwed down, fighting back tears.

"Or maybe the bad guys turned it off," Morgan said.

Again Henry wiped his eyes. "Without the code?"

"Some of these guys are very adept at alarms." Morgan massaged his neck. "Of course that wouldn't explain the unlocked door."

"Unless they broke in."

"No sign of that."

Henry stared at him.

Morgan stood. "I got to get going. We'll talk more later."

Henry walked him to the door. They shook hands.

"Again, I'm sorry for your loss," Morgan said.

"It's going to be tough."

"I still wish you'd consider staying somewhere else."

"Not going to happen."

Morgan hesitated, and then nodded. "Your choice. As I said, I'll have extra patrols through the neighborhood. And you keep things locked up tight."

"You can bet on that."

Morgan climbed in his car and sat for a minute, looking at the house. If Barbara had locked up, set the alarm, would none of this have happened? Maybe. But if she or Henry were the target of a hit, the bad guys would've found a way. That he knew for sure. He cranked up his car but before he shifted into gear, his cell chimed. Caller ID said it was Starks. He punched the "answer" button and brought it to his ear. "Morgan."

"We got a hit."

"On the print?"

"You got it." He sounded excited and spoke rapidly, telling Morgan the story.

The crime scene techs had found that the alarm box on the side of Henry's house was open. Didn't seem pried or damaged or anything. The odd thing was that it looked like it had been wiped clean, the usual dust and dirt on the door, both inside and out, all streaked with swipe marks. They dusted for prints and came up empty until they found a single partial on the inside of the door. Near the bottom. Where someone would grab it to pull it open.

"I take you got an ID on the print?" Morgan asked.

"Yeah," Starks said. "Guy named Raul Gomez."

"Why do I know that name?"

"You'll remember his brother. Santiago Gomez."

"The dude that whacked that drug dealer in broad daylight?"

"That's the one."

"Where?" Morgan asked.

Starks gave him the address, saying he and a couple of units were rolling that way.

"Be there in ten." Morgan said. "Have the units stand off until I get there."

"Already on it. We're gathering at Bud's Burgers. It's a few blocks away."

"See you in there." He slammed the car in gear, tires squealing as he accelerated.

# CHAPTER TWENTY-SEVEN

MORGAN SPUN INTO Bud's Burgers. Three patrol cars huddled at the rear of the parking area near a pair of dark-green trash dumpsters and an ivy-covered fence that separated the property from an adjacent strip mall. Nearby, Starks stood with a half dozen uniformed officers. Starks looked up as Morgan pulled into an empty space and climbed out. He recognized one of the uniforms. Young guy named Jimmy Green. Been on the force a couple of years. Morgan had worked with him before. Good kid. The others, he didn't know though a couple of faces looked familiar.

"I drove by Raul's place on the way over," Starks said. "Looked quiet."

Morgan nodded. "Okay, here's the play. Jimmy, you and your partner climb in with Starks and me. You other guys, I want a car at each end of the block. Out of sight. Around the corner. I don't want this guy to see a unit anywhere around there. Got it?"

The officers nodded as if they were synchronized robots.

"I want this to go smoothly," Morgan said.

"No problem, sir," one of the officers replied.

"We'll assume he's armed. And maybe not alone. Let's make this cool and casual. He doesn't know we have his prints so there's no reason for him to be all amped up, and I don't want him getting amped up. He might turn this into the O.K. Corral and there are too many citizens around for that. Got it?"

"We understand, sir."

The officer who "understood" didn't look like he understood at all. Buzzed reddish-brown hair with skinned sidewalls, freckles over his nose, and a painfully innocent face, he looked young and eager. Dangerous combination. All action, no experience, no common sense, no caution. And caution was a valuable commodity in situations like this. Morgan wondered if he had ever looked so naive. Probably. All rookies did. Took a few years for the scars of the job to make you wary—and a cynic.

"Okay." Morgan gave a quick nod. "Let's roll."

Morgan drove, Starks shotgun, Green and his partner in back. After the two units were in place, he drove by the house.

"Still looks quiet," Starks said.

Morgan pulled to the curb, three doors down and across the street. Then to Green, he said, "You two work your way through the neighbor's yard and get eyes on the back door. Do not approach. Got that?"

"Yes, sir."

"Starks and I'll handle the front."

They climbed from the car. Green and his partner darted across the street and looped behind the house next to Raul's.

"How you want to handle it?" Starks asked.

"Let's try the friendly knock-and-chat approach."

Starks raised an eyebrow.

"I mean, no way he knows who we are or that we're here to take him down. He'll probably think we're trying to sell magazines or something."

"Or Jehovah's Witnesses," Starks said with a half smile.

"That, too."

Starks flipped open his Smith & Wesson .357 revolver and checked the chambers. He snapped the cylinder closed and settled the weapon into its holster in the small of his back. "Let's get it done."

Morgan pressed the doorbell. No answer. He rapped on the door frame. Nothing. Peeking through a gap in the front window curtains revealed only cheap and sparse furniture—sofa, two chairs, a rectangular coffee table with a pizza box on top, and a three-shelf bookcase that supported a small TV, no books in sight. The house seemed empty. They moved around the left side to the back, also quiet with no indication of activity. As Morgan reached a narrow, cracked concrete patio, where an aluminum chair with green plastic webbing lay on its side, he saw that the rear door stood ajar. He stopped, nudging Starks with his elbow.

"What do you think?" Starks asked.

"I think Raul's not tuned into security."

"Or maybe just catching the breeze?"

Morgan looked at him. "There is no breeze."

"Maybe he left in a hurry," Starks said.

"Or he's inside, watching us right now."

"You think he might've known we were coming?"

"Don't see how." Morgan shielded the sun from his eyes and looked around. He saw Green, kneeling in the shrubbery that hugged Raul's backyard. He motioned for him to stay put. "One way to find out."

Morgan pulled his service weapon and held it muzzle down near his right thigh. He rapped on the door frame and again got no response. Using his gun barrel, he eased the door open and entered.

"Mr. Gomez?"

His voice echoed within the house, but he got no response and didn't detect any movement inside.

"Mr. Gomez? Are you home?"

He was talking to himself.

The kitchen was in order. Dining room and living room, too. The only thing out of place was the pizza box. No signs of a struggle, no evidence of ransacking. Quiet and orderly.

Not so the bedroom.

To Morgan, bedroom murders typically fell into one of several general categories. Spouses that killed spouses in fits of rage. Robberies that escalated, maybe when the owner came home, or was there all along, unknown to the thief. Rapes that turned deadly. Those sorts of things. This one was none of those.

The young Hispanic man was folded in a half-sitting position against the bed. Entry wound near the center of his forehead, blood, bone, and brain matter fanned out over the bed, headboard, and wall behind.

"Well, ain't this some shit?" Starks said.

Morgan stood looking down at the corpse. "Looks like he was shot point blank, face to face."

"So he knew the killer," Starks said. "Probably even opened the door for him."

"Looks that way."

"Where's all his stuff?" Starks asked, indicating the open and empty closet.

Morgan glanced that way. "Good question." He knelt and searched pockets. "No wallet or keys. Nothing."

"Shooter took them," Starks said. "Trying to slow down the ID, I suspect."

"Should've dumped the body, then."

"Didn't have time, I suspect. Even if he was so inclined."

Morgan stood and circled the bed, careful not to contaminate any of the blood spatter. "This is fresh. Blood hasn't dried."

"You thinking Raul did Barbara Plummer and then someone cleaned him up?"

"That'd be my guess. Tying up loose ends." Morgan sighed. "Means these guys are pros."

"Shit," Starks said. "That changes everything."

"Sure does."

"I'll get the guys to call this in and get the ME out here."

Morgan nodded.

Thirty minutes later the place was crawling with cops, crime scene techs, coroner's techs, the whole posse.

Morgan was standing in the living room talking with one of the techs when Jimmy Green stuck his head in the front door.

"Detective Morgan," he said.

"Yeah, Jimmy."

"Lady next door might've seen the shooters."

"Shooters?"

"Said she saw two men come by."

"Where is she?"

"On her porch. I told her to stay there."

"Good job."

Morgan saw her as soon as he walked outside. An elderly woman, sitting on her front stoop, looking his way from beneath a floppy sun hat.

"That's her," Green said. "Name's Hattie Shaw."

Morgan walked to where she sat. A half-empty glass of tea sat next to her. She took off her hat, laying it on the porch.

"You doing okay?" Morgan asked.

"Been better."

"I imagine so."

"I hear Raul got shot."

"That's true, ma'am."

"He was such a nice young man."

"You knew him well?"

"Well enough." She glanced past him toward Raul's house. "He's lived there for a while. Couple of years. Maybe longer. I forget exactly. He used to live with his brother Santiago. Back then there were all kinds in and out, but after Santiago went to prison, Raul stayed."

"Raul have all kinds hanging around him too?" Morgan asked.

"No. He was a good neighbor. Quiet and polite. Not at all like his brother."

"No visitors?"

"Rarely. He's friends with these two brothers who come around. I think they're twins. They look like it, anyway. Darrell and Darnell Wilbanks."

"Seen them around here today?"

She shook her head. "Not for a couple of days. Let's see, when was that?" She looked up toward the clear blue sky as if recalling. "Last I saw them was last Saturday. They left around ten that night."

"Did you hear anything? Today?"

"Nope."

"But you saw someone?"

"Saw them. Spoke to them." She took a slug of tea. "They didn't seem like killers, though."

"Tell me about them."

"There were two of them. They said they were looking for Raul. He wasn't home so they left."

"And?"

"And nothing. That's it."

"So you didn't see them go into the house? Something like that?"

"Told you, Raul wasn't home so they left. But they said they'd be back."

"Did they? Come back?"

"Apparently so."

"But you didn't see them?"

"I was napping." She plucked her hat from the porch and began fanning herself with it. "Worked in the yard all morning. When it gets too hot I have my tea and a nap."

"So you didn't see them again?"

"Isn't that what I said?"

Morgan smiled. He liked Hattie. She was one tough bird, he suspected. Didn't suffer fools and right now had placed him in that pigeonhole. "Tell me about the men."

"Like I said, they came around, looking for him. He wasn't there so they said they'd come back." She again glanced toward Raul's house. "Funny thing was they said I shouldn't tell Raul they had come by."

"They say why?"

"Just that they needed to ask him some questions."

"You got names for these guys?"

"The older one, the tough-looking one, said his name was Ray. The other was a big redheaded fellow. He said his name was Pancake. Hard to forget a name like that."

*Ray Longly and his sidekick. Just great.*

"And they said they'd be back?" Morgan asked.

"Sure did."

"But you didn't see them? Come back?"

"You don't listen so good, do you? Ain't that what I said? More than once?"

"Yes, ma'am. Just wanted to be sure."

"Well, now you are." She stood. "I'm tired. I'm going to go lay down. Unless you want to repeat any of the other questions you've already asked."

"No, ma'am. Thanks for talking with me."

She waved as she entered her house and closed the door.

# CHAPTER TWENTY-EIGHT

THE APARTMENT DARRELL and Darnell Wilbanks called home was on the second floor of an older complex a mile or so inland from the beach. Low rent, no view. The brothers weren't home. On the way over, Morgan had called in and had a record search for the brothers. Darrell had one pop for a marijuana possession, Darnell was clean.

The manager wasn't in, but his wife Edith Rucker revealed that they were "nice boys." Never caused trouble or made noise or anything. Paid their rent regularly, even did odd jobs for her from time to time. Especially Darnell. She wished all the tenants were like them. Hadn't seen them in a couple of days. Not unusual as they often had jobs that took them away for days at the time. What type of work? This and that was the best she could say.

Next stop? A chat with Ray Longly.

"They don't look like killers," Morgan said. He and Starks had climbed the back steps to Ray Longly's deck. Ray and Jake sat at the table, stacks of documents before them.

"Better look a little closer," Starks said. "They look stone cold to me."

Ray gathered several pages and slipped them into a folder. "What brings you guys by?"

"Bodies," Morgan said. "Dead bodies."

"Want to clarify?"

"Seems that you two leave behind dead bodies everywhere you go." Starks said.

"Look," Jake said. "I told you Barbara was killed after Nicole and I left."

"What about Raul Gomez?"

"What about him?" Ray asked.

"You and your redheaded sidekick talked to him?"

"Sure did. Didn't have much to say."

Morgan shoved his hands in his pockets. "He'll have less to say now. Being dead and all."

"What are you talking about?" Ray asked. "We were just there. Maybe an hour or so ago."

Morgan sat in an empty chair. "And then he was dead."

"When? How?"

"When I don't know yet. How was a single shot to the head."

Ray looked at Jake and then back to Morgan. "He was alive and well, and downright pissy for that matter, when Pancake and I left."

"Where is he, anyway?" Morgan asked.

"Working."

"I see." He scratched an ear. "So first old Jake here is at the Plummers' and the wife ends up dead and now you and Pancake are at Raul's and he ends up the same way. Hell of a coincidence, don't you think?"

"They do happen."

Morgan gave a slight nod. "Not as often as most folks think."

Ray said nothing.

"Want to enlighten me as to why you were at Raul's place today?" Morgan asked.

"Raul was on our radar. He had a beef with Walter. About his brother going to jail. He blamed Walter for not getting him off. But you know that."

"So, you were simply asking him if he still had a hard-on for Walter?" Morgan asked.

"Exactly." Ray told Morgan of his and Pancake's conversation with Raul ending with, "He said he had nothing to do with Barbara Plummer's murder. Said he had a solid alibi."

"You believe him?"

"Seemed to me he was less than forthcoming."

"Like he knew more than he was letting on?"

Ray shrugged. "Or maybe he simply didn't enjoy our questions."

"Bet you get that a lot."

"I suspect you do, too," Ray said. "So how do you see these two killings connected?"

"Other than the fact that Walter was at the crux of both? Other than they were both done with a single shot to the forehead?"

"Same weapon?" Jake asked.

Morgan looked at him and hesitated before he spoke. As if considering what to reveal. "Doubt it. Barbara caught a .22. This one looked to be a larger caliber. Judging by the damage done. Anyway, the ballistics guys'll tell us for sure, but I'd be surprised if the weapons matched."

"So where are we?" Jake asked.

Morgan raised an eyebrow. "We?"

"We're on the same team here, aren't we? We both want to know who killed Barbara. And now Raul."

"So, any thoughts on who might've done Raul?" Ray asked.

"Not really." Morgan glanced at Starks and then back to Ray. "You know a couple guys, brothers actually, names Darrell and Darnell Wilbanks?"

"Don't sound familiar. Why?"

"Friends of Raul's. According to the lady next door about the only ones that ever visited him. She'd last seen them a couple of days ago."

"You have a sit-down with them?" Ray asked.

"Not yet. Went to their apartment. No one there. I'll check back later."

"You think they might be connected to this?" Jake asked.

"Maybe, maybe not. We'll run them down and see. At least that might connect a few dots. Raul's business, habits, other friends, that kind of thing."

"Anything we can do to help?" Ray asked.

"Yeah. Stay home. I don't want to find any more bodies in your wake."

"Funny."

"That's me. A funny guy." Morgan didn't laugh, or even smile. "But there might be something you can do."

"What?"

"You know a guy named Victor Borkov?"

"Vaguely. Heard the name."

"He's some badass criminal type from down in Naples. Probably connected to the cartels. Don't know that for sure, but that's the scuttlebutt."

"What's his connection here?"

"Probably none. But he and Henry were locked in some bidding war over a piece or property. Down near Panama City. Both want to develop a resort there."

"I see," Ray said.

"And Walter was doing the legal work on the deal for Henry."

"Really?"

"Seems they about had it done when Borkov threw a wrench in the deal. According to Henry he ran off a couple of Henry's investors."

"I take it we're talking adult money here?" Jake asked.

"Eight figures."

Jake whistled. "A motive right there."

"Any connection between Raul and this Borkov character?" Ray asked.

Morgan shook his head. "Not that we know. But, if he was anything like his brother Santiago, and if Victor Borkov is anything like the rumors about him, Raul would be the kind of dirtball Borkov might use for unpleasant work. Expendable. Foreign national. Able to slip back across the border when need be. Who knows, maybe Raul was tied to the cartels and through them to Borkov."

"Any evidence that Borkov's hooked in with the cartels?" Jake asked.

Morgan scratched an ear. "Nothing hard. Not yet, anyway. But such a connection wouldn't be too far in the weeds."

"So what do you want me to do?" Ray asked.

"Check him out. Off the radar."

"He that scary?"

Morgan laughed. "So I hear. But mostly connected. All the way to Tallahassee from what I understand. An official inquiry might raise his hackles."

"Or tip him off?"

"That, too. If he's involved, I'd rather take a run at him after I know more. Catch him off-guard. I was hoping with all your underground contacts you might be able to find out a few things without him knowing."

"So he's a suspect?" Ray asked.

"Everybody's a suspect. Including you two."

"Since you asked so nicely, how could I refuse?" Ray said.

# CHAPTER TWENTY-NINE

THE HOLMAN CORRECTIONAL Facility hung just off I-65 an hour north of Mobile near the town of Atmore, Alabama. It's the home, some temporary, others permanent, of nearly a thousand bad guys, somewhere north of a hundred and fifty of them stacking time on death row. It's not a pleasant place, violence being a staple among the inmates and the basic character flaw that led most of them through its gates, including one Santiago Gomez.

The brilliant Santiago had set up a drug sale of considerable weight in the parking lot of a convenience store. Two kilos at five K per, Santiago paying the cook only two K per kilo. Driven by his entrepreneurial spirit and a healthy dose of greed, Santiago wasn't content with the substantial profit he'd make, deciding he could easily walk away with both the cash and the drugs. Only needed to pump a couple of rounds in the buyer. In broad daylight. Not noticing the three witnesses and the strategically placed security cameras. Even Walter couldn't save him from that degree of stupidity.

I drove, Ray busying himself with phone calls during the trip. Mainly to his connections in the FBI, DEA, ATF, and the rest of the alphabet soup of governmental agencies. Pointing them in the direction of Victor Borkov, asking that they dig into his life. A couple were at least initially hesitant, not wanting to jeopardize their positions, others were "on board" immediately, but in the end all agreed to see what they could uncover.

Ray had earlier reached out to the Holman warden, whom he knew from past cases, and arranged a sit-down with Santiago. A sergeant named Will Moffitt met us at the entrance and introductions were made beneath the watchful eye of a rifle-toting guard in a sturdy tower to our right. Moffitt then escorted us inside the stark facility. It was midafternoon and the yard was filled with gen-pop inmates, some pumping up their tattooed physiques, some tossing a baseball around, most sitting around in racially-segregated groups talking and smoking. Unfriendly eyes followed our every step.

Once we made our way through the clanging doors and snapping locks, Moffitt led us to a windowless, gray-walled interrogation room, where Santiago sat cuffed to an anchored table. He wore loose white pants and shirt, hard sinewy arms covered with black prison tats protruding from the sleeves, which were rolled up to his shoulders. He looked up as we entered.

"Who the fuck are you?" Santiago asked. His eyes were scary black and shifted rapidly between Ray and me.

"These gentlemen have a few questions for you," Moffitt said.

Santiago never looked at Moffitt, as if acknowledging his existence was a sign of weakness. In Santiago's world that was probably true. Instead, he kept his glare focused on Ray and me.

"What if I don't feel like talking?" Santiago said.

"Then sit there and look stupid," Moffitt said, playing his role in the power struggle between guard and inmate. Then to us, "I'll be right outside. Just holler if you need anything." He exited, locking the door behind him.

We took the chairs opposite Santiago. Ray did the introductions.

"So you got names. Don't mean nothing to me."

"We want to chat about your brother," Ray said.

"You the ones that killed him?"

"You know about that, huh?"

"I got my sources."

Interesting. Raul's body had barely reached ambient temperature and Santiago already knew about it. It crossed my mind that the criminal world might have its own Wi-Fi grid. More likely, one of the guards heard about it and used that bit of information to grind Santiago a little bit. Life in the Holman lockup.

Ray nodded. "No, we didn't have anything to do with that but we are trying to find his killer."

"You cops?"

"Private," I said.

"Why're you interested in Raul?"

"We're looking into something else. Something Raul might've known about."

"I don't know anything about Raul's business."

"Wasn't Raul here about a week ago?" Ray asked.

"So?"

"So, maybe he mentioned something he was into. Something that got him killed."

Blank stare punctuated with a smirk. "What? You think I'd tell you anything, anyway?"

"Depends on whether you want to know who killed your brother," I said.

"Don't guess that matters much now." He smiled. "Until I get out of here."

"I suspect that's the kind of thinking that put you here in the first place," Ray said.

"We take care of our own. Don't need no PI, and damn sure don't need no cops to help with that."

I leaned my elbows on the table. "Just a few questions, and we'll be out of here and you can go back to doing whatever you do with your day."

"Not much. Not here, anyway."

"When Raul was here, did he mention any new gig he might have?" I asked.

"Nope."

"Nothing?"

"We don't talk much business in here. The guards listen in on everything."

"He didn't mention any new deals?" Ray asked. "New associates? New suppliers? Anything like that?"

"Suppliers of what?"

Ray leaned back in his chair, crossing his arms over his chest. "Look, Santiago, we can tap-dance if you want but a few answers might crack Raul's murder wide open. Don't you think he'd want that?"

Santiago hesitated, his gaze moving to me and then back to Ray. "Yeah. He had a new gig as you say. But I don't know nothing about it. Just that he expected to make a bunch of coin from it."

"Drugs?"

He shrugged. "Don't know."

"Maybe Darrell and Darnell Wilbanks?" I asked.

Nothing.

"You know them?"

"Sure. They the ones that did Raul?"

"Possible," Ray said.

Santiago shook his head. "Those two could've never got the best of Raul. Too stupid."

"Stupid people do stupid things," Ray said.

Santiago offered a half smile. "That's true. This place is full of them."

"Tell us about the Wilbanks brothers," I said.

"They're friends of Raul's. Not mine. I told him so, too. Told him they would fuck up anything they touched."

"Did his new deal include them?"

"Don't know. All he said was that he'd roll in some cash and maybe get me a better lawyer. Maybe get a new trial."

"You had a good lawyer," Ray said. "Maybe the best."

"Walter Horton? He's a loser. Out for the money. Didn't give a half a shit about me."

"Your case would've required a miracle."

"A good lawyer can do that." His eyes narrowed. "You know Horton?"

"Sure do," Ray said.

"Good. Tell him I won't be in here forever."

"I suspect he knows that."

Santiago cocked his head to one side. "Horton the one that sent you here?"

I ignored the question. Ray did, too. Be cool.

"You know a guy named Victor Borkov?" Ray asked.

"Everybody knows Borkov."

"How so?"

"Can't say."

"But Borkov dabbles in the drug business, doesn't he?"

Santiago shrugged.

"Do you think he was part of Raul's new deal?" I asked.

"I told you, I don't know nothing about it."

"Would it surprise you if he were?"

He raised his eyebrows and one shoulder. "Nothing surprises me."

"He never used Borkov's name when you two talked?"

"Told you. We don't say shit in here." He leaned forward enough to scratch his nose, the cuff chains rattling before stretching taut. "All he said was it was some 'big deal dude.'"

"When did he say this new deal was going down?" Ray asked.

"You don't listen so well, do you? We don't talk details. Might as well tell it to the guards." He yawned. "I'm bored. And that's all I got to say, anyway."

The next ten minutes were filled with questions but no answers, Santiago deciding to be tough-guy quiet.

# CHAPTER THIRTY

"Tell me about this real estate deal you think Borkov blew up,"
Ray said.

"Don't think," Henry said. "Know it for a fact."

"You got proof?"

"Victor Borkov isn't the kind to leave behind proof."

Ray had called Henry as I sped back down I-65 toward the coast.
Told him to round up Walter for a chat. So now Ray, Henry, Walter,
and I were huddled around a teak table on Henry's deck. The afternoon sun hung out over the Gulf, peeking between two wads of
puffy white clouds and laying down a bright reflective strip aimed
in our direction. The breeze was soft and warm.

I tugged my Texas Rangers cap down, shading my eyes from the
sun. "Morgan said something about Borkov running off investors.
Something like that happen?"

Henry nodded. "Sure did. A couple of them backed out at the
last minute."

"Because of Borkov?"

Another nod. "Took a bit of pleading, but one of them told me
that Borkov had sent by a couple of guys to scare him off."

"Scare off with money or threats?" Ray asked.

"Borkov doesn't waste money. Apparently these guys said my guy
would be better off if he dropped out of the consortium I had working. Said his family, particularly his teenage daughter, would benefit
from such a decision."

"These two guys?" I asked. "He say who they were?"

"No. Said both were bad-looking pieces of work. One was tall and thin with shaggy blond hair, the other a muscle-bound, tattooed Hispanic. Both scary."

"So he backed out?"

"Ran away as fast as he could."

"Killing the deal?" I asked.

"Let's say damaging the prospects. I had five guys lined up. Ten million each. With two dropping out, it set things back a bit. Until I can replace them, anyway."

"So Borkov hasn't completely won yet?" I asked.

"No. But he's leading the race." Henry massaged his neck. "This property is special. On the water near Panama City. Right next door to my current development. Perfect for a major resort hotel and a couple of golf courses. The owner prefers to work with me and not Borkov but mostly he wants to turn the property and get his investment back. Plus a healthy profit, of course. So, no, Borkov hasn't won yet."

Walter said nothing, but nodded his agreement.

Ray leaned his elbows on the table. "So, if Borkov could eliminate you, the owner would have to deal with him."

Henry looked out toward the beach, unfocused, before returning his gaze to Ray. "You think Borkov was behind Barbara's murder?"

Ray shrugged. "His name has popped up."

"Why kill Barbara? What would that do for him?"

"Maybe he thought you were home. Or maybe he just wanted to deliver a message. Like he did with your two investors."

Henry's eyes glistened. He stood, walked to the rail, and leaned on it, his gaze out over the water.

I watched him for a minute, trying to think of something comforting to say but coming up empty. Then, to Walter, I said, "Morgan said you did the legal work on this project."

"That's right."

"Any problems on your end?"

"None. We had it all wrapped up when Borkov pulled his stunt."

"Did you ever meet him? Borkov?"

"Couple of times."

"And?"

"Tough character. One of those you just know isn't going to follow the rules. Arrogant, confident. A ruthless negotiator. He did all the negotiations himself. Didn't show up to either meeting with council."

"Was he ever threatening toward you?" Ray asked.

"Not directly. But the way he looked at you, you just knew he wasn't the type you messed with."

Henry sat down again. "If he did do this, how are you going to proceed?"

"Carefully," Ray said. "We'll see what we can dig up on him and then see how it plays out."

"Anything we—Walter and I—can do?"

Ray shrugged. "Sit tight. Stay low. If he contacts either of you, let me know."

# CHAPTER THIRTY-ONE

NICOLE AND I sat on the deck at Captain Rocky's, corner table, nursing a second round of margaritas, Nicole demolishing the better part of a basket of chips and a bowl of salsa. The sun had set and a cool breeze lifted off the Gulf. A smattering of stars dotted the Western sky, now holding only a hint of Prussian blue. Nicole wore a yellow windbreaker over her black tank top, her hair pulled back into a ponytail.

Ray and Pancake showed up and barely got seated before Carla Martinez approached.

"What can I get you guys?" Carla asked.

Ray rum and coke; Pancake a Corona.

"I'm starving," Nicole said. "How about some fish tacos?"

"A basket of chips not enough?" I asked.

She laughed. "Good sex will make you hungry."

"Must have been with someone other than Jake," Pancake said.

"Funny," I said.

"Poor baby." Nicole reached over and massaged the back of my neck. "It was great. Stupendous even."

Carla appeared with the drinks. "Tacos'll be out in a minute."

A group of alcohol-infused women, about a dozen, waved to her, raising empty glasses, and Carla headed that way. They sat at the other end of the deck around three four-tops they had pushed together. Some celebration for sure. From the empty margarita pitchers and glasses that littered the tables, it looked like they were going to make a sizable dent in my rent. God bless tequila.

"To business," Ray said. He nodded to Pancake. "Tell them what we have so far."

Pancake pulled a folder from his canvas bag and flipped it open. "Borkov's a real multitasker. Into drugs, of course. Looks to have cartel connections. The Sinaloa group. And recently real estate. Seems to be new at that game. He's bought up a bunch of property over the past five years or so."

"Trying to play legitimate?" I asked.

"Or launder money," Ray said.

Pancake took several healthy gulps of beer. "You can pick up some fine property on the cheap—below market value—if you slip a million or two into the right pockets. Off the radar as it were."

"That's what he does?" Nicole asked.

Pancake nodded. "Slipped unscathed through a couple of Fed bribery and bank fraud investigations. One in Miami, the other in Naples. The talk was he paid off the presiding judges, but no one could ever prove it." Another slug of beer. "Then there's the hits he's supposedly put together. Never got popped for any of that either. Worse, he's apparently been involved in sex trafficking."

"Really?" Nicole asked.

"Brings girls in from Mexico. Some Mexican, some from Eastern Europe, others from Southeast Asia. I suspect he's tied in with one of the Eastern Bloc scumbags that do that shit. Again, nothing anyone could ever prove."

"I guess morals aren't his strong suit," Nicole said.

"But he's slick as a greased eel," Pancake said. "Hard to get a hold of."

"So, was he involved in Barbara Plummer's murder?" I asked.

Ray shrugged. "Don't know. But it would fit his character."

"What now?" Nicole asked.

"Keep digging," Pancake said.

"Somehow I think the key might be with the late Raul Gomez," Ray said. "Finding his fingerprint at the scene means he was involved in Barbara's murder."

"But is he connected to Borkov?" I asked.

"Haven't found anything to suggest that yet," Pancake said. "But my gut," he patted his belly, "tells me he is."

"But he's dead," Nicole said. "Not going to be able to ask him."

"Which is the reason he's dead," I said. "To make sure he doesn't tell what he knows."

"True." Ray nodded. "But his buddies the Wilbanks brothers might be able to give us something. If we can find them."

"Seems tenuous at best," I said.

"Morgan's looking into any cartel connects for Raul," Ray said. He nodded toward Pancake. "Pancake, too. And tomorrow we'll try to run down the Wilbanks duo."

"What now?" I asked.

"Nothing until tomorrow."

"So Jake and I are off-duty tonight?" Nicole asked.

Ray laughed. "Looks that way."

"Good." She mussed my hair. "I see a hot tub in your future."

I stood. "We're out of here."

"What about my tacos?"

"We'll grab them on the way out."

I heard Pancake say, "Animals," as we headed toward the kitchen.

# CHAPTER THIRTY-TWO

DARNELL WAS FEELING better about things, even thinking that maybe Darrell was right. This could all work out and they just might have a future with Borkov. Which would put them in the game. No doubt Borkov was a player. An unflinching and aggressive player. Whacking some rich chick out on The Point was not something just anyone did. Took huge cojones. And Borkov definitely had a pair. Not to mention that he paid well. Ten grand for popping some sleeping woman. Easiest money he'd ever made.

But Darnell also knew he had crossed a line. A wide and dangerous line. One that could never be recrossed. Something he never thought he'd do. Ever. Kill someone. Well, technically it was Darrell that pulled the trigger, but he had been there. From the beginning, right through the planning, and finally the execution.

Execution? What an ugly word. But that's exactly what it had been. He could still see that beautiful lady lying there. Hair spread over the pillow, relaxed in sleep. Safe and warm. Until Darrell pointed his gun at her head and pulled the trigger. The suddenness of it had shocked him. One second she was alive and the next she wasn't.

He remembered the first time Raul had brought it up. Told them he could make them some good money and secure a future of more money for them. That sounded good. The phone store was a steady job, but he had no real future there. He had gone about as high up that ladder as he ever would. So doing some work for Raul's mysterious boss seemed like a good move. One with a real future. But when Raul said it involved whacking someone, Darnell knew this whole thing was wrong. Way wrong. Yet for some reason he didn't voice his reservations but rather simply followed along. Let Darrell make all the decisions. Not something he often did.

But what was done was done. He couldn't go back, and he had to admit it had all worked out well. He and Darrell were on the road to success and riches. He could feel it in his bones.

The afternoon out on the water, with Joe Zuma and Frank Boyd, chasing fish, catching a half dozen nice ones, had only reinforced his confidence in their new arrangement. Both Zuma and Boyd had treated them with a certain degree of respect. Almost a welcome to the club. Boyd even suggesting that they would work well together. Zuma said that Borkov treated his guys well, paid them well, and could use a couple of guys like Darrell and Darnell. They drank beer and shared stories like old friends.

It helped that Darrell was away from his meth stash and wasn't all wired and crazy. He actually managed not to say a bunch of stupid shit. A major feat for Darrell.

Dinner had been equally pleasant and relaxed. Grilled fish, fried rice, a huge salad, fresh baked bread, dessert of flaming cherries over vanilla ice cream, and several bottles of Champagne. Like a real celebration. Borkov was a gracious host and more than once told Darrell how much he appreciated their work. He even praised their efficiency in carrying out his orders.

Life was good.

But later, Darrell got into his meth and got all crazy again. Saying things like he and Darnell would be the best lieutenants, Darrell's word, Borkov ever had. Borkov seemed to take it all in stride, puffing on a thick cigar, sipping Champagne from a thin flute that the staff kept topped off.

Grace was the life of the party. She wore a silky shift and sandals but nothing else as far as Darnell could see. Nipples spiking through the thin material, no panty lines. Maybe someday he could have a girl like that. Darrell followed her around like a puppy and she seemed to enjoy his attention. Several times Darrell followed Grace below, always to emerge a few minutes later, Grace rubbing her nose with the heel of one hand. No doubt Darrell was sharing his stash with her.

Borkov seemed oblivious to their flirting, but Darnell was sure little really got past him. He didn't seem to care, though. Maybe he and Grace have some kind of arrangement. If it was him, the only arrangement he'd have would be Grace in a bed. A big bed. In a top hotel. He could afford that now.

Now it was late, probably near midnight. The ship cut smoothly through the calm water, heading to port. Borkov said they'd arrive by dawn. Darrell and Grace huddled on the bench seat near the stern, the silvery wake behind them. Their conversation was muted but their laughter was clear. Darnell sat in a thickly padded deck chair, facing Borkov, who was stretched out in a lounge chair, the remnants of a fourth cigar clamped between his teeth.

"You've got it made," Darnell said.

Borkov shrugged.

"I mean, I never knew anyone with a boat like this."

"Comes with the territory." He flicked a long ash into the ashtray beside him. "Didn't come easy, though."

"Does anything worth having come easy?"

Borkov smiled. "You're a smart young man."

"My mom always said I was a smart-ass."

Another smile. "Mine, too. Before she died. My father took off after that. Never saw him again. But that's his loss." He sipped some Champagne. "I actually owe him for all this." He waved his cigar.

"If he hadn't left, passing me off to a distant cousin, I'd never have run away, never left the Ukraine, never come here to the land of opportunity."

"How'd you do it?" Darnell asked. "I mean, coming here?"

"Got a job on a shipping freighter. Out of Poland. Made a few trips back and forth and then one night decided Miami would be a good place to jump ship. Which I did. Literally." He smiled, his gaze to the sky as if remembering. "The drop was a lot further than it looked. The water colder than I imagined. Not to mention the swim around the ship and to shore. Almost didn't make it."

"Very brave."

"Not really. It seemed like the only option I had." He waved away a cloud of smoke. "I worked for a local dealer, a fellow Ukrainian, who was hooked up with one of the cartels. Mostly cocaine but also weed, meth, heroin, GHB, you name it. Big market for all that in South Beach. I did good, but the guy I worked for was small minded, so I moved him out and took over his operation."

"Moved out?"

Another smile. "Let's just say I eliminated the competition. Anyway, by the time I was your age, I'd moved across to Naples and there things really took off."

"So all this came from drugs?"

"At first, but then I realized I needed to be more legit. Too dangerous to stay on the DEA's radar. I used my cash to get into real estate. The only venture in Florida that's more profitable than drugs." More Champagne. "And the rest, as they say, is history."

Darnell was amazed how candid Borkov was. Relating all his illegal activities as if he was talking about a regular job. A normal life. Darnell took it to mean that Borkov trusted him. Truly felt he was part of the family.

From the corner of his eye he saw Grace stand. She stretched and walked toward them, Darrell in tow.

"It's late," she said. "I'm going to bed and leave you guys to talk business or whatever." She kissed Borkov on the cheek and retreated below, her walk unsteady.

Darrell sat in the empty chair next to Darnell.

"You guys enjoying yourselves?" Borkov asked.

"Yes, sir," Darnell said. "We really appreciate everything you've done for us."

"And many more good times to come, I'm sure," Darrell said. "Now that we're on the team."

Borkov crushed the cigar stub in the ash tray. He flipped open the polished humidor and extracted another cigar. He cut the tip and fired it up, waving away the smoke cloud. "So tell me again how it went down."

"The hit?" Darrell asked. "Nothing to it. No sweat."

"Smooth, huh?"

"Very."

Borkov nodded. "I like smooth."

"That's us," Darrell said. "Smooth as a baby's butt."

"And Raul? He do good, too?"

Darrell leaned forward, one knee hopping up and down, getting into it now. "Like I said before, we didn't really need him. He was going to bypass the alarm." He glanced at Darnell. "Me and Darnell don't know much about those things. But since the alarm was off and the back door unlocked, there wasn't much for Raul to do so he took off. He said we could handle the rest. So we did. All we had to do was creep in and do her."

Boyd had been below and he now returned to the rear deck, settling against the bar where Zuma stood. He crossed his arms over his chest.

"What exactly did Raul tell you?" Borkov asked.

Darrell's bouncing knee came to a halt. "What do you mean?"

Darnell felt a note of tension in Borkov's voice. What was the problem? Hadn't they done as they were told? What was Borkov getting at?

"I mean, what were his exact instructions?"

"That we should wait until just after midnight. After everyone out there on The Point was asleep. He told us to park well away from the guard gate and that we should come along the beach. Approach the house that way. But when we got there we decided it'd be best to walk along the dunes. The beach seemed too exposed. We figured the dunes would give us more cover."

"Very good." Borkov puffed on his cigar, the end flaring bright red. "And did anyone see you?"

Darrell laughed. "Not a chance. We're very stealthy when we need to be." He tapped the back of his hand against Darnell's knee.

Borkov nodded but said nothing.

"Anyway, we got to the house and there was Raul. Hiding among some sea oats. Scared the shit out of us when he stood up." Darrell laughed. "Didn't he, little brother?"

"Sure did," Darnell said.

Darnell was only half listening to Darrell's ramblings. He was focused on Borkov. He couldn't shake the feeling that something had changed. Borkov's face seemed tight, his eyes a bit more narrow than before. As if he had undergone some mood shift. But Darnell couldn't figure out why. Hadn't everything gone according to plan? Maybe he was reading too much into it.

Borkov puffed out a cloud of smoke. "So Raul left and you guys went inside the house. What then?"

Darrell looked at him as if he had asked a stupid question. "Like

I said, we shot her and left. Went back up the beach the same way we came. Smooth."

Borkov gave a slow nod, followed by a brief glance toward Zuma and Boyd. "Did Raul tell you who the targets were?"

"Not by name," Darrell said. "He said we didn't need to know that. Just that we should kill everyone in the house."

"And did you?"

"Sure. Why?"

Borkov waved his cigar toward them. "Just wondering what the plan was."

"We searched every room. The lady was alone."

"And that fit with what Raul said?"

Darnell felt confused. What was Borkov getting at? He sensed something was off but couldn't grasp what it might be. So he said, "What are you asking? I don't understand."

Borkov flicked a long ash into the ashtray. "How many people did he say would be there?"

"Oh," Darrell said. "I get it." His knee started bouncing again. "He said it was a couple. At least I think that's what he said." He looked at Darnell. "Isn't that right?"

"Yeah. I think so."

"But she was alone?" Borkov asked.

"Yeah, she was."

"What'd you think about that?"

"Nothing." Darrell shrugged. "We figured he was mistaken."

"Or maybe the husband was away," Darnell added.

"And it didn't cross your mind that something wasn't right. That maybe you should've backed away and waited for another night?"

Darrell stared at him.

Darnell felt pressure rise in his chest. Borkov's face looked like stone as he puffed on his cigar, its glowing red tip aimed directly at Darnell. His mind was blank. He had no response to Borkov's question.

Darrell did. "We were sent to do everyone there. We did. What's the problem?"

Darnell was now aware that Boyd and Zuma had moved behind them. He began to turn to look at them when the jolt hit him. As he lurched forward he was aware of Darrell also falling forward, Zuma pressing something to the back of his neck. The world swirled and he lost consciousness.

He wasn't sure how long he was out, but when the world began to return it was fuzzy and muffled. As if some translucent curtain was partially blocking all sensations, muddying everything. He became aware of movement, of hands holding him and rolling him from side to side, of voices he couldn't quite make out. Then he was prone on the deck, the wood cold against his cheek. He tried to move but couldn't. As if his arms and legs wouldn't follow orders. Then he saw Zuma and Boyd wrapping duct tape around Darrell's chest, trapping his arms to his side. Darnell realized he had been similarly trussed. Wide bands of tape around his ankles, knees, and chest, his arms trapped at his sides. Zuma and Boyd rolled the brothers to their backs. Darnell looked up. Borkov stood over him.

"You stupid fucks screwed everything up. It's the husband I wanted dead. The wife was collateral."

"But—" Darrell said.

"Shut up. I'm tired of your bullshit."

"But we did—" Darrell began again.

Borkov's jaw tightened and his neck veins became thick ropes. "Didn't I tell you to shut your fucking mouth?"

Darrell nodded.

"Now I'm going to ask you a few questions and your answers better be what I want to hear. Clear?"

Again Darrell nodded.

"Good. Now, did you see anyone else?"

"No."

"What about when Joe and Frank picked you up on the beach? See anyone there?"

"No."

"Not a girl in a car?"

"Yeah," Darrell said. "Like I told them, she was just some random chick. Asking for directions."

"Why don't I believe you?"

"It's true. I swear. We don't know who she was."

"Here's my problem. Some chick wondering around lost that time of morning? Doesn't quite gel to me."

"But we'd never seen her before." Darrell's voice was high pitched and strained.

Borkov knelt next to him. Darnell heard a click and a switchblade knife appeared. He aimed the point at Darrell's face. "Let's try it again. Who was the chick?"

"We don't know."

Borkov slid the blade into one nostril and with a flick sliced through Darrell's nose. He screamed.

"Tell me now or I'll cut your fucking nose off and then dig out your eyes."

"Please."

The knife's tip settled against Darrell's cheek just beneath his left eye.

"She's Darrell's girlfriend," Darnell said.

"Shut up," Darrell said.

"She's nothing," Darnell said. "A nobody. She didn't know where we were going or who we were meeting."

Borkov swung on his haunches toward Darnell. "But she knows

you were picked up, on a beach, middle of the night. Kind of thing she'd remember if anyone asked."

"Like who?" Darnell asked.

"Like anyone. I need a name."

Darnell hesitated, deciding what to say. No way he would give up his life for some dumb chick. "Her name is Heather. Heather Macomb."

"See, that was easy. Who is she?"

"Some high schooler Darrell's been screwing. That's all. She's not important."

"She is to me. Where does she live?"

"Gulf Shores."

"And she snuck out to be with you two?"

"That's right," Darrell said. "She just wanted to say goodbye."

"Very prescient of her."

"What?" Darrell said.

"Where in Gulf Shores does she live?"

"With her parents."

"And who might they be?"

"Why?" Darrell asked.

Borkov smiled. Cold without feeling. "I might want to have a chat with her."

"Leave her out of this," Darrell said. "Please."

"You should've thought of that before she showed up on the beach. Now I'm losing my patience here. Who the fuck are her parents?"

"Her dad owns a grocery store," Darnell said. "Mel's. In Gulf Shores."

"Good. Now one more question. And this one is very important. Anyone else know where you were going?"

"Only Raul," Darrell said. "He told us where to meet the boat and what time to be there. Ask him."

"I would but I don't think he'd tell me."

"Sure he would. Why wouldn't he?"

"Raul's dead."

"Oh, Jesus," Darnell said.

"Jesus has nothing to do with this." Borkov stood and nodded to Zuma. "Go ahead."

Zuma and Boyd hoisted the brothers to their feet. Boyd arranged them back to back while Zuma wrapped more duct tape around them, binding them together.

"What are you doing?" Darrell asked, his voice high pitched with panic.

"Cleaning house," Borkov said.

Darnell heard the clanking of metal on the deck. Then Zuma was beside them, a thick chain in his hand. He and Boyd wound it around the brothers, securing it with a padlock, leaving a three-foot tail. Boyd and Zuma left the deck for a minute and returned with a rusted metal disc. Thick, four feet in diameter, heavy enough that the pair struggled to settle it on the deck near the stern. They then shuffled the brothers to the stern, lifting them up on the seat where Darrell and Grace had sat earlier.

"Don't do this," Darrell said. "We won't say a word."

"I know you won't."

"We'll help you find Heather."

"I think I can manage."

Zuma fastened the metal ring to the chain with a clamp. The two men lifted the ring, their heavily muscled arms rippling. He looked at Borkov. Borkov nodded.

They muscled the ring out over the water. Darnell felt a sharp yank and his feet lifted from the seat. He floated over the rail and seemed to hang in the air for a brief moment, then the water was cold and dark. The pressure on his chest built rapidly and his ears popped as they plunged deeper. He felt Darrell writhing against his back. Pain knifed through his head as his eardrums ruptured.

Oh, Jesus.

# CHAPTER THIRTY-THREE

GRACE MADE HER way below deck, through the galley, and down the hallway to the master stateroom. Not an easy journey. She was hammered. She banged into the stair railing, the galley table, and a doorjamb along the way. Why had she drank so much? Not to mention the meth Darrell kept feeding her. She managed to scrub off the sparse makeup she wore and smeared moisturizer on her face, her nightly ritual. Wasn't easy. She eyed the head more than once, stomach churning, thinking she might throw up.

She stretched out on the bed, not bothering to undress. The gentle rocking of the boat seemed more forceful than usual. Her stomach rocked with it. She took a few deep, slow breaths and closed her eyes. It'll pass, she thought. She focused on a single spot on the ceiling and thankfully her nausea began to settle.

She pictured Darrell. He was cute, even hot. Another time, another place, she would have been interested. But not here, not now. She enjoyed his attention, of course—what girl wouldn't?—but that's all it was. A brief flirtation with the help. Victor was her future. She had made that decision a dozen months ago and wasn't about to screw up this gig. She'd seen and done things that she never imagined. Paris, San Francisco, Hawaii. Places she had only dreamed about. Not to mention the days and nights on this amazing ship.

Victor was good to her. Very good. The best of everything. Clothes, food, wine, whatever she wanted, he made happen.

Effortlessly. All she had to do was make him happy. Not an unpleasant task. Victor was the best lover she'd ever had. Not that there had been that many, but he was amazing. Big, hard, and the stamina of an athlete. Even at his age.

No, Darrell was a momentary distraction. A fun little game.

Victor understood. He knew she liked to flirt. Knew it was only a game. Knew she was his and wouldn't do anything stupid. In fact, he encouraged her flirting with the men he brought on board. He said it made them relaxed, unfocused, and more malleable. She remembered he had used that exact word. She had had to look it up to see what it meant. It made her feel good that she could not only make Victor happy but also help with his business dealings. It made her feel needed.

Another wave of nausea rose. A few deep breaths didn't help. She swung her legs off the bed and sat up. That didn't help, either. Everything seemed wobbly, off-balance.

Ginger ale. That's what she needed. Victor always kept it in the fridge. Said it was great for seasickness, settling the stomach. She glanced at the bedside phone, thinking she'd call the staff and have some brought to her. But that would take ten minutes or so. She needed it now.

She stood, her legs wavering. Steadying herself against the wall, she made her way back down the hall to the galley and tugged open the refrigerator. The can she pulled loose from the plastic six-pack ring felt icy in her hand. She rolled it across her forehead, the cold a welcome relief. She snapped open the pop top and took a gulp, the liquid chilling her chest and stomach. Better. Another gulp.

She heard voices. Not normal conversation but high pitched, pleading.

*What the hell?*

She placed the ginger ale on the counter and walked halfway up the steps, just until she could see across the deck toward the stern. She froze.

Darrell and Darnell stood on the rear seat. Back to back. Odd. Then she saw they were wrapped with duct tape. What the hell was going on? Boyd and Zuma crab walked into view, shoulders hunched, struggling with something heavy they carried between them. They turned as one and she saw it was a thick metal ring. They swung it back and with audible grunts tossed it over the ship's stern. Darrell and Darnell seemed to leap airborne, hovered briefly, and then they were gone.

She recoiled, losing her balance, stumbling back down the steps. She crashed to the floor.

"What the hell was that?" Victor's voice.

She scrambled to her feet. Nausea swept over her. Her heart tried to escape from her chest. Sweat popped out everywhere. Cold. She felt the room spin. She staggered to the sink and vomited. Ginger ale, Champagne, fish tacos, and bitter bile rushed upward, burning her chest. She vomited again.

Then Victor was there.

"What's the matter?"

She kept her head down, shoulders rolled forward. "Too much to drink." Her stomach lurched again. "Maybe too many tacos."

Victor glanced toward the stairs. "I see."

He rested a hand on her shoulder. He was suspicious. She could hear it in his voice. Knew the real question he was asking: Had she seen what happened? Maybe he didn't care. Maybe he trusted her. Maybe he didn't. Not a chance she could take.

Play sick. Play dumb.

"I'll be okay. Just give me a minute."

"Want to lay down?" Victor asked.

She nodded and swiped the back of one hand across her mouth. "I think I should before I fall again."

He helped her to the stateroom and she tumbled on to the bed, rolling to her back, one arm over her face. "I'm so stupid."

"How so?"

"Drinking that much. It's Darrell's fault. He kept filling my glass."

"So I saw."

"I hope he's not sick, too."

"I don't think Darrell's having much of an alcohol problem about now."

# CHAPTER THIRTY-FOUR

HEATHER MACOMB WAS pissed. Darrell had said they'd be back early. "At dawn," he'd said. But here she was waiting for nearly two hours and still no Darrell. Yet again she'd cut her morning classes. For this? Not that she minded ditching school, but not to hang around the marina wasting time.

She walked to the end of one of the piers and gazed out toward the Gulf. A few boats cut through the water but they were small fishing rigs, heading out for a day of fishing. Not the massive boat Darrell said he and Darnell were going out on. Surely if it were anywhere out there she'd see it. A bump on the horizon. Something. But the water was flat, the horizon line crisp and unbroken.

What an asshole. She should dump his sorry ass. He treated her like shit. Like a toy. A plaything. She deserved better.

"Can I help you, young lady?"

She turned. The man was old, thin, slightly stooped, and wore khakis, a loose t-shirt beneath a dark-blue windbreaker, and a cap, also dark blue, Marina Staff stamped on it.

"No, thanks. I'm waiting on someone."

"Out fishing? The one you're waitin' on?"

"Yeah."

"Probably got into a hot spot and lost track of time."

"Maybe. But they've been out since yesterday morning."

"Ah, an overnighter." He scratched the stubble on his chin. "Used to do that myself. When I was younger. Not now. My old joints won't take being out on the water that long anymore."

"Sorry."

"Not your fault. But Old Mother Nature can be a bitch." He tilted his cap back. "Course youngster like you don't got to worry about stuff like that."

"You work here?"

"Sure do. Try to keep the boats moving in and out. Keep things clean."

"You get here early?"

"Five thirty. Like clockwork. Been doing it nearly thirty years now."

"Did you see a large boat come in today?"

"How large we talking?"

"I don't know. But from what I was told, very large."

"Nope. Not today. Course we don't get many big ones here. They mostly come and go out of Pensacola. You think they might've docked there?"

"No. He said he'd be here around dawn."

"Ain't been in here. Not no big boats."

"Maybe they didn't dock. They went out on a smaller boat. Out to meet the bigger one. Maybe they came back on that. You seen anything like that?"

He shook his head. "They'd've settled right out there if that was the case." He pointed toward the Gulf. "I'd've seen any boats large enough to have a tender boat. Can't hardly miss 'em. Specially as flat as the water is today."

"Thanks." She walked past him, back up the dock.

"They'll be along before too long, I suspect," the man said.

"Hope so."

She returned to her car. Leaning against it, arms folded over her chest. Now what? Did they go to Pensacola? Or maybe back where she had left them out near the old fort? Darrell would've called if that was the case. Maybe. Reliability and Darrell had never actually met. But she was their ride home, after all. Unless, of course, Darrell the flake forgot that.

She tried Darrell's phone for like the millionth time and yet again it flipped over to voice mail. She didn't bother to leave another message. Twelve should be enough.

She stood there fuming for a few minutes and then decided to swing by their apartment. Maybe they got back middle-of-the-night early and went home to sleep. Well, she'd just go wake his ass up.

# CHAPTER THIRTY-FIVE

GRACE FELT LIKE hell. Her head seemed as if it were stuffed with soggy paper, her eyes and throat dry and scratchy, her mouth sour and metallic. Daylight pressed against the stateroom curtains. According to the bedside clock it was 9:15. Victor was already up and gone. Probably on the deck, making phone calls. She had slept in fits and spurts, but he had no such problem. Moving little, snoring softly, he slept as if all was normal. After tossing two men overboard? What the hell?

Several times during the night she had rolled to her side and stared at Victor's sleeping profile. Trying to decide if she really knew him. Truly understood his nature.

She had met Victor a year earlier, while she waitressed in a Naples resort restaurant. He had been charming and flirty. Handsome in a rugged way and obviously in charge of all around him. Zuma and Boyd hovering constantly, speaking only when spoken to, ready to jump every time Victor so much as nodded. Victor wore wealth and power easily. Heady stuff. She had resisted his advances. At first. But he persisted and she finally agreed to dinner. Innocent, she told herself. But by midnight she found herself in his palatial suite, on her back, him on top, whispering in her ear, taking charge of her body like no one she had ever encountered. Within a week she quit her job and sailed away on his yacht. They had been together ever since.

Her mother had been horrified, but Grace assured her that Victor was kind and generous and offered her a way out of serving tacos and tequila to jerks. Her mother argued but ultimately gave up, saying, "It's your life so do what you wish." More resignation than endorsement.

The past year had been filled with glamorous trips, the best food and Champagne, and parties with celebrities and sports stars and business types. Victor seemed to burn through money like the supply was unending. For him that was apparently true. It had all been dizzying for a girl from a modest background. The boys she had dated were just that—boys. Silly, stupid, and falsely macho. Not Victor. He was a man and he was in complete control of his world. But in the middle of this whirlwind life she had chosen, something happened. Something she never would have predicted. She fell in love with Victor Borkov. Deeply in love.

But now?

She knew Victor was shady. She wasn't stupid. She'd overheard bits and pieces of conversations that hinted of illegality. The Mexican drug dealer that spent a week with them fishing and diving off Cozumel. The three Eastern European types who had unloaded boxes of automatic weapons from the *Sea Witch* and then disappeared across the Gulf in their high-speed boat. The Armani-suited businessmen who brought bags of hard cash to the frequent meetings Victor directed. Not to mention the stream of pro athletes who powered through the bikini-clad blonds that seemed to pop up like weeds at Victor's estate in Naples.

She rationalized this is as simply business in the upper echelon of society. Choosing to ignore the signs she should have taken more seriously. Given what happened last night, much more seriously.

She sat on the edge of the bed, trying to gauge her balance. She realized the ship was no longer moving. Where were they? She stood and pushed back the curtain. The light seemed harsh, but as her eyes adjusted, she realized they had docked. How had she slept through that?

After a quick shower, she slipped on a pair of white pants and a red long-sleeved pullover, sweeping her damp hair back over her shoulder. She swiped on a bit of lip gloss and stared at her reflection in the mirror, steeling her nerves. Could she pull this off? Did she have another choice? Her mother had always said she'd make a great actress and now she would have to prove it. If Victor believed, or even suspected, that she had seen what had happened on deck what would he do? Trust her? Kill her? Either was possible.

She slipped on her sunglasses and headed toward the galley. Zuma and Boyd greeted her when she walked in.

"Have enough to drink last night?" Zuma asked.

"Way too much. My head feels like the drummer for Metallica is having a practice session in there."

Boyd laughed. He handed her a mug of coffee. "This might help."

"Thanks." She cradled the mug and took a sip. "Maybe this and a brain transplant." Another sip. "Where's Victor?"

Zuma jerked his head toward the stairs. "On deck."

She made her way up the steps and took a seat at the table across from Victor. He had his laptop open, the remnants of a Bloody Mary next to it.

"Good morning," he said. "Sleep okay?"

"Sorry. I don't know what got into me. I never drink that much." He smiled. How could he be so relaxed? So unconcerned? "I didn't even know we had docked."

"About an hour ago."

"Where are we?"

"Pensacola."

She massaged her scalp. Even it hurt. "Where's Darrell and Darnell?"

"Gone."

"Gone?" Was he going to confess? If he did, how should she react?

"I had a job for them. They took off as soon as we docked."

Liar, she wanted to scream. Instead she said, "I hope they weren't as hungover as I am."

"They aren't." He drained his drink. "Maybe you should have one of these."

"Oh, no, I don't want to see alcohol for a long time."

"Hair of the dog. It'll help." He waved a hand and Brian Wirtz, the ship's chef, appeared as if by magic. "Make me another. And whip one up for Grace."

Before she could protest, he was gone.

"What's on the schedule today?" she asked.

"I have a couple of potential investors boarding around noon."

"I need to go to the mall at some time," she said. "To pick up a few things."

"Not today. Maybe tomorrow. We'll be here a few days."

She started to protest but thought better of it. "That'll work."

"These guys'll be on board a few hours so you'll be on entertainment duty."

Meaning that she was supposed to look sexy, be flirty, make them feel welcomed and relaxed. Show them what the good life was like. That hooking up with Victor would be a good thing. That opening their checkbooks would buy them a slice of all this. It was the game. Victor had trained her well. She knew what was expected.

Brian returned, two Bloody Marys in hand. He placed them on the table. "Can I get you something to eat?" he asked Grace.

"That would be great. What did you make today?"

"I have a smoked ham and Swiss quiche, croissants, and fruit. Or I can make an omelet. Whatever you want."

"Maybe some fruit, yogurt, and granola?"

"No problem."

# CHAPTER THIRTY-SIX

RAY, NICOLE, AND I easily found the Wilbanks brothers' nondescript Gulf Shores apartment building in a quiet neighborhood maybe a mile as the crow flies from the beach. According to the manager, one Clifford Rucker, a middle-aged, balding guy who wore the mark of alcohol and cigarettes on his creased face, the brothers lived in Number 22, upstairs, back side. He stood in the open door to his unit, a cigarette with a dangerously long ash perched in one corner of his mouth, bobbing as he spoke. Yellowed fingers clutched a glass of amber whiskey and partially melted ice. Getting the day started early.

"You happen to know if they're home?" I asked.

Rucker's gaze devoured Nicole for the third or fourth time until he managed to tear it away and look back at me. "I don't stick my nose in my tenants' business."

"The perfect landlord," Ray said.

Rucker's eyes narrowed. "You being a smart-ass?"

"Just making an observation."

"What you want with them?" Rucker asked.

"Thought you didn't stick your nose in other folks' business?"

"Listen, Jack—"

"Ray. The name's Ray."

"Like I give a hot shit." The ash fell onto his plaid shirt and he brushed it away. "Why don't you folks get on up outta here?"

"As soon as we chat with the brothers we'll do just that."

Rucker had apparently run out of words. He took a step back and closed the door.

We circled the building and climbed the metal stairs. Number 22 was the third door. No answer to my knock.

Nicole cupped her hands around her eyes and peered through the gap in the front window curtains. "Looks quiet in there," she said.

"What now?" I asked.

Ray massaged his neck. "Guess we'll come back later."

I heard footsteps on the stairs and turned that way. A young woman. A very pretty young woman. She stopped when she saw us. Surprise on her face.

"Morning," I said.

She hesitated, obviously confused. "Who are you?"

"I'm Jake. This is Nicole and Ray. You?"

"Heather."

"You know the Wilbanks brothers?"

"Yes."

"Know where they might be?"

"Why are you asking?"

Ray stepped forward. "Need to chat with them."

Her gaze bounced away, then back to him. "About what?"

"Routine stuff."

"You guys cops or something?" Heather asked.

"No," I said. "Private investigators."

Confusion cut deeper into her face.

"We just need to ask them about a case we're working on," Nicole said. She smiled.

Heather seemed to relax a little. "Well, I've got a couple of questions for Darrell myself."

"About what?" I asked.

Another hesitation. "I was supposed to meet him and Darnell at the marina this morning. They didn't show so I thought maybe they got back early and might've come back here."

"Back from where?" I asked.

"Fishing. They headed out early yesterday morning and were supposed to be back at dawn."

"Who are you?" Ray asked. "How do you know them?"

"I'm Darrell's girlfriend."

"Don't you hate it when guys stand you up?" Nicole asked. A woman's touch seemed to relax Heather further.

"Darrell's pretty good at that," Heather said.

"Honey, they're all good at that," Nicole added.

Heather laughed. "Ain't that the truth."

"Who'd they go fishing with?" I asked.

"I don't know. Some bigwig with a big boat's all I know." Now her brow furrowed.

"What is it?" Nicole asked. "You looked worried."

She sighed. "It's all so strange."

"What's strange?" I asked.

"Everything. I mean, I went with them out to the beach yesterday. Early. Way too early to be up and around. Four in the morning. Out by the old fort. Two guys picked them up in a motorboat and took them out to the big boat."

"What big boat?"

"I don't know. Darrell called him the 'boss man' or 'big man.' Something like that."

"No name?" I asked.

"Darrell said I didn't need to know that so he wouldn't tell me."

"Why's that?" Ray asked.

"I don't know. It was all so weird. Darrell made me promise not to say a word to anyone about it." She sighed. "And here I am telling you." She shook her head. "I should learn to keep my mouth shut."

"We can keep a secret," I said.

"And the other strange part—I followed them out there. Darrell was going to leave his car for some guy to use while they were out fishing."

"Any idea why?"

She shook her head. "All I know is that the trip was also business. Some big deal Darrell and Darnell were doing with the boat guy. He wouldn't tell me anything about it. Just said they'd make a lot of money."

"So, let me get this straight," Ray said. "Darrell and Darnell met some guys on an isolated beach, middle of the night, to go on some fishing/business trip with some mysterious dude who owns a big boat?"

"Sounds strange, doesn't it?"

"Sure does. And you don't know who that person is?"

Heather shook her head. "Not a clue."

"Did you see this boat?" I asked. "The big one?"

"No. As soon as we could hear the little boat's engine coming, Darrell ran me off. Said they'd be in trouble if the men in the boat saw me there. So I left."

"Did you see the boat pick them up?"

"No. Like I said, I took off."

"Did you happen to go by and see if Darrell's car was still out there? By the beach?" I asked.

She shook her head. "That never occurred to me. But I know Darrell said someone was picking it up for some job or something. Darrell doesn't tell me a whole lot."

"We'll check it out," Ray said. "What kind of car does Darrell drive?"

"A Honda Accord. It's gray and has a damaged front fender. You know that rust stuff?"

"Primer?" I asked.

"Yeah. Left front fender." A look of concern crept into her face. "Why're you looking for Darrell and Darnell? Are they in some kind of trouble?"

"Not that we know of," I said. "It's a case we're working, and we were hoping they might be able to help."

"I see."

"Do you know Raul Gomez?" Ray asked.

"Not really. I've met him a couple of times. Do you think they might be off somewhere with him?"

"Do you?"

She shrugged. "Maybe. I mean, I know they did some work with Raul."

"What kind of work?" I asked.

A sigh. "I don't know. Like I said, Darrell don't tell me shit about his business."

"Looks like we have a problem here," Ray said. "You see, Raul's dead."

Heather wavered, took a step back. "What? Dead?" Tears welled in her eyes. "I don't understand."

"We don't, either. But someone shot Raul."

Her face screwed down in a futile attempt to control her tears. Didn't work. "Is Darrell in danger?"

"Maybe."

She sniffed. "Who? Why?"

"That's what we're trying to find out," Ray said. "And you're going to have to tell the police everything you just told us."

"No. I can't do that."

"Not much choice. Detective Morgan's in charge and he'll definitely knock on your door."

"I won't do it."

"You will," Ray said. "Otherwise you're obstructing an investigation and you don't want to go there."

"Shit." She sniffed back tears. "My parents will go ballistic."

"Sorry," Ray said.

"Can't you just forget about this? Let me go home?"

"I wish we could but that's not possible." He pulled out his cell phone. "I'll let Morgan know you'll be home. Right?"

She nodded. "Okay."

"And I'll get him on finding Darrell's car." As he dialed, he walked away, his back to us.

"You okay?" Nicole asked. She walked to where Heather stood and placed a hand on her shoulder.

Heather shook her head. "No, I'm not okay. I don't know what the hell's going on." She wiped away tears with the heels of her hands. "None of this makes any sense."

"One more question," I said. "Did you see anyone else that morning? Out on the beach?"

"No." She shook her head, and then hesitated, gaze upward as if recalling something. "Actually, I did. As I drove back up the road I passed a jogger. A woman."

"What'd she look like?"

"It was dark so I couldn't see much. Just a glimpse in my headlights."

"And?"

"She looked like a runner. Lean and fit with long legs is about all I remember. She had on a white top and dark shorts."

"How tall?"

"Maybe my height, if I had to guess. Five-six. I think she had short dark hair. Oh, and she had in earplugs and one of those arm bands that hold an iPod."

"Do you think she might have seen any of this? The men or the boat?"

"It's possible, I guess. She was maybe a mile up the road when I passed her. But she was moving pretty good and was headed that way."

# CHAPTER THIRTY-SEVEN

TAMMY HORTON HAD finished her walk on the beach and an hour of Pilates, and now stood in the kitchen eating an apple and staring at Walter through the French doors. He lay in a lounge chair on the deck, his back to her.

Last night they had had a long talk about Barbara, their marriage, their future, everything. It had actually been good. Cathartic, as they say. In the end Tammy had said that she loved him, forgave him, and even understood how these things happen. Even that she was glad it was Barbara and not some young floozy. That Barbara had been classy and a good person and she could see his attraction to her.

But this morning she felt the anger rising again. Fretful sleep and dreams that held images of Walter and Barbara rolling around together had relit the fire. Her first thought, as she lay there in bed, Walter softly snoring beside her, was to revisit last night's discussion. Say the things she had avoided saying last night. The hateful things that could do irreparable harm. That couldn't be taken back. Didn't she deserve that bit of revenge?

Instead, she decided exercise might be the best medicine. She slipped from bed, careful not to disturb Walter.

She had begun her walk angry, no, infuriated, with Walter. Still creating blistering words in her head. Still wanting to singe his ears, to make him pay for his betrayal. But halfway through her two-mile loop up the beach and back, the sharp edges of her rage began to smooth and then the Pilates tamped them down to a manageable level.

She dropped the apple core into the compactor and stepped out on the deck. Walter apparently didn't sense she was there since he sat quietly, staring out over the beach. To see him there, doing nothing, was odd. Walter never had downtime. Couldn't tolerate it. Didn't believe in it. Had to always be on the move or doing something. Whether in the office or at home, he always had his briefcase open and was reading, writing, studying, whatever it was that lawyers did.

But right now he seemed beaten. Like he didn't have the energy to do anything. Or was it a lack of interest?

Was it Barbara's death that ate at him? Was it guilt for his betrayal of her? Was it the weight of him being a suspect? But that seemed to have died down a bit. Detective Morgan had dropped by just yesterday and said as much. That Walter wasn't completely in the clear but the evidence they had so far suggested that it was someone else.

The only disturbing thing about his visit was that Morgan had asked Walter about Raul Gomez. Had he heard from him and seen him recently? Of course Walter hadn't. Not since he threatened Walter for not being able to get his brother off. That had been a few tense months. Knowing that a cold-blooded killer's brother was pissed at you. Tammy had slept poorly, waking in the night, sneaking to various windows, gently parting the curtains, careful not to move them too much, and checking the street, the beach, anywhere Raul might be sneaking up on the house. Of course, she never saw anything. Eventually, as Raul never did anything or contacted them in any way, the fear lessened and life returned to normal.

"You okay?" she asked.

He didn't move, but said, "I'm fine."

"Not going to the office today?"

"I canceled everything. Don't want to deal with other people's problems just yet."

She walked to his side, resting a hand on his shoulder. "I meant what I said last night. I forgive you."

"Not sure I can forgive myself," Walter said. "It was wrong on so many levels."

Tammy squeezed his shoulder. "I can't argue with that but just know that it's behind us now."

"Is it? Doesn't feel that way to me."

"Give it time." She gave his shoulder another squeeze. "I mean, I'm still mad at you, at Barbara, even at me, but it'll fade with time."

He looked up at her. "You? Why on Earth would you be mad at you? You didn't do anything."

"I must have. Why else would you need someone else?"

Walter reached up and laid his hand over hers. "It wasn't like that. It isn't like that. You know I love you. And I'll make all this up to you somehow."

Neither said anything for a minute.

"Want something to eat?" Tammy asked.

"Not right now."

"Let me know when you do." She pulled her hand from his. "I'm going to hit the shower."

But she never made it that far. As she walked through the foyer toward the curving staircase that led upstairs, she saw a black Channel 16 news truck parked across the street. The side sliding door was rolled back, a cameraman sitting in the opening, working on his equipment. A young female reporter sat in the passenger's seat, checking her makeup in the visor mirror. Tammy couldn't remember her name but had seen her on TV many times.

Were they setting up to do a remote? Right here in front of her house? The hell they were.

She stormed out the door and marched toward them. The cameraman looked up, the reporter stepped out of the van.

"What the hell are you doing here?" Tammy asked.

"Are you Mrs. Horton?" the girl asked.

"Yes. And you're intruding on my privacy."

"I'm Sharon Morrison. Reporter for Channel 16." She extended her hand to shake.

Tammy ignored it. "I don't give a damn who you are. Get out of here."

Tammy now noticed the cameraman was settling his camera on his shoulder and directing it her way. One hand automatically went to her hair. She should have showered first. And put on some makeup. People couldn't see her on TV looking like this.

Then reporter Sharon was speaking to her again. "Mrs. Horton, all I want to do is give Mr. Horton a chance to tell his side of things."

"His side is that he didn't do anything wrong. He had nothing to do with what happened to Barbara Plummer."

"That's what Detective Morgan said when I interviewed him yesterday," Sharon said. "But weren't Mr. Horton and Mrs. Plummer involved?"

"No. We've been friends with the Plummers for years. That's it."

The cameraman now had Tammy in full focus, and Sharon had her handheld mic extended toward her.

"My sources tell a different story," Sharon said.

"Your sources are wrong." Tammy glared at her and then at the cameraman. "Now I suggest you leave immediately or I'll call the police. This is a private community."

Not waiting for an answer, Tammy spun on her heels and headed toward her house.

"But, Mrs. Horton," Sharon continued in her wake, "a few answers from Mr. Horton would clear all this up."

Tammy extended her middle finger over her shoulder as she slammed her front door. She wondered if that'd make the six o'clock news.

\* \* \*

My cell phone chimed. Caller ID said it was Tammy. Answer or don't answer? That was always the dilemma with her. Answering meant a tirade about something trivial, even stupid. Not answering meant a series of calls until by attrition I would answer and go through the tirade, anyway. I answered.

"Jake, get over here."

"Why would I do that?"

"There's a news truck out front. That female news girl and her cameraman."

"Make sure you have your makeup adjusted before you go out, then."

Nicole and I were sitting at a table at Captain Rocky's. She smiled at me. How did she always know when it was Tammy? Could it possibly be me grinding my teeth?

"Damn it, Jake, get over here and run them off." Tammy was getting wound up now.

"I think you'd be better at that than me."

"I tried. They want to talk to Walter."

"Then let them. Old Walter can fight his own battles." I sighed. "Look, I'm a little busy right now."

"Doing what?"

"I have a business to run."

I mean, Nicole and I were at Captain Rocky's. And I do own it.

But I wasn't working. We were having lunch. I saw no need to share that with Tammy.

"But—"

"But nothing. Either have Walter talk to them, or, like I told you before, close your door and don't engage with them. They'll get bored and go away." Tammy didn't immediately respond so I took advantage of the opportunity. "Talk to you later, I'm sure." I disconnected the call.

# CHAPTER THIRTY-EIGHT

HERE'S THE THING about guys—we like watching women undress. I don't mean strip clubs, though I've been to a few of those over the years. I swear, only a few. Never much cared for them. Mainly because of the creeps that hung around in there. And the music was usually too loud and the drinks too weak and too cheap—not in price, but in the brands of alcohol they poured. Then there were the dancers. Not that many of them weren't attractive, or at least had tight bodies, but I always felt uncomfortable. Like I was witnessing a slow train wreck. I figured most of them were there because they lacked the skills or the opportunity or maybe simply the drive to be anywhere else. Of course the money was good so there was that.

But the kind of disrobing I'm talking about is the one-on-one variety. Usually a prelude to sex. Like last night.

But here's the other thing about women and clothes—guys sometimes like watching women get dressed. There's something sexy about it. Seriously sexy. Like now.

Nicole stepped from the bathroom, clad in black panties that didn't have enough material to wad a shotgun, those long legs reaching all the way to the floor, no bra. Me likey. Then she slithered—literally—into a pair of frayed jeans, tugged on a black t-shirt, and pulled her hair back into a ponytail, securing it with a dark-green clasp.

I was stretched out on the bed, jeans, no shirt, no shoes. When she turned toward me, she said, "What are you doing?"

"Watching you."

"You better get your ass dressed. It's three thirty. We have to leave like right now."

Last night we had decided that if the jogger Heather had seen was truly hardcore, she probably ran there often. And running out there near the fort at four in the morning had hardcore written all over it. Since most serious runners were creatures of habit, she likely ran around the same time each day. And if she had indeed seen something the morning the Wilbanks brothers hooked up with whoever met them on the beach, we needed to know.

I just hoped this wasn't one of the days she skipped her morning run.

I rolled off the bed and slipped on my sandals. "Where's my shirt?"

"Living room. Where I pulled it off you last night." She laughed.

"How could I forget that?"

"Easy. All your blood was busy elsewhere and your brain wasn't working."

I had no comeback for that.

With Nicole piloting her SL it only took us fifteen minutes to reach Highway 180, out near Fort Morgan, where Heather left Darrell and Darnell and had seen the jogger. She parked and we climbed out. The odor of the Gulf was strong, the breeze light and warm, and in the darkness I could just make out the white remnants of the waves that lapped against the sand.

"What if she doesn't show up?" Nicole asked.

"Think positive."

"Positively."

"What?"

"The correct way is positively."

"You are positively a smart-ass." I gave her a gentle smack on her rear.

"It's that writer thing."

"Maybe someday we could play teacher and student."

She looked at me. "That could work. I could serve up the appropriate punishment when you misspelled a word." Now she smacked my butt. "You'd like that."

"Bet you would, too."

"Probably."

I pulled her into my arms and kissed her. When the kiss broke she said, "Shouldn't we be watching for a jogger?"

"I am. Over your shoulder."

The smack on my butt was harder this time. "Are you saying I need to kiss better?"

"You couldn't. You're perfect as it is."

Now she kissed me. Long and slow. It was magnificent. Except over her shoulder I saw a form moving toward us. Maybe a hundred yards away, along the road's sandy shoulder, bobbing like a jogger. I broke the kiss.

"I think we have company."

Nicole turned and looked up the road. "Better let me handle this."

"You? Why?"

"Oh, let's see. Woman on a deserted road, middle of the night, and some pervert approaches her? Hard to imagine she wouldn't welcome that."

"So I'm a pervert?"

"That's one of your better qualities. But I know you. She doesn't."

I hated it when she made sense. Which, actually, was often.

As the woman approached, she slowed and moved across the road, wariness creeping into her gait. Nicole gave her a wave and stepped out into the middle of the road. The woman stopped, yanked her earbuds free, and slid a hand into the pocket of her shorts. She came out with a canister. Looked like pepper spray.

"Relax," Nicole said. "We're harmless."

"What do you want?"

"A couple of questions is all."

"About what?"

"You jogged by here a couple of mornings ago?" I asked.

She took a step to her left. "Who are you?"

"I'm Jake Longly. This is Nicole. We're private investigators."

"That doesn't make any sense."

"We only want to know if you saw anything unusual."

"Like what?"

"We have a witness who drove by and saw you. Or someone like you. She was driving along here."

"I remember. I never see anyone out here so a car was unusual. It was just back that way." She pointed back up the road. "Around my four-mile mark."

"Four-mile mark?" Nicole asked.

She seemed to relax a bit. At least her eyes weren't so wide anymore. "I run here every day. Have for years. I have a ten-mile loop and I know every inch of it."

I knew that was true of most distance runners. More so than any other athlete, distance runners have an incredible sense of distance and time. Comes from timing their every step. This lady was no different. She wore a thick black watch that I was sure had stopwatch and lap timer functions. Every runner's favorite toy.

"So seeing a car is out of the norm," I said. "Anything else strange about that morning?"

She nodded. "Actually, something very odd happened." She looked around. "It was about right here." She settled her gaze to her right where several clusters of sea oats dotted low sand dunes. "In fact, it was right here."

"What was?" I asked.

"I heard a boat motor. Coming toward the beach. Not something you hear this time of the morning. I was maybe fifty yards short of here. When the motor died, I heard voices. Male voices. Several of them. Pretty scary out here in the dark."

"What'd you do?" Nicole asked.

"I got off the road. Out of sight." Another wave of her hand. "I ducked behind those dunes to see what was going on. There were five of them."

"What'd they look like?" I asked.

"I was too far away to make out much. Three were fairly tall. One of them had longish blond hair. The other two were shorter. One slight and the other was muscular. Very muscular. Like a body-builder type."

"What were they doing?"

"Standing in a cluster, talking. My first reaction was to turn around and head back home but I felt that might leave me exposed."

"Exposed?"

"Here on the road."

"Were they threatening?" Nicole asked.

"No. I mean, they didn't know I was here. But there was a car parked about right where your car is. So I figured a group of men, some in a car, and some in a boat, meet up out here at this hour?" She shrugged. "Must be a drug deal or something like that. And if so, the last thing I wanted was to be seen."

"Smart move," I said.

She wiped sweat from her face with one hand. "Is that what this is about? Drug deals?"

"We don't know yet. Then what happened?"

"Four of the men got in the boat and took off. The last one got in the car and drove that way." She pointed. "Back toward Gulf Shores."

"And they never saw you?" Nicole asked.

"No. Scared me shitless, though. I ended up on my belly in the sand. My heart was hammering so hard I thought they might hear it."

"The car?" I asked. "Did you get a look at it?"

"Briefly. It was dark gray, I think. Best I could tell, anyway. It was small, like a Toyota or Honda. Something like that. And when the guy turned it around to leave I saw it had what looked like primer on one fender." She hesitated as if thinking. "Left front."

"You could see that in the dark?" Nicole asked.

"Where I was hiding was only about ten or fifteen feet off the road. Saw it when he drove by."

"Did you see the driver?"

"Not really. But I think he was the smaller of the two short ones. I could be wrong."

"Did you see anything else? After they all left?"

"Actually, my route loops around the fort and then back up the other side of this spit. When I got around there the boat—it was like a fishing boat—was approaching a huge boat. Maybe a half mile offshore."

"How big?"

"Massive. A hundred feet. Sleek, white. One of those that cost more than a house. Maybe more than some neighborhoods."

I laughed. "A yacht?"

"Oh, yeah."

"What's your name?"

"I'd rather not say."

"I understand. The problem is that this is also a police matter, and they might need to talk to you."

"Jesus."

"Don't worry. It would all be kept confidential."

"For now, maybe."

I couldn't argue with that. "But if the police do need to talk to you, they'd find you, don't you think?"

"Shit." She propped her hands on her hips and looked out toward the beach. "Doesn't sound like I have many options."

"Not really."

She sighed. "I'm Rachel Weber. I live in Orange Beach."

"Phone number?"

She recited it and Nicole tapped it into her phone.

# CHAPTER THIRTY-NINE

"THAT'S AN UNHAPPY woman," Nicole said. "Not thrilled with the prospect of talking with the police."

We were standing in front of her car and watched Rachel fade into the darkness as she continued her jog around the old fort.

"I imagine so. Goes out for a run and gets involved in all this."

She hooked her arm in mine. "Feed me. I'm hungry."

"Aren't you always?"

"Mostly."

"Not many choices this time of day but I know a place."

She climbed behind the wheel. "Get in."

"Need to make a call first."

"To Detective Morgan?"

"Not at four thirty. Don't want him pissed at me."

I punched in Ray's number. He answered after a single ring. Awake and alert. No morning voice. So Ray. I didn't think he ever slept. I told him what we had learned, including Rachel's description of the car she saw.

"Sounds like Darrell's ride," Ray said. "Like Heather said."

"That was my first thought."

Ray sighed. "Okay. I'll call Morgan and Pancake and get things rolling. Let's meet here by eight."

Next stop, Danny's Diner, an all-hours greasy spoon in Gulf Shores. I had toast and coffee, Nicole the Trucker's Special. Eggs, bacon, grits, biscuits, and a pair of pancakes just in case. Nicole didn't finish it all but she damaged it pretty good.

After the dishes were cleared and our coffee mugs refilled, we sat quietly for several minutes, killing time.

"So what is this?" I asked.

"This case?"

"This me and you? What are we?"

"Two wild and crazy lovers."

I nodded and took a sip of coffee.

"Oh, you mean, where are we going?"

I shrugged. "Something like that."

"Courting, proposal, marriage, kids. I want a dozen."

"You're a smart-ass."

"True." She reached over and took my hand. "Truth?"

"Let's start there."

"I'm not really the settling-down type. You aren't, either. So we keep doing what we're doing."

"Fun and games?"

"Why not?" She squeezed my hand. "But I will say this—you're the most interesting man I've met in a long time. Maybe ever."

"As are you."

"Interesting man? You better take a closer look."

"I did. Remember?"

She laughed.

"But I like your take on it," I said. "Fun and games and see where it goes."

She looked out the window. The sky had lightened considerably. I glanced at my watch. Six thirty.

"Let's take a drive," she said. "Along the beach. We can watch the sun come up."

We did. Nicole lowered the SL's top and we were off. She actually stayed below the speed limit. We held hands and gave each other looks. I felt like a teenager. I think she did, too.

We drove nearly to Pensacola before turning around and making our way back to Ray's. It was right at eight when we parked and climbed the stairs. Out on the deck, Ray, Pancake, and Morgan sat around the table. Nicole and I pulled up chairs and sat.

"I just brought Morgan up to speed on what you guys uncovered," Ray said. He looked at me. "Good work."

Did he really say that? The last compliment I remember coming out of Ray's mouth was when I tossed a one-hitter in Yankee Stadium. That seemed a lifetime ago.

"Borkov has a huge boat," Morgan said. "Got to be as big as the one your jogger lady saw. Not many that size around here."

"You're thinking the Wilbanks brothers were off to hook up with Borkov?" I asked. "He's the 'boss man' Heather talked about?"

Morgan shrugged. "I don't know. But let's look at what we have. The dots are a little loose but we have Barbara Plummer murdered. Gangster style. I believe Henry was the real target, though I can't say that for sure. Henry was locked in some range war with Borkov so money would be the motive. The Wilbanks boys head off to a mysterious yacht in the middle of the night. For some business deal that was going to make them rich. Then their buddy Raul's print pops up at the murder scene and bad luck of all bad luck he takes a slug. Also gangster style."

"So we need to find Darrell and Darnell," I said.

Ray shook his head. "You won't. Not alive, anyway."

I looked at him. "How do you know that?"

"I don't, but it makes sense. I agree with Morgan. All roads seem to head in Borkov's direction. And miscreants like him don't leave loose ends."

"So like Raul, the Wilbanks brothers have become liabilities," I said.

Ray drained his Dew and tossed the empty in the trash can against the wall behind him. "If I had to guess, Raul and the brothers were the ones that did Barbara Plummer. And since it was botched—Henry wasn't home—Borkov had to eliminate anyone who could come back on him."

"He probably would've tied up those loose ends, anyway," Morgan said. "Even if the hit had gone perfectly."

Pancake grunted his agreement.

"But we still don't know this Borkov character is involved," Nicole said.

"Want another connection?" Pancake asked.

Everyone looked his way.

"Raul Gomez definitely had cartel connections. His brother Santiago, too. A cousin who's way up the food chain with the Sinaloas. Pedro Hidalgo, the cousin, comes to the U.S. about every three months. I suspect he meets up with Cousin Raul during those trips. Anyway, Raul got popped for possession a year or so ago. Down in Naples. Charges were later dropped but his attorney was a guy named Rolando Saurez. A cartel-connected attorney who just happens to show up on Borkov's payroll, too."

"Really?" Morgan asked. "How did you dig all that up? I've had my guys working on it and they've come up with *nada*."

Pancake gave him a "get real" look. As if it was a stupid question. And in Pancake's case, it was. He might look like a big old dumb jock, but he was anything but. He could rummage around inside the computer world with the best of them. Find things that shouldn't be found.

"You just have to know where to look," Pancake said.

"And be able to do it outside legal parameters," Morgan said.

Pancake shrugged his massive shoulders. "I'll take the Fifth."

Morgan smiled.

"That tightens up the dots a bit," I said.

"Sure does," Pancake said. "And there's more. We know Walter defended Santiago, Raul's brother. What I found out, and Walter doesn't know this, the money Walter made defending Santiago came through Saurez's firm. Not directly. It went through Santiago's mother. But if the cash was touched by Saurez, it came from Borkov."

"Sounds like Borkov owns everyone," Nicole said.

"Looks that way, doesn't it?" Morgan said.

"And then there's this," Ray said. He opened a folder and pulled out a photograph. He slid it toward me.

It was an aerial view of a harbor.

"After you called this morning, I gave a shout-out to a guy I know. Captain Ira Gemmel with the Coast Guard," Ray said. "Wasn't happy about a call that early, but he's a trooper. Anyway, he ran a location on Borkov's yacht. That's it." He pointed to a large boat hanging near the end of a pier. "Pensacola."

"This is a satellite photo?" I asked.

Ray nodded. "Made about an hour ago."

I knew Ray had connections within connections but this was amazing.

"He also had tracking data for the vessel," Ray continued. "It was definitely off the coast here early the morning the Wilbanks brothers were picked up on the beach. Then out to sea overnight and back to Pensacola yesterday morning." He pointed to the photo again. "Right there."

Pancake picked up the photo and studied it. "I got a buddy who has a boat there. Been out fishing with him many times. His slip's just a couple of slots down from where the dock angles. Puts it fairly close to where Borkov's moored. My buddy's trout fishing up in Montana. I'll let him know we're going to crash on his boat for a day or two."

Ray nodded. "We can set up some surveillance from there."

Pancake nodded. "Consider it done."

"I can do better," Nicole said. Everyone looked at her. "I can get you on that boat."

"How do you propose to do that?" Morgan asked.

She stood, did a full turn, and then waved her hands up and down her body. "With this. Babes and boats. Go together like shrimp and grits, don't they?" No one had a comeback for that so she continued. "I'll put together the right outfit and we'll get invited on board."

"Sure of yourself, aren't you?" I asked.

"Would you invite me on your boat?"

"Sure." Actually I'd invite her on anything I had.

She smiled. "Men are all alike."

Morgan's cell chimed. He answered and listened for a minute, concluding with "I'm on the way." He slipped his phone in his pocket and stood. "We found Darrell's car. Around the corner from Raul's place."

Well, well. The circle gets tighter.

# CHAPTER FORTY

PANCAKE RAIDED RAY'S closets for the equipment he needed and then headed out to set up his friend's boat. Ray said he had some computer work on another case to catch up on but would meet us in Pensacola later, so Nicole and I followed Morgan to check out Darrell's car. It was indeed parked around the corner and a half block down from Raul's. The doors and trunk were open and a pair of crime scene techs were dusting every nook and cranny for prints.

Jeremy Starks stood nearby.

"What've you got?" Morgan asked when we walked up.

Starks shook his head. "Clean. Been wiped down. The boys dusted everywhere and found nothing."

"Who found it?" I asked.

"One of the patrol guys," Starks said. "But it was really Morgan." He nodded toward his partner.

"I played a hunch," Morgan said. "After Ray called this morning and told me about the Wilbanks brothers handing off their car to someone from the boat and that jogger described it just as Heather had, gray with a primer fender, I played a hunch. I suggested a unit snoop around Raul's neighborhood."

"Good call," I said.

"I do know how to do this job."

I raised my hands. "Never said you didn't."

"Anyway, I figured the guy used the car to hit Raul and then dumped it nearby. More or less framing the Wilbanks brothers for Raul's murder. And now the brothers are missing, and, like Ray, I'd bet they'll never be found, so it seems Borkov tied up all his lose ends."

"But we don't know the brothers are dead," I said.

"They are. And it probably went this way—Borkov lured them out to his yacht on the pretense of some business deal. Money being the great motivator. Then out to sea. Shot them in the head and deep-sixed them. Fish food."

"That's cold," Nicole said

"Sure is," Morgan said. "But it's what I'd do—if I were Borkov."

Nicole wrapped her arms around herself. "This Borkov guy is scary."

Morgan gave her a half smile. "The scariest kind. Rich, powerful, ruthless, and connected. All the major food groups."

"One other thing," Starks said. "Got the ballistics back. Different weapon used on Raul than the one Barbara Plummer caught."

Morgan nodded. "I suspect Raul and the Wilbanks brothers did Barbara, dumped the gun, and then Borkov disposed of the brothers while he sent another shooter to take out Raul."

"The pieces do fit," I said.

"More and more." Morgan rubbed his neck. "So it's time to dig deep into Mr. Borkov's world."

"Pancake's on it. He'll have his buddy's boat set up in an hour or so, and we'll have eyes and ears on the yacht."

Nicole stood and stretched. "Then I guess it's time for me to go to wardrobe."

Morgan looked at her.

She laughed. "Rummage through my closet and find an outfit that gets me an invite on board."

"Not sure that would be safe," Morgan said.

"No problem," Nicole said. "Ray and Pancake will be there. Armed and dangerous."

Morgan nodded.

"And I'll have Jake with me."

"What's he going to do, throw fastballs at them?" Starks asked.

"Only if I have to," I said. "My speed's down to only eighty miles an hour so it might not work."

# CHAPTER FORTY-ONE

WHAT AN OUTFIT. Stunning. I checked my chin for drool and shockingly found none.

"You like?" Nicole did a pirouette. The sunlight that filtered through her living room windows highlighted her blond hair and curves. She wore a black string bikini. Micro version. Not enough material to make a hanky. Left little to the imagination. Barely covered her best parts. Well, excluding that face. And those eyes. Those parts were pretty good, too.

"I can't breathe," I said.

"Good. That's the effect I was going for."

"Not sure you can be in public like that," I said.

"That's why I have this."

She slipped on a thin, woven jacket, more air than material. It hid nothing.

"That helps," I said, shaking my head.

"You don't like it?"

"Didn't say that."

She laughed. "Bet the boat crew will, too."

"They'd have to be dead not to."

She kissed my cheek. "That's so sweet." She mussed my hair. "Let's get going."

With Nicole driving her SL, we covered the forty miles to

Pensacola Harbor in under an hour, despite fairly thick traffic. We arrived just after noon.

The main pier gave off four smaller ones that branched at right angles, each with a dozen slips, most filled with buttoned-down fishing rigs, before it elbowed forty-five degrees to the right and jutted out into the water. Borkov's yacht was tied to it beyond the angle by thick ropes. It dwarfed the other boats. Hell, it dwarfed the entire marina.

Nicole parked and we climbed out. From the asphalt lot, we walked down the main pier, the wooden planking weather-worn and uneven, the smell of the Gulf thick.

"Wow," Nicole said. "That looks like a cruise ship."

"Only better, I suspect."

"We're looking for the *Storm Shelter*," I said.

"You mean this one?" She indicated the boat we now stood near. "The one that has big blue letters saying, 'Storm Shelter'?"

She can be a real bitch sometimes.

"Yeah, that'd be it."

Pancake came up the stairs and onto the rear deck. "It's about time you guys got here." Then he saw Nicole. "My, my. Come here, darlin'."

Nicole climbed on board. Pancake enveloped her in a bear hug.

"I could do this all day," he said.

"You are kind of comfy," Nicole said. She pushed him back. "Now get your ass to work."

"This is one tough lady, Jake."

"You don't know the half of it," I said.

"Let's get to it," Pancake said and headed below.

We followed. Ray sat at the galley table, laptop before him, a clear image of the *Sea Witch* filling the screen. I saw two Mac 10s and an assortment of handguns on the galley counter. Ray was ready for anything. I expected nothing less.

"Give me your phones," Pancake said.

"Why?" I asked.

"I'll set them up as mics. So we can listen in. That way I won't have to wire you." He glanced at Nicole. "Nowhere I can see to wire you anyway."

"Sit," Ray said.

We settled across the table from him. He spun the laptop so we could see the screen. He moved the image around, settling it on the rear deck. He zoomed in. Two people, only heads and shoulders visible, appeared to be sitting at an umbrella-shaded table. A girl with large, round sunglasses; a man with a cigar clenched in his teeth.

"That's Borkov and some young lady," Ray said.

The angle seemed impossible from where we were. "Where's the camera?" I asked.

"Pancake strapped it to the top of the radar unit," Ray said. "Best we could do, so this angle'll have to work."

"Here." Pancake returned our cells. "I downloaded an app to each. I can access them from the computer and hear everything that's going on."

"Cool," Nicole said. "Like a real spy." She slipped the phone into the pocket of her jacket.

"That's you," Pancake said. "A real Mata Hari."

"Now all you have to do is get on the boat," Ray said. He looked at me. "Pancake and I'll stay out of sight. You get up top and act like you belong here."

"How do I do that?"

"Swab the decks. Or sit out back with a beer. Either would work."

I laughed. "I'll take the beer."

I wore sandals, a baggy swimsuit, and an oversized t-shirt with a Jack Daniel's logo on front. I grabbed a beer and a magazine, a two-month old *Sports Illustrated*, and settled in the rear well of the boat. I positioned myself so I could pretend to be reading while keeping an eye on Nicole as she worked her magic.

"You ready?" I asked.

"Sure am." She stepped off onto the pier.

"Be cool," I said.

"Is there any other way?"

She unzipped the front of her cover, exposing . . . well . . . everything, and walked up the pier toward the yacht.

As she approached, a man leaned on the rail and looked down at her. Hispanic, dark hair, and muscles on top of muscles.

Showtime.

"That's Joe Zuma," Ray said, his voice coming from below deck. "One of Borkov's bad boys."

Nicole was maybe fifty feet away, but I could hear her shout up to Zuma. "Is this your boat?"

"No. Belongs to my boss."

Nicole laughed that wonderful laugh of hers. "I want your job."

Now Zuma laughed. "It definitely has its pluses."

"Here comes Borkov," Ray said.

Borkov appeared at the railing. I could almost hear his intake of breath when he saw Nicole.

"So you like the *Sea Witch*?" Borkov said.

"Like hardly covers it. It's amazing."

"It is comfortable."

"More than that, I suspect."

"Come on board. Take a look around."

It was just that easy. For Nicole, anyway. Sex sells, no doubt.

"I'm here with my boyfriend," she said.

"Bring him along," Borkov said. "If he wants."

"That's so kind of you, but we wouldn't want to intrude."

"No problem. We were just going to have a bite of lunch. Please join us."

"I'll check with Jake and see."

Borkov nodded. "You do that. We'll set places for you."

Five minutes later we met Borkov, Joe Zuma, and Frank Boyd, obviously Borkov's muscle, and Borkov's apparent plaything Grace. A beautiful young lady. Borkov had good taste if nothing else.

We spent the next thirty minutes touring the ship. It was like nothing I'd ever seen, and I've been on some nice yachts. Not this big and not this expensive, though.

We returned to the rear deck and settled at the table with Borkov and Grace, Zuma, and Boyd disappearing below. I flashed on what Henry had said about the two miscreants who had run off his investors. One tall with shaggy blond hair, the other Hispanic and muscular. Boyd and Zuma definitely fit those roles.

"This ship is amazing," Nicole said. "I could live here."

"Seems we practically do," Grace said. She looked at Borkov. "Victor and I spend as much time here as we do at home in Naples."

"Naples is pretty nice, too," I said.

Grace nodded. "Victor has a place there. On the Gulf."

Two young men appeared, carrying a bowl of salad, another of fresh fruit, a platter of fish tacos, and a sweating pitcher of margaritas.

"Hope this works for you," Borkov said.

"It sure does," Nicole said. "I'm starving."

Borkov laughed. Very casual. He did have charm. "Well, dig in."

We did.

The conversation mostly revolved around the yacht and how we didn't own the boat we were using. I explained that it belonged to a friend and we were simply hanging out on it for a few days. Borkov seemed to buy it.

"Where'd you get those shoes?" Nicole asked Grace, indicating the designer sandals she wore.

"I don't remember." She looked at Victor. "Didn't we get these in Nassau?"

"We?" he said with a smile. "Grace likes to use the royal *we* about her shopping." He drained his margarita. "Which I guess is true. She shops, I pay." He reached over and squeezed her hand.

"I wonder if I could find anything like that around here?" Nicole asked.

"Maybe." Grace glanced at Victor, then back to Nicole. "I need to hit the Cordova Mall later today. Why don't you come along? I bet they'll have something similar if not the same shoes. Besides, Victor hates to shop and I hate to go alone."

"I never knew a man that enjoyed shopping," Nicole said, catching Victor's eye, smiling. "I'd bet I could give you the day off."

"Never a day off, but if I can avoid shopping, you're on."

"Great," Grace said. "It's a date. When do you want to go?"

"Anytime works for me."

Grace glanced at Borkov, as if waiting for his permission, or blessing.

"Joe and Frank have some business onshore," Borkov said. "They'll leave around three. I'll have them drop you ladies at the mall and then bring you back after they finish. In time for happy hour."

"Perfect," Nicole said.

I started to say that I'd take them or that Nicole could drive. That her car was in the marina lot. No reason to inconvenience Zuma and Boyd. Truth was I didn't want her in a car with those two. But

Nicole had already agreed and balking now might raise Borkov's eyebrows. Better to let it lie. For now, anyway.

One of the young men who had served lunch cleared the plates and refilled our margaritas; the other appeared with a burled cigar box, flipping it open for Borkov. He selected one and held it up.

"Do you mind?" He asked Nicole.

A real gentleman.

"No problem," Nicole said. "Enjoy."

"Jake?" Borkov nodded toward the box.

"Sure. I'd hate for you to smoke alone."

After the cigars were fired up, Borkov leaned back in his chair, relaxed. He was in his domain. Master of ceremonies.

"Jake Longly?" he said. "You the baseball player?"

I shrugged. "Was. Seems years ago."

"You were pretty good."

"I had my days. I guess you follow baseball?"

"He's a fanatic," Grace said. "I find it boring, but Victor loves it."

"The purest of sports," Borkov said. He turned to the serving table behind him, picked up the phone, and pressed a button. Then said, "Bring up a couple of my baseballs and bats." He hung up. "You'll love this."

One of the young men reappeared, two baseballs in one hand, a bat in the other. He handed them to Borkov.

Borkov passed a ball to Jake. "Two home run balls. That one by Henry Aaron. This one by Willie Mays." He extended the bat toward me. I took it. "This is the Mick's bat. He hit an upper deck shot at Yankee Stadium with it."

The bat not only had Mantle's signature, it was personalized. To Victor Borkov.

I stood, gripping the bat, and moved onto the deck. Took a

couple of cuts. "I can't believe I'm standing here swinging one of the Mick's bats."

"Sweet, isn't it?" Borkov said.

"Definitely."

"Of course, you were a pitcher. Not a hitter."

I sat down again and returned the bat to Borkov. He leaned it against the table to his left.

"When I was young I was a pretty good stick," I said. "Played shortstop when I wasn't pitching."

Borkov smiled. "That's what I played." He sighed. "A long time ago."

"These are impressive," I said, nodding toward the baseballs on the table.

"Got a couple of hundred of them and too many bats to count." He held up the May's ball. "Show me how you threw that sinking fastball of yours."

I gripped the Aaron one. "I used a cross-stitch grip. Like this." I held it up so he could see.

He mimicked my grip. "That's all there is to it."

I smiled. "That and putting ninety-five miles an hour behind it."

Borkov laughed. "There is that, I guess."

He set the ball on the table and leaned back again. He held me with his intense blue-eyed gaze and then said, "You Ray Longly's boy, right?"

"True." I could feel sweat collect on my scalp. This is not where I wanted the conversation to go.

"He runs a PI firm around here, I understand?"

"That's true, too."

"You work for him?"

"Not a chance."

He raised an eyebrow.

"Ray and I don't always see eye to eye," I said.

"Father and son war?"

"Maybe not war, but he does what he does and I do what I do."

"Which is?"

Borkov was like a good attorney. Didn't ask questions he didn't already know the answer to. Meant blowing smoke up his ass wouldn't work. At least mostly not work.

"I own a bar over in Gulf Shores. Captain Rocky's. Ever heard of it?"

"Can't say I have."

"It's small. Mostly a local following. But it does okay. Drop by sometime and I'll return the hospitality."

"I just might do that." Borkov flicked an ash into the ashtray on the table. "I had a restaurant once. Too much work, so I sold it."

"It is a lot of work. Never enough hours in the day to get everything done."

Borkov nodded. "But you don't work for your dad?"

"Nope. Not that he doesn't try to lure me into his world."

Borkov took a couple puffs on his cigar, exhaling upward, waving away the smoke. "I hear he's investigating that murder that happened over on The Point? The Plummer woman?"

"I wouldn't know. Like I said, Ray and I don't run in the same circles."

"So, the other night. Out on Peppermill Road. Wasn't that you that got a couple of windows hammered out? Right near the Plummer home?"

This was definitely not going as expected. What exactly did Borkov know? That we were scamming him? That Nicole and I weren't simply accidental tourists? How the hell did he know about my confrontation with Tammy? Why would he know? He obviously had connections within the Gulf Shores PD, and, if so, did he know we were hooked up with Detective Morgan? That would be a game changer. Was my face as red and sweaty as it felt?

I glanced toward the pier, almost expecting to see Ray and Pancake storming the Bastille.

"That was my ex," I said. "I was parked near her house. She took offense."

"You asshole." It was Nicole. She slugged my shoulder. "What the hell were you doing over at that psycho's house?"

"I wasn't. I was outside."

Tears welled in her eyes. "You promised me you'd never see her again." She looked at Victor. "He's addicted to her. Can't seem to throw the hook. Every time I think we have a future he does some shit like this." She stood and tossed her napkin on the table.

Damn, she's good. And just might have saved our bacon.

"It's not that way," I said, following her lead.

"Really? What goddamn way is it, then?" She glared at me. "Sometimes I could just strangle you." She stormed off toward the bow of the ship.

Grace stood. "I'll make sure she's okay."

Borkov leaned forward, head down, speaking in a low voice. "Sorry about that. I wouldn't have brought it up if I'd known."

"Not your fault. Totally mine." I sighed. "Tammy, my ex, isn't easy to get over."

Borkov smiled. "Good in the sack, I suspect."

I nodded, then gave a glance forward as if afraid Nicole would hear me. "The best, actually."

"Better not let Nicole hear that."

"She would kill me then. For sure."

Borkov nodded. "So you don't know anything about your father's business?"

"Don't know. Don't care."

God, I hoped he believed me.

# CHAPTER FORTY-TWO

NICOLE REACHED THE bow before Grace caught up to her.

"You okay?" Grace asked.

"No." Nicole turned toward her, wiping away tears with the back of her hand.

She knew all those acting workshops would come in handy. Not exactly the way she had hoped. An A-list actor had been the goal, but wasn't that true of every other young actress in Hollywood? But here and now she appreciated every night class she ever took.

"He can be such an asshole," Nicole went on.

"Can't they all?"

Nicole sighed and looked out toward the water. "Sure seems that way."

"Why not dump him? I mean, if he's still in love with his ex. Those bonds are hard to compete with."

"I've tried. But I always go back."

"Sounds like love."

"His disease is Tammy. The ex. My disease is him. I love the clown. "

Grace looked at her. "You're beautiful. You could have just about anyone you wanted. Why him?"

"He makes me laugh." Nicole shrugged. "Seems like pretty weak glue, doesn't it?"

"I'd say that's the best attraction." She looked toward the stern. "I wish Victor had a better sense of humor."

"He seems all right to me."

"Don't get me wrong, Victor is very good to me."

"How long have you guys been together?"

"A year. I was a waitress. We met at the restaurant where I worked. He swept me off my feet."

"I can imagine someone like him doing that." Nicole waved a hand. "As if this wasn't enough, he does seem charming."

"Oh, he's that, all right."

Nicole noticed Grace's eyes had glistened with the beginning of tears. She reached out and touched her arm.

"Are you okay?"

"I'm fine." She sniffed and looked out over the water. "At least I was."

"Did something happen? Did Victor step out with someone else?"

"I wish it were that easy."

"What is it?" Nicole asked.

"I can't talk about it."

Nicole hesitated, deciding whether to roll the dice or not. Could blow up in her face. Could get them killed. But what she saw in Grace's face was more than jealousy and grief. It was fear. Time to go all in.

"Can I ask you something?" She glanced around to make sure they were alone. "Darrell and Darnell Wilbanks?"

Grace's intake of breath was audible. Now she looked around as the fear on her face blossomed. "I don't know anyone named Wilbanks."

"I think you do. I think you met them here on this boat."

"Who are you?" Grace asked.

"Jake lied. We are working for his father. We're trying to find those brothers. We know they boarded this boat in the middle of the night and were never seen again."

"I can't talk about this."

Grace turned to walk away but Nicole grabbed her arm. She tried to pull away but Nicole tightened her grip.

"Jake and I will be off this boat soon, and you'll still be here. If Borkov did something to those brothers, you're in danger. Don't you think?"

Grace hesitated and then sighed. "Victor will kill me."

"Not if we have anything to say about it."

"You don't."

"You might be surprised. Ray, Jake's dad, is a very bad dude. He can go up against anyone, I'd imagine. But not until we get you to safety. Now tell me what you know."

Grace shook her head. "I can't."

"You can't not. Right now is your chance to extricate yourself from this. If you don't, you could get swept away in Borkov's shit."

"Can you really do that? Get me away from him?"

"I promise."

"How do I know I can trust you?"

"You don't. But you have to."

Grace shook her head. "I don't know."

"Look," Nicole said. "I trusted you. I exposed who we are and what we're doing. You could get us both killed." Grace looked at her. "So trust me. Okay?"

Grace wiped her eyes. "Okay. But not here. When we go shopping, can I simply disappear with you?"

"My plan, exactly."

# CHAPTER FORTY-THREE

WE THANKED BORKOV for his hospitality. He waved it away saying it was "his pleasure." He continued. "I'll have more interesting food for happy hour."

"This was marvelous," Nicole said.

Borkov smiled. "We can do better. And I have some very nice wines on board."

Nicole laughed. "You're making me hungry again."

"Hold that thought. And think lobster thermidor and Château Lafite Rothschild."

"How do you stay so thin around here," Nicole asked Grace.

"Sometimes it's not easy."

"Of course, she mostly eats fruit and yogurt," Borkov said.

Grace smiled. "True. But for lobster, all bets are off."

Borkov and Grace walked us to the gangway and watched as we descended the steps.

"See you at three," Grace said to Nicole.

"I'll be ready."

We returned to the boat. Ray and Pancake sat at the table, the computer before them.

"That was dicey," Pancake said. "Thought we might have to come on board."

"That thought crossed my mind, too," I said.

"You did good," Ray said.

What? Two compliments in one day? Was Ray going soft? "Thanks."

"But it was you, young lady," he said to Nicole, "that really did the job."

I looked at her. "True. The whole Tammy scene was outstanding. Couldn't have scripted it better."

"Don't think I could have either," Nicole said with a smile. "But you got lucky."

"Me? How so?"

"I thought about giving you a good slap across the chops." She smiled. "Since I had more or less a free shot."

"Free shot?" I laughed. "Glad you reconsidered."

"But I thought that might be too melodramatic."

"The Tammy thing's not what I'm talking about," Ray said. "Though that was handled to perfection. And it sounded like Borkov bought it."

"What are you talking about?" I asked.

Ray nodded to Pancake, who worked the keyboard. "Best if you hear for yourself."

Pancake played an audio file. Nicole and Grace talking. I listened, looking at her in awe more than once.

When it finished, I said, "That's amazing. You're amazing."

"And you doubt that?" Nicole asked.

"Not for a minute." I smiled. "She almost broke. At least it sounded like she wanted to say more."

"She will," Nicole said. "As soon as we can shake her free. She's scared. We're her lifeline now."

"Unless she's had a change of heart," Pancake said.

Nicole shook her head. "I don't think so. I think she feels trapped. She's looking for an exit door. And we're that."

Ray looked at her. "You're an amazing young lady. Even if old Jake here won't work for me, I just might hire you. You have some very good assets."

She laughed. "I'm sure you're talking about my brain."

Ray smiled. "Actually, I was. Though your other assets come in handy, too."

"Girl's got to use what she has."

Ray glanced at his watch. "Another hour or so and we'll know what side of the fence Grace is on, I suspect."

"I'm going with you," I said. "To the mall."

"Why?"

"Because I don't want you in a car with Zuma and Boyd alone."

"Grace will be there."

"And if she flips on you?" I asked. "You'll be at their mercy and we know what that can mean."

"I agree," Ray said.

He stood and rummaged through the collection of weapons on the galley counter. He picked up a small revolver and handed it to Nicole.

"You know how to use that?"

"Sure do."

"Is this necessary?" I asked.

He handed me a matching weapon. "I want you both armed. Just in case."

"Isn't that a bit of an overreaction?"

"You have car insurance, don't you?" Pancake asked.

"Of course," I said.

"Then there you go. This is insurance."

I didn't like this. None of it. I mean, I knew these were bad guys. No doubt about that. But the image of the gun fight that formed in my mind somehow seemed suddenly real. Not that I was uncomfortable with guns, or even a good old fashioned fistfight, but to put

Nicole in the middle of a potential gun fight was a different thing all together.

"Maybe we can find another way to get her off the boat without this," I said.

"I'm listening," Ray said.

I thought for a minute but came up empty. I hate it when that happens. I sighed. "It's just that if Grace does roll over on this, it puts Nicole in a bad place."

"That's why you'll be there," Ray said. "And you'll be armed."

"So are they," I said.

"I'd do it myself," Ray said, "but I don't think that'd go over well."

"Just make sure you guys are in the back seat," Pancake said. "That'll give you the advantage if things do go south."

"So you agree this could blow up?" I asked,

Pancake shrugged. "Anything can blow up. Best laid plans and all that."

"You're not making me feel any better about this."

"I don't read it that way," Ray said. "I honestly believe Borkov bought the program. Doesn't know you're actually working for me."

"Grace does," Nicole said. "I told her as much."

Ray sighed. "True. That's the hook in all this. And that's what the guns are for."

"I still don't like it," I said.

"Want to back out?" Ray asked. "Find another way to get Grace off that boat?"

Now I sighed. "No. If Grace can put a finger on Borkov, it's worth the risk."

"Okay," Ray said. "Pancake and I will hang in the lot and follow you. Make sure Zuma and Boyd do indeed drop you guys at the mall."

"I'll tap into your phone with mine," Pancake said. "If anything goes wrong or even smells funny we'll know and come running."

This seemed loosely thrown together to me and I said so.

"In the field," Ray said, "you have to make fluid plans. No time to button up all the holes."

"I know."

"All you need to do is find a way to go along with Grace and Nicole," Ray said. "Something that won't ping Borkov's radar."

"Probably best to keep it simple," I said. "I just like hanging with beautiful women."

"That would be in character," Nicole said.

"Funny."

"Just remember the goal here," Ray said. "First thing is everyone walks away unharmed. Be cool. Secondly, get Grace away from them as smoothly as possible."

"Okay," I said. "Where do we meet in the mall? They have a Victoria's Secret, don't they?"

"Perv," Nicole said. "Belk is better. It's large and always crowded, and near the parking area."

"I like her answer better," Ray said.

"I'm more partial to old Jake's suggestion," Pancake said.

"You would be," Nicole said.

"There's just something about skimpy women's undies, I guess," Nicole laughed.

"Okay, Belk it is." Ray nodded to Pancake. "Let's get moving."

"What if they see you guys leaving?" I asked.

"Got it covered."

Of course he did.

He rummaged in his black canvas bag and began pulling out clothes. Pancake slipped on a gray hoodie, flipping the hood up to cover his red hair. Ray tugged on a windbreaker and a floppy fishing hat, complete with an array of lures. Ray retreated to the front of the boat and returned with a couple of fishing rods, handing one to Pancake.

"How do we look?" Pancake asked.

"Like two old fisher dudes," Nicole said.

Ray checked the computer. He adjusted the zoom and scanned the *Sea Witch*. "Looks quiet. Let's get to it."

Ray and Pancake quickly climbed onto the dock and then casually walked away. Fishing rods on their shoulders, Ray carrying his black canvas bag. They did indeed look like two old fisher dudes.

# CHAPTER FORTY-FOUR

I HAD A great cover story. Needed to buy some aftershave, maybe a new razor. Maybe some socks. I rehearsed it in my head until I was satisfied that it would come off as casual. No big deal, but thanks for letting me tag along sort of thing. But I didn't need any of those lies. Turned out that riding along with Nicole and Grace proved to be amazingly simple.

At three o'clock sharp, Grace, Zuma, and Boyd descended the gangway and walked to where Nicole and I waited on deck. Nicole had changed into jeans and a loose gauzy green shirt; I wore jeans, a black t-shirt, and a gray jacket.

"Mind if I go along?" I asked.

"Not at all," Grace said. "You can carry our bags."

"Glad to be needed."

Neither Zuma nor Boyd flinched, Zuma saying, "Let's get going."

We walked up the dock and angled into the parking lot. Zuma chirped open the locks of a black Lincoln SUV with the key fob. He and Boyd climbed in the front, Zuma driving, the three of us in the back. So far so good. As we left the lot, I saw Ray's pickup fall in behind us. At an inconspicuous distance. Still, I kept my hand on the gun in my jacket pocket.

Took ten minutes to reach the mall. During the ride over, neither Zuma nor Boyd said a single word. They seemed distracted as if focused on something else. Probably whatever errands Borkov had assigned them. Nicole and Grace chatted, but very little. Their shared tension was evident in their voices and in the way Grace sat straight up, eyes ahead, and clasped her white-knuckled hands together in her lap. I imagined she was mentally urging the SUV forward, willing it to reach the mall more quickly, wishing she was out and free. I know I was.

Finally Zuma slid to a stop near the entrance to Belk. We climbed out.

"We'll be back at four thirty," Zuma said. "Right here. Don't be late." Then without waiting for an answer, he drove away.

As we walked inside I could still sense Grace's apprehension. Hands clenched at her sides, head on a swivel, she looked as if she expected disaster.

"You're safe now," I said.

"Am I?"

"Definitely."

"You don't know Victor Borkov," she said. "His reach is long."

"Not anymore."

She glanced at me. "Confidence is a good thing. Overconfidence not so much."

"When you meet Ray, you'll feel differently."

"That's your father?"

"Yep."

Grace glanced at Nicole and then back to me. "Nicole said he's some kind of badass."

"He is. So is Pancake."

"Pancake?"

"You'll see."

We found Ray and Pancake near the cosmetics counter. Pancake was sniffing various perfume bottles, as would any fourteen-year-old boy. Most men remain fourteen-year-old boys all their lives, never seeming to advance beyond that level of maturity. As if certain parts of the male brain refused further evolution. Pancake was a prime example. Most people, Ray for sure and probably Nicole, would say I fit that mold, also. Can't fight evolution.

"Looking for a new fragrance?" Nicole asked.

"Something for the young lady I've been spending time with lately."

"Spending time? Is that what they call it now?"

"Enough chitchat," Ray said. He extended his hand to Grace. "I'm Ray. This is Pancake."

"Glad to meet you both."

"I understand you have some information for us," Ray said.

Grace glanced at Nicole.

"They heard our conversation," Nicole said.

"How?"

"That's not important." Ray said. "What is important is that you are away from Borkov." Ray looked around. "Let's find somewhere we can talk."

Pancake of course led us to the food court. Since it was the afternoon lull between lunch and the dinner hour, only a few tables were occupied. We settled at one toward the back, no one nearby.

"So tell us," Ray said.

"Tell you what?"

Ray leaned his elbows on the table and looked directly at her. "Grace, don't play coy. You know what I want to know. The Wilbanks brothers. What happened?"

"And if I tell you, what happens to me?"

"Depends on what you have to say."

She hesitated and then said, "What if it's something that could land Victor in jail? And make my life more or less worthless."

"What do you mean worthless?"

"Look, I'm not stupid. I know Victor is involved in a bunch of shady things. I always tried to stay away from it." Her gaze swept the room. "I didn't really want to know."

"But?"

"The other night. Something happened that changed everything."

"The Wilbanks brothers?"

She nodded. Tears collected in her eyes. She pulled a napkin from the table dispenser and dabbed them away.

"Take a breath," Ray said. "Relax. Tell me what happened."

She told them of Darrell and Darnell coming on board. Of how Victor treated them well. Went fishing. Ate and drank. All very casual. How she had drunk too much and even dipped into Darrell's meth stash. "Not something I've done very often."

"And something happened?" I asked.

She told of going to bed but becoming dizzy. A trip to the galley for ginger ale. How she saw Darrell and Darnell wrapped in duct tape and chains and attached to a large iron ring.

"Zuma and Boyd simply tossed the ring overboard," she said. "Took Darrell and Darnell with it. In the middle of nowhere."

"They were alive?" Nicole asked.

Grace nodded. "Yes." She covered her face with her hands. "It was horrible."

"Did anyone know you saw anything?" Ray asked.

"No. Not really."

"What does that mean?" Pancake asked.

Grace sniffed and again dabbed her eyes. "I was pretty messed up. Alcohol and the meth. And when I saw that I became ill and vomited in the sink. Tried to control it, but out everything came." She massaged her temples. "Victor heard the commotion and came downstairs. Asked what was wrong. I told him I had had too much to drink."

"And he believed you?"

"I think so."

"Was Victor there?" Ray asked. "On deck when all this happened?"

She nodded again. "Victor gave the order."

This was much worse than I thought. Not Victor killing the brothers. I figured that was a given. But tossing them overboard alive? Weighted down? How does someone do that?

"Okay," Ray said. "Here's the plan. We'll take you to see Detective Morgan. He's looking into the Wilbanks brothers' disappearance and a couple of likely related homicides."

"That woman who was murdered out on The Point?" Grace asked.

"That's one of them."

"And you think Victor was involved in that?"

"I do. As well as the murder of a guy named Raul Gomez."

Grace's eyes widened. "Raul? He's been murdered?"

"I take it you know him?" Ray asked.

"He's been on the boat a few times. Hangs out with Carlos Fernandez."

"Who's that?"

"Some guy who does work for Victor at times. I don't know him well. Just met him a couple of times."

"What kind of work?"

"I don't know. Every time they had something to discuss—Carlos, Raul, and Victor—Victor would always ask me to leave them alone."

"Did that seem odd?"

"Not really. Victor has a lot of private conversations."

"Planning a hit would probably fit that category," I said.

Tears reappeared. Grace dabbed them away again. "My mother warned me about Victor. She said he was no good. Even said he was dangerous. I figured she was upset because he was so much older than me." She sniffed. "I guess she saw something I didn't."

"Mothers can be very intuitive," I said.

Grace hung her head, staring at the tabletop. I could only imagine the crap spinning inside her head about now. Second guessing her decision to hook up with Borkov. Putting herself in this situation. Probably second guessing being here. Afraid Victor would get to her regardless of any assurances we might make. Probably trying to figure some way to extricate herself from all of this.

Finally, she looked up, her gaze on Ray. "I have to tell the police what I saw?"

"Of course," Ray said. "They're the ones that'll have to arrest Victor and his crew."

"And then what? Testify against him in court?"

Ray nodded.

Grace shook her head and her lips trembled as she spoke. "I'll never get the chance. Victor is very capable if nothing else."

"He'll be in jail," Nicole said.

Grace let out a short, harsh laugh. "Like that would stop him. He has connections all over. Even the governor has been on the *Sea Witch*."

"You'll be safe," Ray said.

"I wish I could believe that." She sighed and straightened her back, her unfocused gaze moving around the food court. Then her shoulders sagged and she looked at her hands, clasped on the table before her. "Guess it's too late to back out now."

Ray stood. "I'll call Morgan and arrange a meet."

# CHAPTER FORTY-FIVE

GRACE LOOKED UP at the man who walked out on the deck. He looked tough. No nonsense. Must be the detective Ray had called. What was his name? Martin? Morgan? Something like that.

She sat on the deck of a beach house. Apparently it was the head-quarters of Longly Investigations. Ray's company. It didn't seem all that professional to her. Instead, it looked more like an after-thought. Who puts a PI firm in a vacation home? Were these guys real? Had she made an incredibly stupid mistake signing on with them? Going against Victor? If Victor was anything, he was professional, not to mention focused and relentless. Nothing was ever an afterthought to him.

The man introduced himself as Detective Bob Morgan. He sat across from her, his forced smile meant to relax her. It didn't. Not that anything could right now. The tightness in her throat and the sweat that slicked her palms spoke to the fear that bumped around inside her.

"Tell me," Morgan said. No hello or how are you. Right to it.

"I don't know," Grace said. "Maybe this is a mistake."

Morgan glanced at Ray, hesitated, and then propped his elbows on the edge of the table, leaning forward. "I know you're scared, and fear gives everyone second thoughts. But I need to hear what you witnessed directly from you."

She forked her fingers through her hair, looked up at the few clouds that hovered in the otherwise clear blue sky, and sighed. Too late to back out now. She told Morgan what had happened. He listened, thankfully not interrupting with questions, and let her get it all out. It came out much easier than she thought it would. Sort of like exhaling a long-held breath.

Morgan seemed to let the story lay there, brow furrowed as if digesting everything she had said. Then he asked, "And Borkov gave the order? You're sure of that?"

She nodded. "He was right there. He gave a signal to Zuma and Boyd."

"What kind of signal?"

"Victor's usual. A slight nod and brief wave of his hand. He's good at that. Giving orders."

"Did Borkov say anything?"

"Not that I heard. But he wouldn't have to. Those two do anything Victor says, and they do nothing without his approval."

"Anyone else witness this? Any of the crew?"

"I don't think so."

Morgan nodded, the creases in his brow deepening.

"Is that a problem?" Grace asked.

"Maybe." Morgan scratched an ear. "It'll be your word against the three of them."

"I saw what I saw."

"I know. But you were drinking and had used some meth. Am I right?"

Tears welled in her eyes, blurring Morgan's face. "I knew this was a bad idea." She looked around. "I should go back. Pretend nothing happened."

"Not an option, I don't think," Jake said.

She looked his way. "Why not?"

"First off, it's after five. Zuma and Boyd will have come to the mall. Looked for us, and called Borkov. He'll know something's up."

"I can just say that we lost track of time. That I looked for them but couldn't find them. I could say I got a ride back to the *Sea Witch*."

"And not call Victor?" Jake asked. "Not ask him where Zuma and Boyd were?"

She squeezed her eyes shut, trying to push back her tears.

"Do you honestly believe Borkov would buy that?" Jake continued.

He was right and she knew it. Victor would see right through it. She had somehow miraculously pulled off deceiving him about what she had seen on deck that night, but this would definitely be pushing her luck. God, how did she get in this mess? She knew what her mother would say, could even hear her voice: *Our troubles are of our own making.* That seemed so true right now. Why didn't life have a rewind button?

"Obviously, you can do what you want," Morgan said. "But I'd advise against going back."

She stared at him, but said nothing.

"For one thing, we can't protect you if you're on the *Sea Witch*."

"Can you, anyway?"

Morgan shrugged. "If you let us."

There it was. Frying pan to fire. How had she gotten here? Stuck between Victor and this cop who she didn't know? Didn't know if she could trust. Didn't know if he could do what he said or was just blowing smoke so he could nab a big fish. Make a name for himself.

Victor's reach had no limits. She had no doubts about that. He had said as much. Just a couple of months ago, she had shared lunch with Victor and some guy she'd never seen before. A very bad-looking dude. Tall, thin, acne-scarred face, and eyes so dark they looked black. Like a shark's eyes. Eyes that seemed to stab at her, seemed to rip away the bikini and thin cover she wore. Victor acted as if he hadn't noticed, but he had. He always did. But he said nothing. Why would he? That was her role. The eye candy, the distraction, the shiny thing that divided the attention of whoever Victor happened to be manipulating at the moment. She'd played that part dozens of times.

After the dishes were cleared and the two men fired up cigars, Victor waved her away. A simple flick of his wrist. She knew what that meant. Time for business. Time for her to leave.

She had excused herself, climbed the stairs one level to the sundeck, feeling those black eyes on her. She then shed her cover jacket and stretched out on a lounge chair. The sea was calm without a breath of breeze. Victor obviously hadn't known their voices would carry up the stairs. She couldn't make out everything that was said, especially from the visitor who had a low, raspy voice, but it was clear the guy was nervous. In some kind of trouble. Victor reassured him that all was okay, that an indictment would never happen, that he had friends in the attorney general's office, even the governor's office, and, if need be, he could intervene.

And if Victor could do that, finding her, regardless of how deep a hole she crawled into, would be a snap.

Morgan pulled her back to the present, saying, "Look, Grace, we're going to start digging deep into Borkov. We'll try to keep it on the down low, but I suspect he'll get wind of that fact. Victor Borkov's a slippery guy. He has fingers everywhere. He'll know he's the target of a police inquiry. Two plus two. He dumps two guys in the Gulf, you were on board, now you're gone—or at least behaving a bit odd." He shrugged. "I suspect Borkov keeps fairly close tabs on you and ditching his muscle would raise his antennae. Don't you think?"

"I am so screwed," Grace said.

"Or saved," Jake said.

"Yeah, right. You don't know Victor."

"We'll set up a safe house for you," Morgan said. "Police protection."

"That won't stop him."

"We're pretty good at this," Morgan said.

"Not good enough." Grace shook her head. "And what about my mother?"

"We'll arrange the same protection for her if need be."

Grace leaned forward, her face in her hands, and let the tears out. Jake laid a hand on her shoulder, causing a momentary flinch.

"You'll be fine," he said.

She straightened her shoulders. "I don't think so. Neither will you and Nicole." She looked at Nicole and then Jake. "Victor always cleans up messes. He never leaves anything to chance."

"Trust me," Morgan said. "It'll all work out."

Was he insane? Did he really understand who he was dealing with? He seemed tough and competent, but was he? Or was he just another dumb ass cop who thought he could fix any problem?

"But if it's three against one, what use is my testimony?" Grace asked.

"We have other witnesses," Morgan said.

"Who? One of the crew?"

Morgan shook his head. "No. Not that lucky. But Darrell's girlfriend took them to the beach that morning. She heard the boat that came for them. She didn't see who was on board but a jogger saw the brothers and two other guys, who, by her description, were Zuma and Boyd, leave in a small boat that went out to a very large yacht."

"And we know the *Sea Witch* was in that area at that time," Ray said.

"How do you know that?"

Ray shrugged. "Let's just say, I know."

"So you see," Morgan said, "we have a few witnesses that can put Darrell and Darnell on the *Sea Witch* and that helps corroborate your story."

"So go arrest Victor," Grace said. "And Zuma and Boyd."

"All in due time. We need to dig up a little more if we want the charges to stick."

"Like what?" Grace asked.

Morgan offered a thin smile. "Won't know until we snoop around. But there is always evidence waiting to be uncovered."

"So what do I do?" Grace asked. "Hide out in a witness protection program?" She shook her head. "Just great."

"Doubt it'll come to that," Morgan said. "But if so, that can also be arranged."

"Just dump my life? My friends and family?"

Truth was she didn't have any friends. Not really. She had walked away from all that when she hooked up with Victor. She hadn't talked to any of her high school buddies in over a year. Would she even be missed if she disappeared? And her only family was her mother. Would she go into protection with her? Was that even fair? This was all her doing. Her choices. Was it right to ruin her mother's life over her mistake? Did she have a choice?

"Like I said," Morgan responded, "I doubt it'll come to that."

"Why not?"

"Borkov is a bad dude, but he isn't the mafia. He can't reach that far."

"Really? I can't prove this but I think Victor is involved with drugs out of Mexico. With one of the cartels."

"That's true," Ray said. "But by their standards, he's small potatoes. Not big enough for them to expose themselves."

"How do you know that?"

"I have my sources."

"And if they're wrong?" Grace asked.

"They aren't." Ray shrugged. "Truth is that if the cartels thought Borkov was a problem they'd take care of him. Borkovs are a dime a dozen for them."

"Maybe that's the best answer," Grace said. "Let one group of criminals kill another group."

"I wouldn't mind that," Morgan said. "Meantime, I'll get a place set up for you. Maybe you can stay here until it's ready?" He looked at Ray.

"No problem," Ray said.

Grace sighed. "This is too much. I still think the best thing is for me to go back. Pretend all is okay."

Ray nodded toward Pancake who flipped open a folder and shuffled through the pages inside. He then slid an eight-by-ten photo across the table toward Grace. She picked it up and looked at the face of a very pretty blond with a nice smile and bright blue eyes.

"Know her?" Pancake asked.

"No. Never seen her. Who is she?"

"The old you."

"What?"

"Her name was Marianne Butler. A grad student at Florida Central until she hooked up with Borkov. Dropped out of school and took off with him. Two years ago. Six months later she disappeared. Never seen again."

"What happened to her?"

"Don't know," Pancake said. "My guess is she's swimming with Darrell and Darnell."

She shook her head and tears again gathered in her eyes. "That was only six months before I left my job for Victor."

"You see a pattern here?" Pancake asked.

Was this true? Did Victor really kill his previous girlfriend? Or were they making this up to cement her cooperation? But she remembered seeing a photo. In a small frame in the bedside drawer at Victor's place in Naples. It was few weeks after she had moved in. She had asked him about it. He'd said it was photo that came with the frame and had removed it and torn it into pieces. Was this the girl in that picture? She remembered blond hair but little else.

Morgan's phone chirped and he answered. He listened for a beat and disconnected the call. He stood. "Looks like we have one less witness."

"Oh?" Jake asked.

"That was Starks. Looks like someone clipped Heather Macomb. And her parents."

"Who's that?" Grace asked.

"She was Darrell's girlfriend. The one that drove them to the beach."

# CHAPTER FORTY-SIX

MORGAN PULLED TO the curb near where Starks stood, cell phone clapped to his ear. Ray and I slid in just behind him. We had left Grace at Ray's with Pancake and Nicole. Pancake for protection; Nicole for comfort. Besides I didn't want Nicole to see what I knew we'd find.

The upper middle class neighborhood appeared quiet, well tended, orderly. By contrast, the Macomb house, a white stucco, ranch style, with slightly sloped gray tile roof, was a hive of activity. Several uniforms stood in the front doorway and looked at us as we climbed from the vehicles.

Starks disconnected his call and slipped his phone into his pocket as we approached.

"What've you got?" Morgan asked.

"Three dead. Mrs. Macomb out back, the mister and the daughter inside. Each shot. Execution style."

"Show me," Morgan said.

We followed Starks around the right side of the house, where thick shrubbery marked the property line and isolated the home from the neighbor on that side. The backyard was large and embraced by similar shrubs. A concrete patio stretched the width of the house, shaded by a green-and-white-striped retractable awning. A pair of round wrought-iron tables, each with four chairs, sat at one end, a massive stainless steel grill at the other. Family time at the Macombs had probably been a fun deal. Not anymore. Not ever again.

A pea gravel path split the yard in half. Flowers, mostly roses, red, yellow, white, and lavender, filled the right side and added a sweet aroma to the air. The left side contained a vegetable garden, neatly rowed with chest-high cornstalks, knee-high tomato plants, and ground-hugging squash vines.

And then there was the body.

The late Mrs. Macomb.

She laid face down, a single entry wound at the base of her skull, a dirt-encrusted trowel near her gloved right hand. Looked like she never saw it coming.

Nearby a crime scene tech had boxed a shoe print in the soft soil and was pouring dental cement into the rectangle. A coroner's tech walked up, body bag in one hand.

"You ready to move the body?" Starks asked.

"As soon as you give the word," the tech replied.

Starks nodded. "Go ahead."

"The tracks show two of them," Starks said. "Came around the left side of the house." He jerked his chin that way. "Looks like they simply walked up behind her and popped her."

"Neighbors see or hear anything?" Ray asked.

"Nope. Probably used silencers. And the shrubbery might've helped muffle any sound."

"This definitely wasn't random," Ray said. "And these guys definitely aren't amateurs."

Starks shrugged. "Sure looks that way." He sighed. "Let's go inside."

He headed that way. We followed.

"No forced entry," Starks said. "And nothing disturbed inside. Disturbing but not disturbed."

That was true. Heather Macomb's body lay on its side, next to the dining room table. An open history text, spiral notebook, and purple ballpoint on the table, each spattered with blood, bone, and brain fragments. As was the tabletop and the pale-gray carpet near her body. I walked around her corpse, carefully avoiding the blood-stains. Heather had a single entry wound to the back of her head, slightly right of center. Left forehead shattered as if it had exploded from inside. Which is exactly what had happened.

"Doesn't look like she saw it coming either," I said.

"That's why I think they used silencers." Starks rubbed his neck. "I hate this shit."

"Where's Mr. Macomb?" Ray asked.

"Upstairs. In the shower."

We climbed the stairs and then down a hallway to the master bedroom. Nothing out of place. Nothing overturned or ransacked. Not that I expected it would be. This wasn't a robbery. This was a hit. This was Borkov's doing. No doubt.

The bathroom wasn't so pristine. Macomb lay crumpled in the corner of the white-tiled shower, the wall behind him sprayed with the same crap I had seen around Heather's body. Blood, bone, and brain tissue. Blood covered his face and an entry wound was visible just beneath his left eye. A blood-soaked towel lay across his chest.

"Looks like he saw the killers. I suspect he had finished his shower and was drying off when they came in. Tried to protect himself with that towel. There's a hole in it. Like he raised it to cover his face when he saw the muzzle staring at him." Starks shrugged. "Didn't help much."

The definition of an understatement.

"Now we know what Zuma and Boyd were up to while we were at the mall," I said.

Ray nodded. "And why they waited until after three o'clock to drop you guys there. Had to wait until Heather was home from school."

"Cold blooded," Morgan said.

"All that and more," Ray added.

"What now?" I asked.

Morgan jangled what sounded like keys in his pocket. "I think it's time we had a chat with Borkov and his crew."

"You think that's a good idea?" I asked.

"No need for stealth any more. Just jump in his face. I want to put pressure on him. Want him to do something stupid."

"Like what?" I asked.

"Won't know the answer to that until he does it. But one thing I know, criminals make mistakes. And they make big mistakes when under big pressure. Time to apply that pressure."

# CHAPTER FORTY-SEVEN

VICTOR BORKOV WAS his usual gracious self. Eventually. When Morgan, Ray, and I arrived at the *Sea Witch*, we were greeted by the dynamic duo of Zuma and Boyd. Acting tough, playing the gate-keepers at the foot of the gangplank, Zuma flexed out trying to look badass. Which I figured he was. Boyd, too. Even Morgan showing his badge got little response. But finally, Borkov came to the rail and invited us on board. Zuma and Boyd turned like saloon doors, allowing us to pass before following us up the ramp. I didn't like them behind me but I felt better with Ray and Morgan there. Particularly Ray. He was badass, too.

We settled at the rear deck table where Nicole and I had sat earlier sharing lunch with Borkov. Borkov offered us drinks, which we declined, so he asked what he could do for us.

"A couple of questions," Morgan said.

"Always glad to help the law," Borkov said as he lit a cigar and leaned back in his chair. Casual and relaxed.

"That's good to know, Mr. Borkov," Morgan said.

"Please. Call me Victor."

"What I really want to know, Mr. Borkov," Morgan said, looking at Zuma and Boyd who stood behind Borkov like good little soldiers, "is where your guys were this afternoon?"

"Here and there," Zuma said.

"I'm more interested in the there than the here," Morgan said.

"After you dropped Grace, Nicole, and Jake at the mall, where'd you go?"

"Don't remember," Zuma said. He looked at Boyd. "You remember?"

Boyd shrugged. "Shopping."

"For what?"

"This and that."

Morgan nodded. "So you were here and there shopping for this and that? That about sum it up?"

"More or less." Zuma smiled.

Borkov puffed his cigar and waved away a cloud of smoke. "What's this about?"

"I think you know," Ray said.

"I do? What is it you think I know?"

"How a family ended up dead."

"What family might that be?"

Borkov was cool. I had to give him that. I looked for signs of stress in his face but saw none. He was in charge. Home court. No fear of a mere civil servant like Morgan.

"The Macombs," I said. "You know, Darrell Wilbanks' girlfriend and her parents."

"Don't know them."

I looked him in the eye. "But you know, or should I say knew, Darrell and Darnell."

"Don't believe I know them either."

"So they weren't on board a couple of nights ago?" Morgan asked.

"Don't know them."

Morgan leaned forward. "Look, Borkov, let me lay it out for you. A woman gets killed on The Point. The wife of a guy you're in some real estate competition with. Then the Wilbanks brothers disappear. From this boat." Borkov started to say something, but Morgan waved him off. "Then a guy named Raul Gomez absorbs a bullet in his brain. And now, a family goes down."

"And this is supposed to mean something to me?" Borkov said through another cloud of smoke.

"All roads lead to Rome," Morgan said. "Seems that all these folks end up connected to you."

"I don't think so. I don't know anything about any of this."

"We have witnesses that say otherwise."

Borkov tapped a long ash into the ashtray near his left elbow. "Where's Grace?"

"I thought she was here," I said.

Borkov leveled a cold gaze at me. "Last I heard she was with you."

"We lost her in the mall," I said. "I figured she hooked up with these guys and came back here. You're telling me she didn't?"

Borkov stood. "I think we're done here."

"A few more questions," Morgan said.

"I don't like you or your tone. Coming on my property and making accusations."

"I haven't accused you of anything, Mr. Borkov. At least not yet."

"Sure you have. Now, I'm going ask you guys to leave. You want to talk more, snoop around in my business, I suggest you get a warrant."

"Will do," Morgan said. He stood. "We'll be seeing each other again, Mr. Borkov. Soon."

As I reached the top of the gangway, Ray and Morgan already halfway down, Borkov stepped up behind me.

"So, you don't work for your father," he said in a low voice. "Fucking with me is the biggest mistake you've ever made."

I turned to him. "I've made worse mistakes. I remember one married woman I hooked up with. Her husband tried to run me off the road one night."

"Too bad he didn't."

"He overestimated his driving ability. He's the one that ended up in the ditch." I smiled. Borkov didn't. His face was like cold granite.

Time to vacate the premises.

# CHAPTER FORTY-EIGHT

EARLIER, AFTER WE had left the *Sea Witch,* we headed over to Ray's where we brought Nicole, Grace, and Pancake up to date on our visit with Borkov.

"Where's Morgan?" Pancake asked.

"He swung by to chat with a friendly judge," Ray said. "Hopefully he'll come back with a warrant for the *Sea Witch.*"

"Think we'll find anything of use there?" I asked.

Ray shrugged. "Won't know till we look."

"It'll at least rattle him a little more," Pancake said.

Since Grace left for the mall with only the clothes she wore and her purse, she and Nicole worked out a list of things Grace might need and Nicole and I left. We swung by a discount clothing store and then a pharmacy. Nicole was a fast shopper, spending only ten minutes in each store. Then, with two stuffed bags, we returned to Ray's.

"I grabbed everything on the list and a few other things I thought you might need," Nicole said as she placed the bags on the kitchen table.

Grace rummaged through the clothes and toiletry items Nicole had chosen. "Looks like you covered the essentials. Thanks."

"Let me know what else you need and we'll pick it up."

"I guess this is my new life." Grace sighed. "Living out of plastic bags."

"It'll get better," Ray said. "And, in the meantime, you'll be safe."

"Doesn't look that way from where I sit." Grace hesitated and then shook her head. "I'm sorry. That wasn't called for." Her eyes glistened as she looked at each of us in turn. "I'm really grateful for everything you guys have done."

"We did the easy part," I said. "You did the heavy lifting. You took the risk. I'm just glad we could get you off the boat and away from Borkov."

Grace fought back tears. "Me, too. In spite of my fears and reservations, I know this is what I have to do." She sniffed. "I might not like it, I might be scared to death, but inside, deep inside, I know it's right."

I hugged her to my chest. "It'll be okay."

The dam broke. Grace collapsed against me, her body shaking as she let it all out. I felt her tears soak through my shirt. It took a couple of minutes for her to compose herself, and I held her the entire time. Finally, she pushed back and looked at me.

"I feel so silly," she said.

"No," I said. "Maybe scared, but not silly."

That's when Morgan showed up. He looked at Grace. "You okay?"

"I'm fine. I just had a ninny moment. Had to get it out of my system, I guess."

"It'll get better."

Grace shrugged. "That's what everyone keeps telling me."

"What's new?" I asked Morgan.

He said he'd reached out to a colleague with the Pensacola PD about securing a warrant to search the *Sea Witch*. The ship was not only out of Morgan's jurisdiction, it was even in another state. Where he had no standing. He and the Pensacola detective then visited the judge. A cop-friendly one it seems.

"And?" Ray asked.

"After I went over the evidence we had, he said he was leaning toward a warrant but made it clear that the probable cause statement needed to be airtight. Not that he didn't believe that Grace saw what she saw, just that he didn't see any corroboration of her statement and she might not be the most reliable witness."

"What the hell does that mean?" Grace said. "Victor and his two clowns killed Darrell and Darnell. I saw it. I didn't make it up."

"We talked about this," Ray said. "You were intoxicated. It's still your word against three."

Morgan said that's why he'd asked one of the local assistant DAs to work on the probable cause wording. "Figured I'd get one of the legal types to write it up since he speaks the same language as the judge."

"What's the turnaround time here?" Ray asked.

"I told the judge we'd have it ready by nine, ten at the latest, tonight and we'd stop by his home then. He wasn't happy, saying it could wait until the morning, but I said since the location we needed to search could move at any time, that we'd rather have it tonight."

"But he agreed?" I asked.

Morgan nodded. "Reluctantly. So, as soon as it's ready, I'll pick it up and head over to Pensacola."

Starks and two uniforms showed up to take Grace to the safe house Morgan had arranged.

"Where is it?" I asked.

Morgan shook his head. "All I can tell you is it's a house, up near Mobile."

"But we might need to bring some things over," Nicole said.

"Call me. I'll handle it."

"But—" Nicole began.

"But nothing," Morgan said. "The whole idea is to keep it a secret. The more people who know the greater the chance it'll leak."

"We won't talk," Nicole said.

"Talk all you want," Morgan said. "Because you won't know."

Nicole started to respond, but I touched her arm. "That makes sense. If we need to reach Grace we'll go through you."

"Ready?" Starks asked.

"As ready as I'll ever be," Grace said.

Starks nodded. "Okay. Grab your stuff and let's get going."

Grace picked up the two plastic bags. "This is it. I'm traveling light, it seems."

We walked Grace down to Starks' car. Hugs and tears followed. Even Nicole shed a couple. I think she and Grace had connected on one of those woman to woman levels. We watched as Starks drove away, Grace looking back at us with big eyes as he turned toward the highway. The uniforms in their patrol car followed.

"She'll be okay, won't she?" Nicole asked.

"She will," Ray said.

"What now?" I asked.

"Wait for the warrant," Morgan said. "I have a half a dozen Pensacola PD guys and their evidence team standing by so we can pay Mr. Borkov a visit as soon as the paper comes through."

"Anybody else hungry?" I asked.

"Me," Nicole said.

"Me," added Pancake.

"Let's head over the Captain Rocky's," I said. "I need to check in with Carla, anyway."

And that's what we did. Even Morgan joined us. After we settled at a deck table and ordered drinks and food, Carla and I went into the office. Took us maybe ten minutes to go over the week's numbers. A good week. Seems we had attracted a bunch of tequila drinkers and that's always good for the bottom line.

While we ate, Morgan was fidgety. Constantly checking his cell phone for messages. Maybe he wasn't so sure the warrant would go through.

"Maybe Nicole, Pancake, and I should venture over to the dock in Pensacola," I said. "To keep an eye on Borkov's boat."

"And spook him?" Morgan shook his head. "I suspect Borkov's already nervous, probably all the way to paranoid, and if he sees you guys, or anyone, snooping around it'll only feed that. I don't want anyone near there until we show up with the warrant."

"Can we at least come along when you do your search?" I asked.

"Not a chance."

"Why?"

"Let's see. You aren't cops. It's a crime scene. I'm only getting in there as a favor from the Pensacola PD. I don't think they'd welcome spectators. And since Borkov's already tweaked, this has the potential of going badly. People like Borkov are used to doing what's necessary and that makes him dangerous. He might do something stupid and . . . all sorts of bad things can happen."

I shrugged. "Since you put it that way, I guess Nicole and I are off-duty."

"I'll keep Ray in the loop," Morgan said. "He can pass it along to you if he wants."

"Jake's not big on answering his phone when he's with Nicole." Ray winked at her.

She laughed. "I'll make sure he keeps it close by."

"So now you're all going to gang up on me," I said.

"Poor little Jake," Nicole said.

"What do you want to do now?" I asked her.

"You."

I stood. "That's my cue."

# CHAPTER FORTY-NINE

TURNED OUT IT didn't take long for Borkov to do something stupid. Or smart. Or scary. I guess it all depended on your point of
view. For Nicole and me, it was definitely the latter.

After we left Captain Rocky's, we swung by Orange Beach and
Nicole parked her SL facing the Gulf. Top down, a cool breeze off
the water. I was glad I had my jacket with me. Nicole didn't and
chided me about being such a wimp, saying something about me
needing my blanky. She can be so pissy sometimes.

Regardless, it was a perfect evening. The sun was just settling on
the water and we sat quietly until it dropped from sight, leaving
behind an orange sky.

Then Nicole got frisky. Or is it handsy? In public. People strolling by. Woman had no brakes.

"Let's go," she said.

"Where?"

"My place."

"Why?" I asked, smiling.

"Really?"

"What if I want to stay here?"

"You don't." She squeezed me through my jeans. "Or at least he
doesn't."

Hard to argue with her when she was right.

She fired up the engine, spun backwards, and we were off. Soon
we were cruising down Perdido Beach Boulevard toward Peppermill

Road and The Point. The road, not exactly what you'd call a boulevard, was two lanes and fairly straight as it rose and fell with the rolling terrain. Clusters of houses here and there but mostly open and uninhabited, only sand dunes and sea oats on either side. I leaned back in the passenger seat, my head lolled against the headrest, and looked up into the darkening sky. A few stars had appeared, and as I watched, more popped into existence. I had a feeling tonight was going to be epic. Of course, every night with Nicole was epic. Everything was perfect.

Then it wasn't.

It all happened so fast. As Pancake would say—as quick as a hiccup.

To my right, an ominous shadow reared, followed by the roar of a large engine. My head whipped that direction just in time to see a black Lincoln SUV launch from behind a dune. More reflex than thought, I extended my arm to stop its progress, but in a split second reason prevailed, and I yanked it back.

I was right about one thing: the night was epic. At least the impact was. The SUV T-boned the SL in an explosion of twisting, screeching metal. The door cracked into my ribs and my head actually bounced off the SUV's oversized bumper. Not standard issue, the wide, deep slab of black metal had been designed for just this.

My ears rang and more stars appeared. Not celestial ones but rather those little electrical flashes that often accompany concussions. My first thought was that this was all a horrible accident. Drunk teenagers out for an illegal romp over the sand dunes in daddy's SUV. But just as quickly the thought that this was something way more sinister entered my mind. Borkov's minions.

But it wasn't over. The SUV wasn't ready to relent. Its tires chirped as it grabbed the pavement, driving the Mercedes sideways and into a four-foot-high sand dune.

Then everything stopped. Or went into ultra slow motion. The

SUV backed away a few feet, still blocking the road, still aimed directly at us. Helpless would be the word. I glanced at Nicole. She was wide-eyed but didn't appear hurt. At least I didn't see any blood or protruding bones.

"You okay?" I asked.

"I don't know." She looked confused. As was I.

I expected the SUV to attack us again, but then the doors swung open and Zuma and Boyd stepped out. Suspicions confirmed.

I tugged my cell from my pocket and thumbed in a quick text to Ray. One word: *Borkov.* As I pressed send, cold metal pressed against my cheek.

"Drop the phone," Zuma ordered.

I did.

"Get out."

Neither door would open. My side was trashed and the driver's door was jammed against the dune. We climbed out over the doors.

"What the hell is this?" I asked.

"Shut up." Zuma waved the gun. "Turn around."

"And if we don't?" Nicole said.

Did I say the woman had no brakes?

Zuma smirked. "I'll shoot you and we'll just take Jake."

"Where?" I asked.

"Mr. Borkov wants a word."

"He could've called."

Zuma stepped forward. He pressed the muzzle into my chest. "Don't give me a reason. I don't like you, anyway."

"But you aren't going to shoot me," I said.

"Why not, smart-ass?"

"Because Borkov wouldn't get his chat. And the way I see it, you clowns aren't allowed to think or act on your own."

That seemed to confuse him. Guess he didn't expect any resistance. He quickly recovered. "We can always say you resisted."

"I'm sure that would play well with your boss."

Boyd eased up behind me. "Hands behind your back."

I hesitated so he twisted one arm behind me. Physical resistance crossed my mind. After all, it would be the manly thing to do. Not smart, but manly. But, not seeing any realistic way of challenging these two, I gave up and let him slip on plastic cuffs. He did the same to Nicole and we were shoved toward the SUV. Back seat. Boyd driving, Zuma riding shotgun, twisted in the seat so he could watch us. His gun rested on the edge of the seat, aimed directly at Nicole.

The ringing in my ears settled into a raspy buzz, but the throbbing behind my eyes remained in full force. I looked at Nicole. Surprisingly, she didn't appear all that scared. More pissed with her jaw set and her gaze stabbing at the back of Boyd's head.

Soon we were on the highway, heading toward Pensacola. Zuma punched a number into his cell and after a minute simply said, "It's done. Be there shortly." He disconnected the call, returning the phone to his pocket.

"You don't think you'll get away with this, do you?" I asked.

Boyd looked at me in the rearview mirror. "Looks like we already did, pretty boy."

"So far. But I suspect that'll change."

"Not for you two," Zuma said.

"Look—" I began.

"Shut up," Zuma said.

I did. I mean, he had the gun.

Nicole on the other hand had different ideas.

"I've got to pee," she said.

Zuma laughed. "Go ahead."

"What about your fancy leather interior?"

Zuma shrugged. "Like I give a shit."

The glare she now aimed at him could have melted the fancy interior, but it had no effect on Zuma. He simply smiled and shook his head.

"Speaking of pissing, if I was you, I'd be careful who I pissed off," Zuma said. "The boss only needs Jake. You're expendable. Truth is, he'll probably leave it to Boyd and me how it all goes down. Easy or hard. Your choice."

"I'm not scared of you," Nicole said.

Woman had balls. Figuratively speaking, of course.

Zuma's smile thinned and his eyes narrowed. "You better be. We might decide to have a little fun with you before we take care of business."

Boyd laughed. "The boss gives us a lot of perks for a job well done."

"Is it?" I asked. "A well-done job?"

Zuma twisted a bit more in his seat, now looking directly at me. "Seems that way from where I sit."

"Except I suspect with this little maneuver you've unleashed the dogs of war."

"Really?" Zuma said, a note of sarcasm in his voice.

"You have no idea what Ray's capable of," I said.

"We'll deal with him later."

"Or he'll deal with you."

"Remind me to be scared."

"I just did," I said. "Whether you believe it or not is up to you."

Zuma let out a little snort and turned back toward the road.

The traffic was light so thirty minutes later we arrived at the dock, Boyd sliding the SUV into a slot at the far end of the lot near the *Sea Witch*. Borkov greeted us at the top of the gangway.

"Welcome," he said. "Glad you could make it."

"Not much choice," I said.

We settled on the rear deck at the same table where we had had such a pleasant lunch. I was sure this sit-down would be less so. Where the hell was Ray? Did he even get my text? Did he understand it? I wished I'd had time to say more. Maybe something like, "We're in deep shit. Come running." But I was lucky to be able to fire off the single word.

"So, what do you want?" I asked.

Borkov smiled. "All in due time."

Two crew members came from below, one turning aft, the other forward. Then I heard and felt something even more ominous. The rumble of the engines cranking to life. I couldn't see the guy who went forward, but the aft guy tossed lines and the ship began to move.

The fate of Darrell and Darnell Wilbanks crossed my mind.

# CHAPTER FIFTY

RAY WENT FOR a long run on the beach. He loved night runs. Cooler and quieter. Fewer people around. Mostly strolling couples and a few shell hunters. After thirty minutes, he turned and made his way back toward home. Leaving his sandy shoes on the deck at the top of the stairs, he headed inside to a hot shower. Refreshing.

In the kitchen, he snagged a beer and a hunk of cheddar cheese from the fridge and sat at the table. He picked up his cell phone from where he had left it on a stack of papers. It indicated he had received a text. Nearly an hour earlier. From Jake. He read it. One word: *Borkov.*

He tried Jake's number. It rang a few times and then jumped over to voice mail. He left a message to call back. He munched on the cheese and drained his beer. What did the message mean? Did Jake have some new information on Borkov? If so, Jake would have called. Left a message. Jake wasn't much for texting. And yet he had. Why?

Hairs raised on the back of his neck. Something was wrong.

He dialed Pancake's number. He answered almost before it rang.

"Yeah," Pancake said.

Ray told him about the text. "What do you think?"

"I think Jake's in massive trouble and Borkov's behind it."

"I agree. Meet me at the dock in Pensacola."

"On my way."

Just as Ray merged onto Highway 182, his cell chirped. It was Morgan.

"What's up?" Ray asked.

"I was going to ask you the same thing."

Ray told him of Jake's text and that he and Pancake were meeting at the Pensacola Harbor.

"That clears things up," Morgan said.

"Clears up what?"

"Just got a call from one of the patrol guys. Charlie Coffman. He got a report of an accident."

Ray's pulse increased. Not something that happened often.

Morgan continued. "Nicole's red SL was found trashed off Perdido Beach Boulevard. Looks like it was T-boned by something big and bad."

"You sure it's hers?"

"No doubt. Coffman recognized the Mercedes from the Plummer scene. When she and Jake dropped by the other morning. Besides, her purse and Jake's cell were inside."

The text now made perfect sense. Borkov had made his play. Not exactly what Ray had expected, but the facts couldn't be denied.

"Call your guy at the Pensacola PD and get him down to the harbor."

"Will do."

Ray then called Pancake, relaying this new information to him.

"I'm ten minutes out," Pancake said.

"I'm twenty. Stay low until I get there."

"You got it."

Twenty minutes later, Ray pulled into the harbor lot. Pancake was there. The *Sea Witch* wasn't. A knot swelled in his gut. There were maybe two dozen vehicles in the lot. Pancake stood near a black Lincoln SUV. Ray parked next to it and jumped out.

"Check this out," Pancake said, the tight beam from his Maglite scanning across the massive front bumper.

Definitely not stock, the bumper was thick metal, painted black to match the SUV. The light beam reflected scrapes and dents and smears of red paint.

"Looks like Borkov's upped the ante," Pancake said. "And now it looks like he's in the wind." He nodded toward the empty stretch of planking where Borkov's floating palace had been docked.

Ray looked around. "Don't see any potential witnesses."

"I got one," Pancake said.

"Who? Where?"

"There." He pointed toward the *Storm Shelter*, his friend's fishing boat. "Before we left yesterday, I set up the camera and the computer with a six-hour recording loop."

"You're a freaking genius."

Pancake grunted. "You ever doubt that?"

Ray didn't. Never had. "Let's take a look."

Once inside, Pancake sat down at the table and began working the laptop. He accessed the video file and began to run it backwards. At first all was still, then the *Sea Witch* appeared, moving backwards, gobbling up its own wake, and then nudging against the dock. Two guys tossing lines. Then Jake, Nicole, Zuma, and Boyd backing down the gangway and out of the screen. Pancake paused the video and then played it forward. As the quartet climbed the gangway, Borkov appeared at the rail and waved them on board. The lines were tossed and the *Sea Witch* angled away from the dock and into the darkness.

Ray walked up on deck. He gazed out toward the Gulf. So Borkov wanted a war. Okay, so be it. War was Ray's favorite pastime. He pulled out his cell and punched in a number.

"Who you calling?" Pancake asked as his massive body lumbered up the steps and onto the deck.

"Ira Gemmel. My guy at the Coast Guard."

Pancake started to say something, but Ray held up a finger.

"Ira?" Ray said.

"Ray, you got a bad habit of calling at night," Ira said.

"I need your help."

"I'm shocked." He did sarcasm well.

"It's Borkov. He kidnapped my boy Jake and his friend Nicole."

"What do you mean, kidnapped?"

Ray gave him a two-minute thumbnail of what he knew.

"You sure?"

"Got it on video."

Ira sighed. "Okay. I'm on it. I'll round up my crew and get to tracking the *Sea Witch* down."

"Thanks. One thing. We'll be in the field so let your guys know that."

"What do you mean in the field?"

"I'm not going to sit by."

"Let us handle it," Ira said. "It's what we do."

"No can do, Ira. You know that."

"Unfortunately I do." Another sigh. "Just don't do anything stupid."

"Wouldn't dream of it." He disconnected the call.

"What now?" Pancake asked.

"Go after them."

"Billy Ray?"

"You got it."

Next call was to Billy Ray Tucker. Ex-Navy Seal. Tough son of a bitch. True warrior. When Billy Ray answered, the background noise sounded like he was in a bar.

"You sober?" Ray asked.

"More or less."

"I need your crew."

"Now?" Billy Ray asked.

"Ten minutes ago."

"What is it?"

Ray gave him the same thumbnail, adding that he was at the dock in Pensacola.

"I'm all over it. I'll grab Tommy Patton and give Megan Willis a call. She has a new boat and I'm sure she'd love to open it up."

Tommy Patton had spent fifteen years with Delta Force. Mostly as a sniper and long-range recon but could do just about anything. Anything lethal, anyway. And had over and over again.

Megan Willis had served with the Marines. Two tours in Afghanistan and one in Iraq. Flew close air support helicopters, among other things. Things she never talked about. Toughest woman he ever knew. And she loved fast boats. Very fast boats.

"See you in twenty, max," Billy Ray said.

\* \* \*

Carlos Fernandez squatted in the hedges that separated the lot from the adjacent strip center. He watched as two men, one average sized, the other massive, sniffed around the SUV. He recognized them immediately as the pair he had seen on Raul's front porch. Why were they here? What were they doing?

Borkov had said grab the vehicle and make it disappear. No problem. If these two didn't screw it up. He eased his gun from his jacket pocket. Not that he wanted to use it. That would attract unwanted attention. But he was on a short timeline. Borkov had also said it wouldn't be long before things led back here and the local police got involved, and he wanted no breadcrumbs left behind.

What to do?

Then the men walked toward a boat and disappeared inside.

Perfect.

Carlos worked his way across the lot, head on a swivel, staying near the smattering of parked cars as best he could in case he had to duck for cover. He quickly reached the SUV, but as he placed his thumb on the fob's unlock button, first one and then the other man came back on deck. Couldn't be more than fifty feet away. The smaller guy had a cell phone to his ear.

Carlos scratched his cheek with the gun's muzzle. He calculated the distance. Not likely he could take them both from this distance. He'd have to charge them. Hope surprise gave him enough time to close the gap and pop them both.

He set his feet, up on his toes, ready to go. His heart raced and his breath was shallow and quick. Now or never, he thought.

But just as his legs tensed, ready to spring, the two men descended below deck.

Carlos waited, expecting them to reappear but when they didn't after a couple of minutes, he punched the unlock button. The SUV's light flashed and a soft chirp came from beneath the hood. The interior lights sprang to life. He tore open the door and scrambled inside.

# CHAPTER FIFTY-ONE

THE SHORELINE AND then the lights of Pensacola disappeared quickly as the *Sea Witch* headed for deep water. Borkov had said little, and, in fact, had gone below, leaving Nicole and me trussed and sitting at the table. Sort of rude but I guessed we weren't in any position to complain to the management. Zuma and Boyd stood near the stern, talking too low for me to hear, glancing our way from time to time.

"This is not good," I said.

"You think?"

I shrugged.

"What does he want?" Nicole asked.

"I don't know. Maybe trade us for Grace. She's the one that can sink him."

"We can, too. She told us what happened."

"Hearsay. She's the witness. She actually saw it go down."

"That might be true," Nicole said. "But we still know too much." She looked at me. "Somehow I don't see Mr. Borkov being overly forgiving of our role in this."

"Maybe he just wants to scare us. See what we know. And once he sees we don't know anything, he'll talk trade."

"Then why are we headed out to sea?" Nicole asked. "Why not hide us somewhere until a trade can happen?"

I had no answer to that so I simply stared at her and then glanced back toward Zuma and Boyd. They were watching the ship's wake, backs toward us. What to do? My inner superhero said I should charge them, try to shoulder them over the back. I mean, isn't that what Bond, James Bond, would do? But that wouldn't solve our problems. Not even close. With Borkov and his entire crew to deal with and us still cuffed. Not to mention that I'd probably bounce off Zuma, him being built like a brick outhouse.

"Know what I think?" Nicole asked.

"What?"

"I think they'll whack us around and try to get us to tell them where Grace is."

"But we don't know," I said,

"Which is exactly why Detective Morgan wouldn't tell us."

"Doesn't make for a very good bargaining position."

"Wouldn't matter, anyway," Nicole said. "Once he knows where Grace is, or figures out we don't, we're expendable."

She seemed too calm considering our situation. Did she think this was a movie or something? Was her heart pounding as hard as mine? Then she looked at me, tears glistening her eyes. I wanted to hug her, assure her that all was okay, even if it wasn't. Not even close.

"So what are we going to do?" she asked.

"Delay and deny as long as we can. And hope Ray understood my text."

"What text?"

I told her.

"You're pretty smart."

"Let's hope."

Borkov appeared. He sat across from us, while Zuma and Boyd positioned themselves behind us.

Borkov nodded toward Zuma. "Cut them loose. They aren't going anywhere."

Zuma pulled a switchblade from his pocket and snapped it open. He cut our cuffs free.

I rubbed my wrists. Borkov lit a cigar and settled back in his chair.

"We have a bit of a problem here," Borkov said.

"You mean like kidnapping?" Nicole asked.

Borkov shrugged. "That's the least of your troubles."

"What do you want?" I asked.

"Grace. Where is she?

"I thought she was here?" I said.

He knocked an ash onto the deck and clamped the cigar in his teeth. "Cut the bullshit. You know she isn't here. But I suspect you know where she is."

"I don't." I looked at Nicole. "We don't."

"Why don't I believe you?" Borkov asked.

I don't think he wanted an answer; his question was purely rhetorical. I answered anyway. "Because if we don't know, all this was a massive mistake on your part."

"And bad news for you."

"Maybe for you, too," I said.

"Ray? You think that washed-up PI is going to ride in on a white horse and save you?"

"Probably won't be a white horse," I said. "Not out here."

"You're a funny guy," Borkov said.

But he didn't laugh. Not even a little smile.

"But if I were you," he continued, "I wouldn't count on Ray Longly saving the day."

But that's exactly what I was counting on. How the hell else were we going to get out of this? Please, please, Ray, I hope you understood my text.

"Folks who underestimate him usually regret it," I said.

He shrugged. "And I'd suggest you don't underestimate me."

Now I smiled. "Wouldn't dream of it."

He sat silently for a minute, puffing on his cigar, clouds of smoke catching the wind and swirling aft. Behind him, far in the distance, beyond the ship's bow, I saw lightning light up a cloud bank. A huge, black cloud bank. Was a storm coming in? Guess I should watch the Weather Channel more often.

Borkov leaned forward, forearms resting on the table edge. "What I know is that Detective Morgan has her squirreled away somewhere."

"Then you know more than we do," I said. "We last saw her at the mall. Figured she made her way back here with those two." I nodded toward Zuma and Boyd who had retaken their position near the stern.

"What did she say to you?" Borkov asked.

"Grace? What did she say about what?"

"Me."

"She didn't say anything." I glanced at Nicole. "Not to us, anyway."

"Nothing about Darrell and Darnell?"

"Who?"

"A couple of guys I'm going to introduce you to."

"Always like making new friends," I said.

"Are they hot?" Nicole asked. "I love hot guys."

Borkov was not amused. He sighed. "Is that the way you want to play this?"

"Mr. Borkov, I'm not sure what we can tell you," I said. "We don't know any Darrell or Darnell. And we don't know where Grace is."

He stood, pulling his cell from his pocket. "I have a couple of calls to make. I think you two should sit here and reevaluate your situation."

"You get reception out here?" Nicole asked.

"Got to love satellites." He headed below.

After he descended the stairs, Nicole asked, "What are we going to do?"

"Not sure. Pray for Ray to show with the cavalry."

"Will he?"

"He'd better."

I looked around, searching for something, anything, that could be used as a weapon. Chairs, an umbrella pole, and a heavy glass ashtray. On the table behind Borkov's chair, the two baseballs he had gloated over when we were last here were nestled in a bowl, the bat leaning against its edge. None of it offered much help against the well-armed Zuma and Boyd.

I looked at Nicole. "Okay, here's the deal. Wait for my play."

"Your play?" she asked. "You sound like Bogart."

"And you look like Bacall."

She managed a half smile. "Okay, I give. What play?"

"I don't know yet."

"Never mind. You're definitely not Bogey. He'd have a real plan."

I shook my head and rolled my eyes. "All I know for sure is that if you see duct tape and a big metal ring, you'll know it's coming."

"You mean what happened to those brothers?"

"Exactly."

She squeezed back tears again. "I'm scared."

"Me, too. But if I yell jump, do it. Right over the side. I'll be right behind you."

She looked at me as if I was insane. And maybe I was.

"Out here?" she said. "Are you crazy?"

"Would you rather hit the water with your arms and legs free or tied to an anchor?"

"Then what? We drown?"

"Maybe. But it'll take a while. You can swim, can't you?"

"Of course. I was on the swim team in high school."

"Hold onto those skills. They might save you."

"Okay, so we jump," she said. "Then what?"

"Swim and pray."

She took a deep breath and let it out slowly. "I don't like this."

"I'm open to other suggestions."

She looked out over the water. "It'll be cold."

"It will. Not to mention a pretty long fall."

"And they'll probably shoot us."

"They'll try. But hitting someone from a rocking boat at night isn't as easy as it is in the movies."

"That makes me feel so much better." She shook her head. "Let's hope it doesn't come to that."

"Let's hope. But if I say jump, don't hesitate. We won't get a second chance."

"Maybe not even a first," Nicole said.

"One more thing. When, if, you have to jump, leap as far away from this beast as you can. If you get sucked under this thing the props will turn you into chum."

She stared at him. "I'll say one thing, Jake Longly, dating you isn't without its thrills."

I shrugged. I had no comeback for that one. I looked out toward the black water. Lightning again flittered in the clouds. They seemed much closer now. The breeze kicked up and now carried a definite chill. Or was it fear?

*Where are you, Ray?*

# CHAPTER FIFTY-TWO

"How many times you going to look at your watch?" Pancake asked.

Ray shook his head. "You know me. I hate waiting."

"They'll be here any minute."

"And every minute Borkov gets further out to sea. With Jake and Nicole."

Pancake nodded. "True. But I hear Megan's new boat is a screamer. Some insane amount of horsepower."

"I'd expect nothing less," Ray said.

Pancake started to say something but abruptly stopped, cocking his head to one side. "What was that?"

Ray had heard it, too. A chirp, then the roar of an engine coming to life. They scrambled up the stairs in time to see the SUV spin a wide U-turn and race toward the exit.

"One of Borkov's guys," Pancake said.

"No doubt. Covering tracks."

The SUV flew out the exit, made a hard, tire-squealing left, and disappeared.

"I'll call the local cops," Pancake said, pulling his phone from his pocket.

"No need."

Ray nodded toward the entrance where a pair of patrol cars turned in. They had just missed the SUV. He and Pancake stepped off the boat and waited until the units stopped nearby. Two officers stepped out of one car, the two in the other unit remained inside.

"What's the story," the young uniform asked. His name tag said he was P. Brewster. "We got a call from Detective Bob Morgan. He said to meet a couple of guys here."

"That's us," Ray said. "I'm Ray Longly. This is Pancake."

That got a raised eyebrow from Brewster. Pancake's moniker always did that.

"We have a kidnapping of two people," Ray said. "They were taken aboard a large yacht that left here maybe a half hour ago."

Brewster looked out toward the water. "That's what this is about? What's Morgan's involvement here?"

"He's investigating a series of murders and the kidnappings are part of that."

Brewster nodded. "I see. So what do you need us for? This sounds like a situation for the Coast Guard."

"Already on it," Ray said. "We're waiting for a boat to go after the yacht."

Pancake punched a couple of buttons on his cell and held it where Brewster could see the photos of the SUV Pancake had taken. "This is the vehicle involved in the kidnapping." He punched another button. "Here's its license plate."

"It was involved in an accident with the kidnapping victims' vehicle," Ray said. "Over in Perdido Bay. Someone involved with the kidnappers just took off in it. Headed toward the highway, I suspect."

"When?" Brewster asked.

"Two minutes before you arrived."

"Can you send me those photos?" Brewster asked Pancake.

"Sure," Pancake said. "I'll text them. What's your number?"

Brewster gave it to him and Pancake sent the images.

"Okay," Brewster said. "I'll get an alert out."

The two officers climbed back in their patrol unit, and, while his partner began working the dashboard computer, Brewster spun the car around and headed toward the exit, the second cruiser in tow.

Ray turned as the high-pitched, high-speed churn of a marine engine came toward them. A sleek shadow with a moonlit wake sped into the harbor. The engine lowered its pitch, the boat slowed, and Megan Willis executed a perfect sideways slide up to the dock. Headlights washed across them. Ray turned to see a large dually pickup enter the lot and race toward them.

The cavalry had arrived.

Ray decided that it was best for Pancake to remain behind as sort of a communications center. Man the computer, the boat's radio, and cell service onshore in case they were needed. Ray and the others would run down the *Sea Witch*. While Billy Ray Tucker and Tommy Patton loaded two heavy canvas duffels, no doubt filled with weaponry, into the back of Megan's brand-new, dark-blue Willard Assault 43, Ray called Ira Gemmel. His office patched him through Ira who was on his Coast Guard vessel tracking the *Sea Witch*.

"Any news?" Ray asked.

"The *Sea Witch* is maybe eight miles south of the harbor doing twelve knots on a south, southwest course. We're maybe fifteen miles away making twenty-five knots."

"Okay, thanks," Ray said. "We're leaving the harbor now. I think we'll be doing a bit more than twenty-five so we'll beat you there."

"We?" Ira asked.

"I have a few friends."

"Listen up, Ray. This is the Coast Guard's jurisdiction and problem. Let us do our job."

"Glad to do just that, but right now time is critical. A few minutes here or there could make the difference whether Jake gets out of this alive or not. That's the key here."

"I know arguing with you will do no good, so all I ask is that you find them and track them but don't engage. Understand?"

"Will do. Unless they force our hand."

"Guess I'll have to live with that," Ira said.

"I'll get you on the radio as soon as we know something."

Ray disconnected the call and climbed on board Megan's new ride. The Willard was just over forty feet and rode low in the water. Painted dark blue, it would be all but invisible at night. It had four seats, two front, two back. Ray settled in the front seat next to Megan, Billy Ray and Tommy in back.

"They're about eight miles south of our current position, making twelve knots," Ray said. "How fast will this thing go?"

"They say sixty, but I know how to squeeze out a bit more if needed. We'll be on them in no time." She glanced over her shoulder. "Hold on."

She eased away from the dock, aiming the bow toward the Gulf, and shoved the throttle forward. The engines spun up and the boat jerked forward. It took about a minute to reach top speed and they seemed to fly over the water.

She had killed the running lights so the vessel was completely dark, except for the faint green glow of the digital dashboard and radar screen. Ray saw she was doing fifty-eight knots.

Megan tapped the wireless headset she wore and indicated another hanging from a hook in front of Ray. He placed it over his head, adjusting the single earpiece in place and lowering the mic arm so that the pickup was near his lips. Then he heard Megan speak.

'Everybody five by five?" she asked.

"Got it," Billy Ray said.

"Copacetic," Tommy added.

"I'm good," Ray said.

"Okay," Megan said. "Everyone get ready. At this speed we'll catch them in fifteen or so."

"That quickly?" Ray asked.

"We're doing nearly five times their speed and they don't have that much of a head start. Eight miles is nothing at a mile a minute." She tapped the radar screen in front of her. "There's the *Sea Witch* right there."

Ray saw several blips on the screen. "How do you know that's her?"

"Unless there's a U.S. Navy destroyer out there, it's her. Nothing else that big out and about tonight."

Ray nodded. "Let's go get some bad guys."

"We have a weather front moving in," Megan said. "Looks like a good one."

"Just when I thought things couldn't be worse."

"What?" Megan said. "You afraid of a little rain and wind?" She smiled at him.

Ray turned in his seat and watched as Tommy removed his sniper rifle from his duffel and began the assembly process. Something he could do blindfolded or in the pitch darkness of the cold Afghan mountains. Billy Ray lifted a semiautomatic weapon from his own duffel.

"What've you got there?" Ray asked.

"An HK G36. In case I need to spray the walls."

"Hopefully not," Ray said.

Billy Ray smiled. "You spoil all the fun."

# CHAPTER FIFTY-THREE

THE PITCH OF the *Sea Witch*'s engines dropped an octave and I felt the massive vessel slow. No way that was good news. It could only mean that Borkov had reached his destination. Middle of nowhere; very deep water. Cold, black, deep water. I suspected the Wilbanks brothers were several hundred feet below us.

Nicole and I still sat at the table, saying little as there was little to say. I held her hand, her fingers delicate and cold. Guilt climbed inside me and took root. But for me, she wouldn't be here. Shouldn't be here. Probably shouldn't even know me. Maybe that was Tammy's fault. If she hadn't trashed my Mustang that night, Nicole might have simply driven on by, hooked up with her bartender boyfriend, and never even known I existed. No, that wasn't fair. This one was totally on me. I wanted to assure Nicole that everything would work out, but in truth I had little to offer.

In the distance, the storm had moved closer, lightning flickering inside the thunderheads, faint rumbles of thunder now audible. The air temperature dropped a few more degrees and the wind buffeted my hair. The waves now had mini whitecaps. As if jumping overboard wasn't going to be dangerous enough, why not throw in a churning Gulf? I mean, could our situation really get worse?

Yes, it could.

Borkov had gone below again, Zuma and Boyd hadn't moved, and Nicole and I sat like we were waiting on the hangman. Which I guess we were.

Did I really believe Ray could pull this off? That he actually received and understood my text? That he wasn't curled in bed asleep? That he had somehow figured out we were on board Borkov's boat miles from shore in water so deep our bodies would never be found?

Never found.

Like Darrell and Darnell.

Borkov returned and sat down heavily across from us. He placed a Glock on the table, its muzzle pointed in our direction. He said nothing, only stared at us, his eyes like Antarctic ice. Cold and hard. I felt as if we were now seeing the real Victor Borkov. No anger, no passion, not even a hint that this was personal. For him, this was a simple business decision. After all, isn't that how all this began? A business dispute with Henry Plummer? Over a goddamn piece of dirt?

I think he expected me to say something, maybe beg, maybe cry and whine. I simply stared back. What the hell else could I do? Ray had always said I was stubborn. In his view, to a fault. Right now I grabbed that and held it tight. If this was our last hour on Earth there was no way I would give Borkov even a sliver of satisfaction.

Finally he spoke. "So what's it going to be? Easy or hard?"

"Does it matter?" I asked.

He shrugged.

"We don't know where Grace is or anything else for that matter," I said. "But you won't believe me regardless of what I say."

"Try me."

"I wish I could tell you something that would resolve this. But we really don't know anything."

Borkov laced his fingers and rested his hands on the table but said nothing.

"Even if we did," I continued, "I don't see it helping here. You've made your decision and we can't really change that."

"What decision might that be?" He smiled. Not a friendly smile, but a tight, thin one. Like a shark circling its prey.

He actually reminded me of Auric Goldfinger telling Bond, James Bond, that he didn't expect him to talk, that he only expected him to die. Which is pretty much how I assessed our situation. Of course, James got out of it. Dodged that deadly metal-cutting laser and took old Auric and Odd Job down. I didn't feel much like 007 right now. Nicole might be able to play Pussy Galore, but I feared it would be her final role.

Cut, fade to black, roll the credits. That's a wrap.

"Mr. Borkov," I said, "I'm sure I have no idea what you've decided."

"Fair enough," he said. "Let me enlighten you."

Over his shoulder, a long stutter of lightning danced in the mountain of clouds that minute by minute marched our way, the following thunder even more ominous.

"I believe you," Borkov said. "I don't think you know where Grace is. I don't think Detective Morgan would hand over that information."

"At least we agree on that," I said. "But does that matter now?"

He shrugged. "Not really."

"So what now?"

"The easy way is I have Joe Zuma shoot you both in the head. Clean and quick." His eyes narrowed. "The hard way is I weight you both down and toss you overboard. Alive."

"Neither sound very good to me."

"Then there's the ugly." He leaned forward, his glare like an ice pick to my chest. "I let Zuma and Boyd take a run at Nicole and make you watch before you get tossed."

Nicole's nails dug into my palm, and when I looked down, her knuckles were iceberg white.

Borkov continued. "So, last chance. Convince me I'm wrong. That you actually do know where Grace is."

"I wish we could, but we can't tell you what we don't know."

He leaned back in his chair and eyed Nicole. "You're a lucky young lady."

She looked up at him, her face etched with fear.

"We don't have time for the ugly option so we'll go with the hard way."

He nodded to Zuma. He and Boyd went below.

Borkov picked up the Glock and pushed back his chair, its legs grating across the wooden deck, and stood. He waved a hand indicting we should follow him. I looked at Nicole. Her pale face was now set in grim determination.

She was ready.

Was I?

Borkov grabbed Nicole's arm and tugged her toward the rear deck. Panic swelled in my chest. I needed some kind of weapon, anything that would at least slow them down. Give us time to make the leap. If it came to that.

I looked around, my gaze falling on the two baseballs and the bat. The bat would be best, but Borkov would definitely notice me carrying that. But maybe not the balls. I scooped them from the bowl where they rested, slipping one into each pocket of my jacket. It wasn't much, I mean baseballs against guns, but I didn't see any other options.

As I walked out to where Nicole now stood, the wind kicked up and began to swirl and rain began to fall. Fat drops slapping against the wooden deck. The water to either side churned with increasing force.

Not a good night for a swim.

# CHAPTER FIFTY-FOUR

RAY AIMED THE binoculars Megan had given him at the faint lights on the horizon. High tech and then some, the binocs had zoom, image stabilization, and a button to switch between regular and night vision. Right now he was on night vision. The world appeared green, and when he zoomed in, the outline of the *Sea Witch* became clear.

"It's them," Ray said.

"That's what I thought," Megan said. "Glad we haven't been chasing the wrong radar image." She glanced at the console. "Got them at four miles and they've slowed. Speed only about six knots now."

Ray felt acid swirl in his stomach. Only reason Borkov would slow down out this far was that he had reached where he was headed. Where he would dump Jake and Nicole. Just like Darrell and Darnell. He had no illusions that there would be any kind of negotiation. Borkov simply couldn't let Jake and Nicole survive. Grace either, for that matter. But right now she was Morgan's problem; Jake and Nicole were his.

"Can you get Pancake on the radio?" Ray asked.

"Give me a sec." Megan worked the radio and soon had Pancake patched into our headsets.

"Did you reach Ira?" Ray asked.

"Sure did. They're under sail, as it were. Said he had the *Sea Witch* located and was maybe thirty minutes behind. Making twenty-eight knots."

"Good. We'll beat them there by a good margin. I'll get back to you as soon as we know more. Keep us up to date on Ira's progress."

"Will do. One more thing. The Pensacola PD tracked down the SUV. Bit of gunfight erupted. The bad guy's down and the vehicle's in custody."

"Any ID on the driver?" Ray asked.

"You're going to love this," Pancake said.

"Tell me."

"Carlos Fernandez, according to his driver's license."

"One of Borkov's crew," Ray said. "No surprise there. Okay, we're closing on the *Sea Witch*. The shit's getting ready to go down."

"Be cool," Pancake said.

"Always." Ray looked at Megan. "Let's go get my boy and Nicole."

"All over it."

Megan angled the boat to starboard, positioning the boat directly astern of the yacht. She eased back to port so that she was now in line with the *Sea Witch*.

"I'll come straight up their wake," Megan said. "They'll never see or hear us until we're in close." She glanced back over her shoulder. "You guys ready?"

"Absolutely," Tommy said.

Tommy stood and handed Ray his sniper rifle. "Hold this a sec." He climbed around the cockpit and onto the long, flat bow. He retrieved the rifle from Ray and stretched out, flipping down the support arms and leveling the rifle toward the yacht.

Billy Ray slung his assault rifle over his shoulder and followed. He settled into a prone position to Tommy's left.

Megan dropped down to fifteen knots, the ship now only a mile ahead. Through the binocs, Ray saw Jake, Nicole, and Borkov walk out on the rear deck.

"It's going down," Ray said. "Borkov has them on the stern deck." He moved his visual field around. "I don't see Zuma and Boyd."

Now only 200 yards behind and sitting smack in the middle of the yacht's wake, Megan dropped their speed to six knots, matching the *Sea Witch*'s speed.

"I got Borkov locked," Tommy said, his right eye fitted against the massive scope. "I can take him anytime you want."

"Water seems a little rough," Ray said.

It was. Rain fell at an angle, the wind came directly at them, and waves had jumped to a good three feet. Maybe more.

"No problem at this distance," Tommy said. "Center of mass is a piece of cake from here."

"If you say so," Ray said. "But not until we know where his two stooges are. Or until he does something stupid."

"Oh, he'll do something stupid." Tommy said. "It's in his nature."

# CHAPTER FIFTY-FIVE

THE SWELLS HAD increased to the point that even a ship the size of the *Sea Witch* rose and fell and wobbled, its gyrations now to our benefit. Not that it would make swimming any easier, but it would make hitting us with handguns fired from her deck nearly impossible. That was the hope, anyway. I briefly wondered if Zuma and Boyd spent much time at the firing range.

I hugged Nicole, pulling her tightly against me, my mouth near her ear.

"I'm sorry," I whispered.

"For what?"

"For involving you in this. For putting you in this situation."

"I'm a big girl. I put myself here."

"No, it was . . ."

"It was nothing. But I'll let you get me out of this if you can."

"Same plan. When I say *go*, you go."

"Which way?"

"Whatever seems the shortest path." I gazed over her shoulder toward the rear. "Try to go straight off the back. But jump far. Less likely to get sucked underneath than off the side, I think."

"But you don't know?"

"No. Just makes sense. Besides, the wake's bubbles and foam should help hide us once we're in the water."

"Or drown us."

"Well, there is that. But the center of the wake will be calmer. Swim straight away as far and as fast as you can. I'll be right behind you."

"I love you," she said.

"You're scared."

"Yes, I am, but I do love you, Jake Longly."

I hugged her more tightly. "Love you, too."

"Okay, let's break it up," Borkov said.

Something slapped the deck nearby. A thick, silvery roll of duct tape. I saw Zuma, standing near the top of the stairs. He smiled. "A little something for your journey." He disappeared below deck.

Borkov picked up the tape. He looked at it, spun it in his hand, and then tossed it to me. "Why don't you make yourself useful. Wrap her ankles and wrists."

Behind him, Zuma and Boyd struggled up the stairs, awkwardly carrying a thick metal ring between them. Looked about the size of a manhole cover and was obviously very heavy. Our ride to the bottom.

"You do it, asshole," I said.

I underhanded the roll at his head. Startled, he failed to get a hand up quickly enough and it struck him near his right eye.

Before I settled on baseball, back in high school, I played a couple of years of football. Wide receiver and punter. And the kick I delivered would have been an eighty yarder, I'm sure. Probably set some kind of high school record. Two steps and a perfect leg swing, the top of my foot driving Borkov's nuts somewhere near his diaphragm. He bent, grabbed himself, and collapsed on all fours, gagging.

Zuma in front and Boyd behind were just reaching the top of the stairs. Bent under the weight of the metal ring, Zuma looked up, shocked, momentarily frozen.

"Go," I shouted,

As I extracted one of the baseballs from my pocket, I peripherally saw a flash of blond hair go airborne over the stern. I didn't have time to see how or where she landed, but rather focused on Zuma.

While in the bigs, I threw a bunch of great fastballs. Blew them past guys with gaudy batting averages. Always loved to hear the ball pop into the catcher's mitt. This was maybe my best ever. I put my entire body and soul behind it and released it on a straight line toward Zuma's wide-eyed face. Like David and Goliath, it cracked against his forehead. He staggered, dropping his half of the ring. The weight now shifted toward Boyd and I heard bones and metal crash down the stairs. Zuma recovered somewhat and took a step toward me, Borkov still retching on his knees. The next fastball was also perfect. It struck Zuma's throat with a sickening slap.

Then I was gone. The leap was perfect. Over the stern railing, far out over the water, well beyond the props that sliced and diced the Gulf into a churning wake. I immediately curled into a knot, my arms yanking my knees as tightly against my chest as possible. Perfect in every way.

As I seemed to hover in midair I realized the first of my miscalculations. The drop. Seemed to take forever. For some odd reason I flashed on a physics class I took during college. Why I had signed up for it remains a mystery but I think I thought it would be interesting. Even fun. It was neither. It was hard. I didn't grasp most of it and, shock of all shocks, I didn't do well. What I did remember, right now as I plummeted toward the water, was that some egghead had worked out a formula for the acceleration of falling bodies. The falling body in question here was me. I didn't remember the formula on the final exam and damn sure couldn't recall it here, but I did remember that crazy speeds were achieved very quickly.

The result was that I hit the water hard. It felt like concrete. My breath escaped in a harsh whoosh and then I was underwater, lungs empty, nose filled with seawater. That's when Mr. Panic introduced himself.

Lungs begging for air, the natural urge was to gulp in a breath. Common sense screamed, "Are you crazy?" I managed to hold on, kicking at the water with increasing ferocity, until I broke the surface. Gagging and coughing followed.

That's when my second miscalculation reared its head. From the deck of the *Sea Witch*, the swells seemed fairly large but not really massive. Down here among them, they seemed like angry mountains. What I had estimated as three feet or so was actually closer to six. A thrill ride of ups and downs.

Where was Nicole? Did the fall take her breath? Fill her lungs with water? Was she floating facedown? Or worse settling deep in the water never to be seen again?

I rode up another swell, my head on a swivel. Nothing. Down and then back up. Still nothing. On the third ride up the marching swells, I saw her. Fifty yards away, treading water.

"Jake," she yelled, waving at me. I swam toward her.

Then I heard a pop and a bullet sailed past me and slapped the water five feet away. Then another, a little farther away. By the time I reached Nicole, another half dozen shots flew past us, creating little water spouts in the already angry water. I looked back. Zuma and Boyd, standing on the stern, Boyd pointing our way, Zuma leveling his gun. Then we were down in a trough and out of sight. Briefly. Back up and three more shots came our way.

Then the world lit up. Two large lights on the back of the *Sea Witch* had snapped on.

That was the bad news. The good? I saw a boat, a hundred yards ahead.

Ray.

# CHAPTER FIFTY-SIX

"Borkov's down," Ray said.

He had the binocs trained on the *Sea Witch*'s stern. They were now only one hundred yards behind the yacht, apparently not yet detected.

"And there goes the girl," Tommy said, his eye still plastered to his scope.

Ray saw. Nicole took a leap off the back and hit the water hard. He followed her leap. She bobbed to the surface and began swimming in their direction. Megan pushed the throttle forward, angling the boat toward her.

Ray swung back toward the yacht. Jake threw something at someone Ray couldn't see. And then another pitch and Jake too was over the back. Gunshots followed. Then two lights snapped on. The water between them and the yacht lit up. In the wash of light between the two high candle-watt searchlights, Ray saw Zuma point in their direction.

"We're on their radar now," Ray said.

A bullet slammed into the front of the boat. Megan zigged to starboard, and then back to port. Two more muzzle flashes and a bullet whizzed past Ray's head.

"Take them," Ray said.

Tommy didn't hesitate. His sniper rifle spit, and through the binocs Ray saw Zuma's chest blossom with a dark stain. Zuma staggered and fell to the deck. Boyd appeared, handgun pointed in their direction. Another pop from Tommy's rifle and he too went down. Amazing. Two for two from a hundred yards in a choppy sea. No wonder the Taliban never had a chance with Tommy in the field.

"Take out those lights," Megan said.

"Take out everything," Ray barked.

"Yeah, baby," Billy Ray said as he opened up with his automatic assault rifle, its staccato burst ripping through the night air. First one light and then another exploded in a cascade of fireworks, but Billy Ray didn't let up. He chewed up the rear of the *Sea Witch*.

Ray saw Borkov turn and retreat but he only managed a couple of steps before Billy Ray cut him down.

Megan cut the engines.

Then all was silent. It was as if the air had been sucked up into the ionosphere.

"Where are they?" Ray asked.

Tommy rose to his knees and scanned the water. "There." He pointed. "Ten degrees port, fifty yards."

Ray looked that way and saw Jake and Nicole bobbing in the water.

Took only a couple of minutes to get them on board.

"You okay?" Ray asked.

"Freezing," Nicole said.

"Not to mention scared," Jake added.

"You're such a ninny," she said.

"Me?"

"I wasn't scared at all. I knew Ray would show up."

Billy Ray remained up front while Tommy dug a couple of blankets from the rear locker and handed them to Jake and Nicole. "These'll help."

Jake wrapped one around Nicole and the other around himself.

The rain was now hard, the swells even bigger. Lightning streaked overhead.

"The *Sea Witch* has come to a stop," Megan said.

"Guess the captain decided running wasn't in his best interest," Ray said. "With the admiral down and all."

"What now?" Megan asked.

"Wait on the Coast Guard," Ray said. "Ball's in their court now."

Ray sat down next to Jake. "You guys okay?"

"Now we are," Jake said.

"That text was a stroke of genius."

"I was hoping. Didn't know if you got it or understood it."

The radio crackled to life. Megan patched it into the headphone system. It was Pancake.

"What's the story?" Pancake asked.

"All good," Ray said. "We have Jake and Nicole and three bad guys are down for sure. Maybe more."

"Excellent. The Coast Guard is maybe ten minutes away."

"Make sure they know we're the friendlies," Ray said.

"Already done. I'll let Ira know the *Sea Witch* is all his."

A few minutes later, the lights of the cutter appeared off the port side, headed toward the yacht.

"Can you get them on the radio?" Ray asked.

Megan flipped a couple of switches and spun a dial to another frequency.

"Coast Guard vessel," Megan said. "This is the *Hot Pursuit*. We're off your starboard."

A voice came back. "We have you, *Hot Pursuit*. Do you need assistance?"

"No. We're good. We have the two hostages and they're good, too. At least three down on the *Sea Witch* but might be others. Consider them armed."

"Copy, *Hot Pursuit*. Clear the area. We have it from here."

"Roger that," Megan said. "We're returning to port."

"Home sounds good," Jake said.

"I'm hungry," Nicole said.

Jake put an arm around her. "Of course you are."

# CHAPTER FIFTY-SEVEN

THREE NIGHTS LATER, Nicole and I met Ray and Pancake at Captain Rocky's. By the time we arrived, Pancake had already consumed a platter of ribs and three PBRs, to "tide him over," Ray two Coronas.

We were late because we had stopped by to see Walter and Tammy. Walter had called, saying he had something for me. Wanted to thank me for solving the murder of Barbara Plummer and clearing him. I tried to tell him I did little and that it was Morgan that tied it all up. He'd have none of that. So we swung by.

Walter gave me two bottles of wine. Not just any wine. Screaming Eagle. Goes about two grand a bottle. I tried to explain that I didn't know good wine from bad, but he said, "Try this and you will."

Tammy, for her part, was actually pleasant. For her. I mean she didn't rip Nicole's head off or suck out her blood or anything like that. She even shared a laugh or two with her and hugged her when we left. Amazing.

Her and Walter? Tammy's take was along the line—men do stupid shit. Even Walter. And compared to me, Walter was a saint. So all was forgiven.

I did my best not to take offense, but my feelings were hurt. Really, they were.

"What's happening?" I asked, after Nicole and I sat.

"Ribs," Pancake said, indicating the pile of completely cleaned bones before him. They looked like something a pride of lions would have left behind. Or maybe an anthropological research project. "Might get me some more," he added.

"More what?" Carla Martinez said from behind me. I hadn't heard her walk up.

"More ribs," Pancake said.

Carla nodded. "Figured as much." She looked at Nicole and me. "Anything for you guys?"

I nodded to Nicole. She pulled one of the Screaming Eagles from her purse. "This," she said.

Carla examined the bottle. "This is definitely the good stuff."

"A gift from Walter," I said. "For some reason he thinks I solved Barbara's murder."

Carla nodded. "I'll open it. And bring out the good wine glasses."

"Get one for yourself," I said. "Wouldn't want you to miss the celebration."

"Will do." She walked away.

"You did," Ray said.

"Did what?" I asked.

"Solve the murder."

I shook my head. "Not sure I agree with that. I think there were a lot of moving parts in this."

"But you two," Ray indicated Nicole, "grabbed the video that got the ball rolling. That made the connection between Borkov, Henry, and Walter. You found the jogger that witnessed the Wilbanks brothers hooking up with Borkov's guys. You went on board the *Sea Witch* and got face to face with Borkov. And you got Grace off the yacht." Ray shrugged. "Without all that, we wouldn't be sitting here celebrating a victory against the bad guys."

"I could've skipped that last part on Borkov's boat," I said.

"Wimp," Nicole said.

"Me? I seem to remember a few tears and some cold, shaky fingers."

"I knew you were scared. Just wanted to commiserate."

"Commiserate? Is that what it was?"

She shrugged.

Carla returned with five glasses and the open bottle of wine. She poured and we all toasted.

"To a job well done," Ray said. Then he took a sip. His eyes lit up and he examined the deeply red wine in his glass. "My, this is good."

Nicole nodded. "Best wine I've ever had."

"Ribs should go fine with this," Pancake said. He looked at Carla and smiled. "Bring us a few racks."

"You got it."

I saw Bob Morgan come through the front door, his gaze scanning the crowd until he saw me. He wound through the tables and sat down.

"Wine?" Nicole asked.

He shook his head. "Still got an interview to do back at the station."

Carla appeared with a platter stacked with racks of ribs and a basket of hush puppies. She placed both in the middle of the table. "Anything else?"

"I suspect this'll do it," Pancake said. "For now."

She nodded and left.

After everyone tore off a few bones and began to eat, Ray asked Morgan. "So, what's the latest?"

Morgan wiped his hands on a napkin. "A lot, actually. The guy who got himself shot up just outside of Pensacola? The one that snagged the SUV from under your noses?" He nodded toward Ray and Pancake.

"We were a bit busy," Ray said.

Morgan laughed. "Just giving you some shit. Anyway, he was indeed Carlos Fernandez. He is definitely connected to Borkov and likely a cartel hitter. It seems Borkov's attorney got him out of a couple of scrapes. On Borkov's dime."

"Figured as much," Pancake said around a mouthful of rib. Sauce circled his mouth but he didn't seem to notice, or care.

"His gun wasn't the murder weapon in the Barbara Plummer killing, but the firearms guys matched it to the one used in the killing of Raul Gomez."

"So Borkov ordered that killing?" I asked.

Morgan nodded. "No doubt. The FBI has taken over since all this went down on the high seas. And crossed state lines a few times. They're being fairly closemouthed about it, but my guy over there filled me in. Of course, Borkov, Joe Zuma, and Frank Boyd are history. Your guys chewed them up pretty good."

Ray shrugged. "Nothing they didn't deserve."

"True," Morgan said. "The Feebies took in the entire crew of the *Sea Witch*. Apparently they had little to say. Except for a guy named Brian Wirtz. He was Borkov's chief cook and bottlewasher from what they could glean."

"We met him," I said. "He was Borkov's chef."

"Well, he was fairly quick to sing. Said he had nothing to do with any of Borkov's stuff. Just a simple employee."

"Reliable?" Ray asked.

"The Feebies think so. Anyway, he says he met Carlos a couple of times. When he was on board. Said he was a real reptile. Cold was the word he used. Said he overheard a lot during his years with Borkov and that he heard Borkov tell him to take out Raul."

"Did he say why?" I asked.

"Apparently Borkov was furious that Raul had botched the killing of Henry and Barbara. Yes, the plan was to whack them both and, no, Borkov didn't know Henry was away. The idea was to make it look like a simple B and E with a killing. Random. But Raul apparently farmed it out to Darrell and Darnell Wilbanks. Seems he was trying to build his own crew. Thought the brothers would make good soldiers."

"From what I know of those two, I'm not sure that was a wise move." I said.

Morgan nodded. "Apparently Borkov agreed with that. So he sent Carlos to take out Raul while he handled the Wilbanks guys."

"You said Carlos' weapon did Raul," Ray said. "What about Heather Macomb and her family?"

Morgan smiled. "I was getting to that. Two shooters there. We knew that early on. The bullets found there matched the guns the Coast Guard and the FBI found on board the *Sea Witch*. Near the bodies of Zuma and Boyd."

"So they dropped us at the mall," Nicole said, "and then drove over and killed an entire family?"

Morgan raised an eyebrow. "Sure looks that way."

Nicole shook her head. "I guess their 'To Do' list was a little different than mine. Let's see, drop Grace at the mall, pick up laundry, kill family."

That got a laugh from everyone.

"What about Grace?" I asked.

"She's fine," Morgan said. "Moving to Denver with her mother. Apparently she has a few friends there. She's actually looking forward to making a fresh start in a new place."

"Good. She's been through a lot," I said.

"Haven't we all," Nicole said. "I'm still cold from that jump off the *Sea Witch*."

"Don't worry," I said. "I'll warm you up."

"Confident, aren't you?"

I smiled. "Of course I am."

Nicole took my hand. "I do see a hot tub in your future."

I looked at Ray. "We're out of here."

"Of course you are," he said.

Nicole and I stood, said our good-byes, and turned toward the front.

"Jake?" Ray said.

I turned back and looked at him.

"Good job."

I stared at him for a beat, nodded a thanks, and led Nicole out of my restaurant.

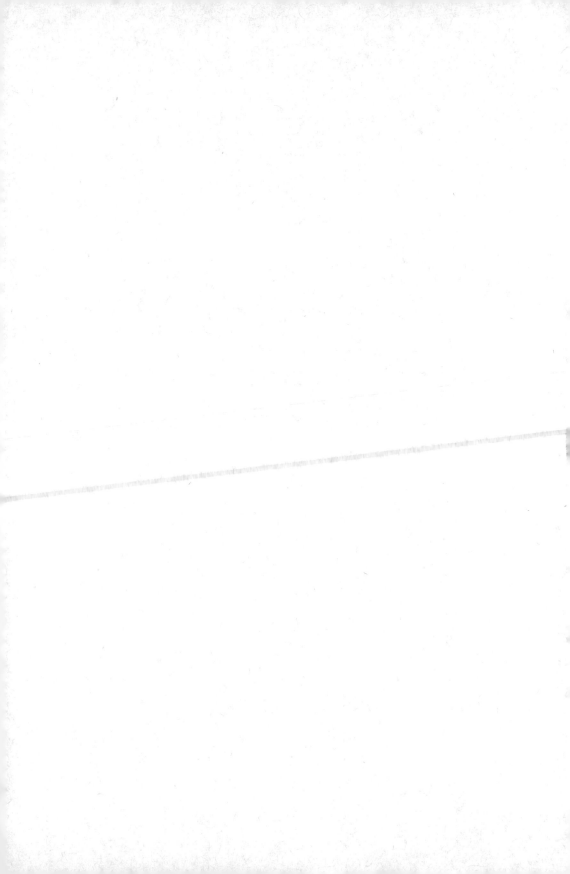